THE BEGGAR
OF VOLUBILIS

THE ROMAN MYSTERIES
by Caroline Lawrence

Also available:

— A Roman Mystery —

THE BEGGAR
OF VOLUBILIS

Caroline Lawrence

Orion
Children's Books

First published in Great Britain in 2007
by Orion Children's Books
a division of the Orion Publishing Group Ltd
Orion House
5 Upper St Martin's Lane
London WC2H 9EA
An Hachette Livre UK company

3 5 7 9 10 8 6 4

A catalogue record for this book is
available from the British Library

ISBN 978 1 84255 189 9

Typeset by Deltatype Ltd, Birkenhead, Merseyside
Printed in Great Britain by Clays Ltd, St Ives plc

www.orionbooks.co.uk

To Victoria Lee
with thanks for her insight and input

ITALIA

Rome
Ostia

Pillars of
Hercules

Tingis
Lixus
Volubilis   Caesarea

Middle   MAURETANIA   Carthage
Atlas   CAESARIENSIS
                                     AFRICA
                                     PROCONSULARIS
MAURETANIA
TINGITANA

SICILY

Sabratha Oea
                                     Lep
                                     Mag
SAHARA   Cydamus

N
W   E
S

ROMAN AFRICA CIRCA AD

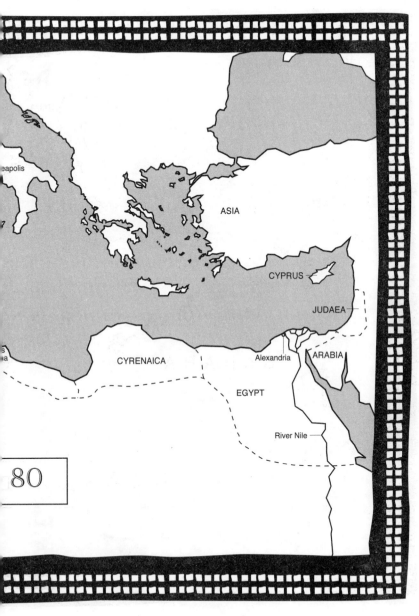

eapolis

ASIA

CYPRUS

JUDAEA

CYRENAICA

Alexandria

ARABIA

EGYPT

River Nile

80

COIN PORTRAITS

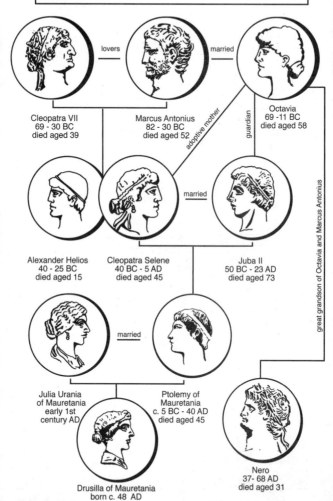

Cleopatra VII
69 - 30 BC
died aged 39

lovers

Marcus Antonius
82 - 30 BC
died aged 52

married

Octavia
69 -11 BC
died aged 58

adoptive mother

guardian

great grandson of Octavia and Marcus Antonius

Alexander Helios
40 - 25 BC
died aged 15

Cleopatra Selene
40 BC - 5 AD
died aged 45

married

Juba II
50 BC - 23 AD
died aged 73

Julia Urania
of Mauretania
early 1st
century AD

married

Ptolemy of
Mauretania
c. 5 BC - 40 AD
died aged 45

Drusilla of Mauretania
born c. 48 AD

Nero
37- 68 AD
died aged 31

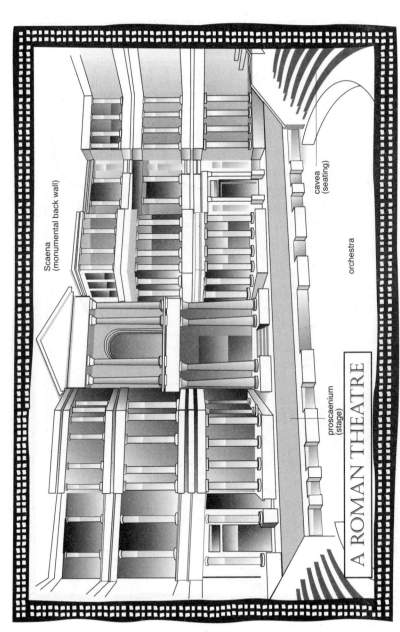

Scaena
(monumental back wall)

cavea
(seating)

orchestra

proscaenium
(stage)

A ROMAN THEATRE

This story takes place in ancient Roman times, so a few of the words may look strange.

If you don't know them, 'Aristo's Scroll' at the back of the book will tell you what they mean and how to pronounce them.

At the beginning of this book you will find coin portraits of some of the historical people mentioned in this story, as well as a drawing of a Roman theatre and a map of Roman Africa in the first century AD.

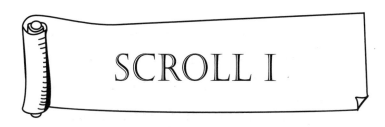

SCROLL I

Diana the huntress crouched by the myrtle bush and examined the footprint of a deer. Her short scarlet tunic glowed in a beam of early morning sunshine. In her left hand she grasped a polished bow. Green-feathered arrows rattled in her painted quiver.

She looked over her shoulder at the two girls and their dogs waiting silently behind her. One girl had fair skin and light brown hair, the other was dark-skinned with golden-brown eyes.

'Do you see it?' whispered Diana. 'The fresh hoof-print in the earth? That means our prey is close at hand. Come, Flavia. Come, Nubia. The hunt is on!' She stood and pushed through the myrtle bushes, causing drops of morning dew to sprinkle the girls.

Flavia – the fair-haired girl – laughed and caught hold of Nubia's hand and the two of them followed. After two months of rain and tears, this last day of February was sunny and warm. After two months of black garments, Diana's red tunic was a welcome touch of colour.

They followed the huntress through the dappled groves.

Presently Diana stopped them with a silent raised hand. They all saw the deer, standing in a sunlit clearing by an acacia tree.

Carefully, almost lovingly, Diana notched the arrow in the string and slowly pulled it back. A heartbeat's pause, then a deep, sweet thrum. Unhurt, the deer vanished into the myrtle bushes.

Diana laughed. 'It doesn't matter,' she said, her eyes shining. 'It's the hunt that counts. Being out here in the woods. Being free. Being alive!' She led the girls to the spot where the deer had been and stopped beside the acacia tree. Her green-feathered arrow was embedded in its trunk.

Diana gave the arrow a tug. 'When my sister Cartilia died of the fever last winter,' she said, 'did I don black garments of mourning and spend my days weeping? No! I honour her by living!'

Flavia gazed in admiration. Diana Poplicola's silky hair was the colour of partridge feathers, her long limbs lightly tanned and smooth. She looked just as Flavia imagined the goddess Diana must look. She also had the goddess's courage and independence. And her hatred of men.

The huntress grunted as her arrow came free. 'And I will have nothing to do with men. They kill you as surely as this arrow can kill, by getting you with child, like your poor dead friend.' She dropped the arrow into the quiver on her back. 'And even if you survive child-birth, marriage leaves you bloated and trapped, with runny-nosed brats clutching your knees. No, I would rather die than ever marry.' Her long-lashed brown eyes blazed with passion.

'Me, too,' said Flavia, and looked at Nubia. 'Us, too! Will you teach us to be huntresses like you, Diana?'

'Of course,' said Diana, and looked them over. 'But you need to look the part. First, pull up your tunic to allow your legs free movement. And cut off your sleeves at the shoulder. Here, let me show you.'

She helped Flavia and Nubia belt their tunics so that the hems skimmed their knees. Then she took a sharp hunting knife from her belt and cut off the long sleeves of Flavia's sky-blue tunic. 'Here,' she said, handing Flavia the sleeves. 'You can use the fabric as a headband.'

'Oh!' Flavia's face grew hot. 'It feels strange to have my arms and legs all bare and cool. I feel almost naked!'

'Don't worry.' Diana tossed her hair. 'Nobody will see us out here in the woods.' She turned to Nubia, made a few swift cuts and pulled away the mustard-yellow sleeves of her tunic. 'Look how beautiful you are in your short golden tunic, with those long mahogany arms and legs. How old are you?'

'Twelve,' said Nubia shyly. 'I am twelve.'

Diana laughed. 'I'm nineteen and you're almost as tall as I am. You look like an Amazon. And you,' she turned to Flavia, 'you remind me of Diana herself, with your courage and love of the hunt.'

'I do?' said Flavia, feeling her cheeks grow hot again.

'Yes. But if you want to hunt with me in the resin-scented pine woods of Ostia and Laurentum, you must renounce men.'

Flavia looked at Nubia. 'Diana's right,' she said. 'We don't need men. Look what happened to Miriam. We want to live and be free and have adventures.' She turned to Diana. 'If we renounce men, will you teach us to hunt? Will you show us how to use your bow?'

'Better than that,' laughed Diana. 'I have two smaller

bows at my house. I'll give you each one and I'll teach you this very morning. But first you must make your vows at the Temple of Diana. I have some traps in the next grove. I usually catch a few rabbits in them. Are you willing to offer a rabbit each as your vow?'

'Yes!' cried Flavia, and nudged Nubia.

After the merest pause, Nubia nodded.

'Then follow me!' cried Diana. 'Your new lives are about to begin!'

Jonathan ben Mordecai gave a coin to the ferryman and stepped down into the small boat. His friend Lupus followed. Wordlessly, the two boys joined a workman in a one-sleeved tunic near the front of the boat. The man was covered with white marble dust and he looked like one of the lemures, or spirits of the dead. Jonathan shuddered. Ten-year-old Lupus gave his friend a sympathetic look and patted him on the back.

Dawn had been sunny, but now a high film of clouds dulled the February morning and flattened the colours. The mouth of the River Tiber was swollen and brown from over two months of daily rain. Jonathan absently watched it flow towards the grey sea.

With the arrival of two veiled women, the boat had its full complement. Lenunculus the ferryman pushed off from the south bank, then settled himself and began to row. The Tiber was only a few hundred feet wide at this point, but the current was particularly strong. Jonathan knew the journey would take almost half an hour.

He closed his eyes and listened to the silky swish of the water, the plop of the oars, the peevish cries of seagulls overhead, and the soft murmuring of the women. After the constant wails of babies and grieving women at home, the relative silence was a relief.

When the boat reached the other side, Lupus scrambled out and up onto the riverbank. He caught the rope thrown by the ferryman and moored it to the post. The ferryman was the second out, reaching down a muscular arm to his passengers. Jonathan waited for the powdery stonemason to disembark and then helped the women up to Lenunculus on the muddy bank. Jonathan was in no hurry. He knew what he would find here.

The Isola Sacra was a flat triangle of land between Ostia and its new harbour Portus. It was the site of market gardens, warehouses, a marble yard, and – along the road from Ostia to Portus – a growing necropolis. The land was cheaper here than along the roads outside Ostia, and it was becoming a popular site for tombs of the poor.

The road to Portus, Ostia's new harbour, was straight and well-paved. For a short time Jonathan followed the two women, but as his pace slowed they drew far ahead. He passed a tomb with a small lighthouse mosaic, and one with a clay relief of a ship.

'Arghhh!' yelled Lupus, leaping out from behind a large red-brick tomb. He had no tongue and could not speak, but he made convincing animal noises.

'Not now, Lupus,' sighed Jonathan. 'I'm not in the mood to play beast-hunters and bears.'

Lupus looked at him for a moment, then shrugged and ran off to explore more of the graveyard.

Jonathan left the road and found his father slumped at the opening of the family tomb.

Mordecai ben Ezra had not cut his hair or beard since

the day of his daughter's funeral ten weeks earlier. His long tunic was muddy at the hem. He wore no cloak.

'Father?' Jonathan bent and gently shook his father's shoulder.

'Susannah?' said Mordecai. His voice was slurred and when he opened his red-rimmed eyes, Jonathan saw that his pupils were huge and black. 'I didn't mean to. I tried to help her. I didn't mean to. Should have said no. No, no, no. Why did I do it? Why did I let her marry him?' He closed his eyes again.

'Father, it's me. Jonathan. Time to come home.'

'Who?' Mordecai blinked up at him, then shook his head angrily. 'No. She was too young. I should have said no.' Tears began to run down his gaunt cheeks and into his beard.

Lupus appeared from behind the tomb and looked down at Mordecai. Suddenly he grunted and pointed at Mordecai's feet.

'I know,' said Jonathan. 'He's put his boots on the wrong feet. Like a child.' This – more than anything else – made him want to cry. He took a deep breath and swallowed the familiar tightness in his throat. 'Come, Father! Time to go home. Mother is worried.'

Lupus frowned at Mordecai and then made the sign of someone drinking and raised his eyebrows at Jonathan.

'No,' said Jonathan. 'He's not drunk. Not on wine, at least. But I think he's been taking poppy-tears again. Look how black his pupils are.' Jonathan sighed. 'Come on, Lupus. Help me stand him up and let's take him home.'

The gongs of Ostia were clanging noon when Flavia

knocked on the back door of her house. It was built into the city wall and had no outside latch for security reasons. Presently, Flavia's old nursemaid and house-slave Alma opened the door. Her eyes widened as she looked the girls up and down.

'Great Juno's peacock! The two of you are practically naked! What have you two done to your tunics?' she cried. 'Hacked them all to bits!' Without waiting for an explanation she muttered, 'Well, you'd better get upstairs quickly and change! You have a visitor.'

'I don't care who sees me!' said Flavia, as she bent to undo Scuto's lead. 'I want the world to see me like this.'

'Are you sure? It's that nice young lawyer. Flaccus.'

Flavia stood up. 'Floppy? Floppy's here?' She stood on tiptoe and peered anxiously over Alma's shoulder. 'Is pater here, too?'

'No, your father is out. It's just Floppy ... I mean Flaccus. Juno! You have me saying it now!'

Flavia caught her friend's hand. 'Come on, Nubia. Let's see what he wants.'

Flavia had met the handsome young patrician the previous spring on a voyage to Rhodes. Gaius Valerius Flaccus had become a good friend and had recently stayed with them in order to plead a case in Ostia's basilica.

Now he was standing in her father's tablinum with his back to them, pretending to examine the shelves of scrolls.

Flavia cleared her throat. 'Hello, Gaius Valerius Flaccus,' she said politely.

He turned with a smile. 'Hello, Flavia,' he said. 'Hello, Nubia.' And then: 'Good gods! What are you wearing?'

Flavia quoted Virgil: '*A painted quiver on her back she wore, and at full cry pursued the tusky boar.*'

'You what?'

She lifted her chin a fraction. 'Nubia and I have just made offerings at the Temple of Diana. We have taken vows of chastity and we are now virgin huntresses!'

Flaccus stared at her for a moment, then muttered: 'That's going to make this more interesting.' He cleared his throat. 'Flavia. I was hoping to speak to your father first ... But now that you're here, I have something to ask you.' His eyes flickered towards Nubia and he smiled at her.

Nubia gave him a shy smile in return.

'Flavia, could we speak privately?' And then to Nubia: 'Do you mind?'

Flavia caught Nubia's hand. 'Nubia is my best friend. She always stays by my side. Whatever you want to tell me, she should hear, too.'

For a long moment he looked at her in consternation, and she could see the tips of his ears grow pink. Finally he took a deep breath and said. 'Flavia Gemina, I love you.'

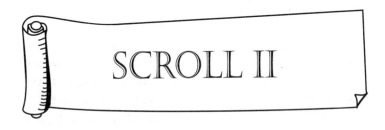

SCROLL II

Without taking her eyes from Flaccus, Flavia said, 'Leave us alone, please, Nubia,' and added under her breath. 'But don't go far.'

Nubia gave Flaccus a little smile, then whistled for the dogs; they were busy sniffing the young man's boots. Tails wagging, Scuto and Nipur followed her out of the tablinum. Flavia watched the three of them disappear through the inner garden in the direction of the kitchen. When they were out of sight she turned back to Flaccus.

'What did you just say?'

Flaccus took a breath. 'Flavia Gemina,' he said. 'Since I first met you last year I have come to realise something. You are the bravest, most intelligent girl I have ever – is that blood on your cheek?' He squinted at her.

Flavia's mouth opened but no words emerged.

Flaccus gave his head a little shake, glanced up at the ceiling and whispered to himself: '... bravest, most intelligent ...' Then he cleared his throat. 'But what makes me love you is your courage, and your hunger for justice and truth.'

Flavia stared at him.

'Flavia,' he said, his voice deep with emotion. 'Flavia, will you marry me?'

Flavia closed her mouth.

Flaccus smiled and moved out from behind her father's desk. 'We won't have the betrothal ceremony until June,' he said, 'when you come of age. And we don't have to have the actual wedding until you're fifteen or sixteen.' He took another step towards her and now he was so close that she could feel the heat radiating from his muscular body.

'I just want to know that one day you'll be mine,' he said softly, and added, 'I know you have feelings for me. I can see it in your eyes.'

Flavia's heart was pounding and she could feel her resolve wavering. Floppy loved her. He loved *her*!

He looked at the floor. 'The death of your friend Miriam reminded me that life is short. I want to marry and raise a family. I want to have children.' He looked up at her again. 'Flavia, I want to have *your* children.'

From the house next door came the sudden thin cry of a baby. It reminded Flavia of why Miriam had died so young.

Flavia swallowed and shook her head. 'I'm sorry, Gaius Valerius Flaccus,' she said. 'But I have just this morning taken a vow of chastity. I made a vow to Diana. Nubia and I have renounced men forever.'

He tried to smile. 'Bad timing on my part, then. I suppose I shouldn't have lingered in Rome this morning to make those offerings to Fortuna and Spes.'

He looked so crushed that Flavia's heart melted. 'Oh, Floppy!' she cried. 'I'm sorry. If I were ever to marry, you would be my first choice. My only choice! I think you're marvelous. Any girl would be lucky to have you. You're rich, and handsome, and highborn ...'

From the house next door, the cry of a second baby had joined the first.

She took a step back. 'But I can't marry you. I can't. I'm sorry,' she whispered.

After a pause, he pulled a ring from his little finger. 'If you ever change your mind, will you put this on?' The ring was gold, and showed two clasped hands.

'Oh!' she cried. 'A betrothal ring.' She reached out to take it, then drew her hand back. 'I can't wear that.'

'Don't wear it,' he said. 'But take it. And if you ever change your mind, put it on.' He took her left hand and turned it so that the wrist faced the ceiling. 'They say,' he touched the base of her ring finger, 'that a nerve goes from this finger right to the heart.' He slowly traced a line from her finger across her upturned palm and her wrist and up her bare arm to the crook of her elbow and then to her shoulder and finally down over her chest.

He was standing very close to her now, looking down at her upturned face with his long-lashed dark eyes. She could feel her heart pounding under the tip of his finger. Presently he moved his hand slowly back up towards her collarbone, then plucked an arrow from the little wicker quiver slung over her left shoulder. Without taking his eyes from hers, he snapped the arrow with a crunch.

He bent lower and now his mouth was so close to hers that she could smell the faint sweet smell of mastic on his breath. 'Your arrow has pierced my heart, Flavia.'

And then he was gone.

Her knees gave way and she sat heavily in her father's leather and bronze armchair. When the blood had stopped rushing in her ears and when her heart had stopped pounding, she saw the two objects he had left on the desk. The gold betrothal ring, and the feathered shaft of the arrow.

He had taken the pointed half with him.

Later that day an imperial messenger banged on the door of Jonathan's house, the house next door to Flavia's. All the women inside were occupied with babies, and his father was still in a drugged stupor, so it was left to Jonathan to answer the door.

'Quiet, Tigris!' said Jonathan to his dog. 'You should be used to messengers by now.' He glanced at the man. 'Even imperial messengers.' He studied the seal, nodded, then turned the folded papyrus over to see to whom it was addressed.

'Master of the Universe,' he muttered, and showed the letter to Lupus, who had just come into the atrium. 'It's addressed to us. To me, you, Flavia and Nubia.'

Jonathan thumbed open the seal and quickly scanned the letter. 'I don't believe it!' He handed the letter to Lupus and turned back to the messenger. 'Does the emperor want an answer right away?'

'By tonight if possible,' said the messenger. 'I'll wait at the Grain and Grape Tavern for your response.'

'I need to discuss it with my parents,' said Jonathan. 'I'm only twelve, you know.'

The messenger nodded. 'It's a great honour for someone as young as you to be asked to go on such a mission,' he said. 'I would advise you to accept. If you do, I am authorized to give you enough money for your passage as well as four imperial passes.' He glanced at the cypress branch hanging over Jonathan's front door.

'Who died?' he asked. 'If you don't mind my asking.'

'My sister,' said Jonathan, 'and her husband. She died in childbirth and he disappeared a week after she died. We found his cloak and sandals on the beach. We think he drowned himself from grief.'

Nubia, Flavia and their two dogs were hunting in the dunes south of the Marina Harbour. The high thin glaze of clouds had thickened, and now it was beginning to drizzle.

'Oh, it's so nice to be out,' sighed Flavia, pushing aside a clump of juniper. 'Out of the house and away from those crying babies.'

'I am liking babies,' said Nubia quietly.

'I like babies, too,' said Flavia. 'But not ones that cry all the time.'

'Behold,' said Nubia, looking up. 'It is beginning to rain.' She sneezed.

'We need to get used to the elements,' said Flavia briskly, 'if we are going to be virgin huntresses.' She let the juniper branch spring back and glanced down at her wax tablet. 'Diana said you can sometimes find deer down here, where the woods meet the beach. I want to kill a deer. I want to prove we're worthy to be her companions.'

Nubia sneezed again, and sighed. Although she was no longer Flavia's slave, she sometimes felt like it; Flavia rarely considered Nubia's wishes, or asked her opinion. Nevertheless Nubia was going to offer her opinion now.

'Flavia,' she said. 'Flaccus loves you and is wanting to marry you. Do you not want to marry him?'

'I have taken a vow,' said Flavia firmly. 'Alma says the

gods often tempt you after you've taken a vow. The goddess Diana was testing me. But I passed – Shhhh! Scuto, Nipur. Quiet! Did you hear that, Nubia? I heard a twig snap. Come, faithful hounds!' she said to Scuto and Nipur, who were busy sniffing the base of a pine tree. 'Come, faithful maiden companion! The hunt is on!' Flavia ran towards a grove of oak trees, then crouched behind a rotting trunk near another clump of juniper.

'Flaccus is kind and handsome,' panted Nubia, crouching down beside Flavia and catching Nipur's collar. 'And I know he pleases you. You told me once you imagine kissing his lips.'

Flavia ignored Nubia's comment. 'Now that we are virgin huntresses,' she mused, 'shall we live in the resin-scented woods of Ostia and Laurentum? Or shall we catch a boat to a faraway country?' She looked up at the sky. 'Oh, not again! It's rained every day since Miriam died. I can't remember such a wet winter in my whole life. Wouldn't it be wonderful to be somewhere sunny? Shhhh! There. At the foot of that big oak! I saw something brown!'

Flavia pulled an arrow from her quiver and notched it on her bowstring. A moment later the arrow sped from its bow.

'Aaaaah!' came a voice from the foot of the oak tree. 'I've been shot!'

'Oh, no!' cried Flavia. 'I shot a person, not a deer!'

Flavia pushed through the juniper bushes and emerged into a sandy clearing within sight of the beach. There were a few ancient oak trees here and a man in a brown tunic and leggings stood beside one. He had just pulled the arrow out of his calf and was examining it with interest. 'Ow!' he said. 'That stung.'

'Oh, I'm so sorry, sir!' cried Flavia. 'I thought you were a deer. Scuto! Get away. That's not your lunch.'

'I'm not a deer,' said the man, rescuing his cheese and bread from the dogs' interested sniffing. 'Just a sailor trying to eat my lunch.' The man squinted down at her. 'Oh, it's you, Miss Flavia.'

'You know me?'

The man nodded and grinned. 'I know your father. Sailed with him once a few years ago. My name's Gorgias.'

'Pleased to meet you. And sorry about shooting you.'

'Doesn't matter. Wasn't much force behind it. Only went in a little. Fleshy part of the calf.' Gorgias looked down at the spot of blood on his left legging. 'See? It's almost stopped bleeding already.'

'Here.' Flavia pulled off her blue linen headband. 'Let me bind it up.' She knelt and wrapped the cloth around his calf, then tied it off neatly. She stood up and brushed away a stray strand of hair. 'If it festers, Gorgias, you must visit Mordecai ben Ezra on Green Fountain Street. I'll make sure he treats you gratis.'

'So is he back from his travels, yet?'

'Doctor Mordecai?'

'Your father. Only I'm looking for work.'

Flavia frowned up at him. 'My father's at home. Right here in Ostia. What makes you think he's gone travelling?'

'Thought I saw him embarking last December,' said the sailor, scratching his head. 'First day of the Saturnalia, it was.'

'Don't be silly,' said Flavia. 'Ships don't set sail in December. It's not the sailing season. It would be suicide!'

'That's why I remember it. She was bound for Sabratha in Libya, carrying members of the Pentasii beast-hunting corporation. I saw your father going up the gangplank an hour before she set sail.'

Flavia turned to Nubia, a puzzled expression on her face. 'Did pater go on a voyage last—' Then understanding dawned: 'Did my father have a broken nose?'

'Now that you mention it, yes…' said Gorgias. 'I remember thinking he must have been in a fight recently. Oh, and he was barefoot.'

'Great Juno's peacock!' cried Flavia. 'It must have been Uncle Gaius. My father's twin brother,' she explained to Gorgias. 'We all thought he drowned himself. Oh, thank you, Gorgias! That's wonderful news! My father is here in Ostia, but he'll be sailing to Alexandria tomorrow or the next day. He usually posts details of his voyages in the Forum of the Corporations. I'll put in a good word for you, if you like.'

'Much appreciated. Oh. Here's your arrow. Only a little blood on it.'

'Thank you.'

Flavia caught Nubia's hand and pulled her away. 'This is Diana's doing!'

Nubia frowned. 'Diana Poplicola?'

'No! Diana, the goddess of the hunt,' cried Flavia. 'She doesn't want me to hunt deer. She wants me to hunt men. She wants us to find Uncle Gaius and she's put us on his scent! It's her reward for my resisting temptation.'

As they emerged from the woods onto the tomb-lined road, the dogs began to bark.

Nubia pointed. 'Behold!' she said. 'It is the Jonathan and the Lupus!'

The boys had just appeared from the Fountain Gate and were hurrying towards the girls.

They ran towards each other, and when the two boys finally stood before the two girls, Flavia and Jonathan opened their mouths and said in unison: 'We have to go to Africa!'

SCROLL III

'A letter from the Emperor!' breathed Flavia. 'A letter asking us to go to Africa, land of exotic cities like Leptis Magna, Carthage and Volubilis, and oasis towns scattered like leopard spots on the tawny skin of the desert!'

The four of them had taken shelter from the rain under some umbrella pines near the synagogue. From here they could see the beach and the Marina Harbour. Jonathan had bought a papyrus cone of pistachio nuts and was passing them round.

Flavia took a nut. 'And the letter arrives the very day we learn Gaius is there! It must be the goddess Diana rewarding me.'

'Are you certain it was your uncle the man saw?' asked Jonathan, cracking a pistachio shell with his teeth.

Flavia nodded. 'He looked like my father, but with a broken nose,' she said. 'That's a perfect description of Uncle Gaius. Also he was barefoot. Remember how we found his sandals on the beach?'

'How could I forget?' said Jonathan. 'We thought he must have been so overcome with grief that he just walked into the sea and drowned.'

'But he didn't!' cried Flavia. 'He didn't drown himself. He just ran away, and the goddess Diana has put us on his track. She's rewarding me for my faithfulness,' she said.

'What faithfulness?' said Jonathan with a frown. 'Why do you keep going on about Diana?'

'Nubia and I have renounced men and taken a vow of chastity,' said Flavia, lifting her chin a fraction.

Lupus almost choked on a pistachio nut, so they all patted him on the back. When he stopped coughing, he looked at Flavia and raised his eyebrows questioningly.

'Nubia and I have sworn never to marry,' said Flavia, 'and I have already resisted great temptation.'

Jonathan spat out a shell. 'What temptation?'

Nubia answered: 'Gaius Valerius Flaccus asks Flavia to marry him. She says no.'

'Floppy asked you to marry him?' cried Jonathan and Lupus gave Flavia his bug-eyed look.

'Yes,' said Flavia. 'But I turned him down.'

Jonathan raised an eyebrow. 'You turned down the most eligible bachelor in the Roman Empire?'

'It was the goddess testing me,' said Flavia, flicking away a pistachio shell. 'And now she has rewarded me for my resolve. How else can you explain Titus giving us money for passage and four imperial passes to travel anywhere in the Roman empire?'

'Simple,' said Jonathan: 'He has a mission for us.'

'I long to go to Africa, my home,' said Nubia. 'But I still do not understand why the Titus wants us to go there.'

'He wants us to find a valuable gem,' said Jonathan, 'and bring it back here to Rome. Apparently the Delphic oracle prophesied that whoever possesses the gem will rule Rome for a long time. The only problem is he's not sure exactly where the gem is. He's sending other agents to parts of Asia, but he wants us to go to Africa.'

'Why us?' said Flavia. 'Has he run out of agents?'

Jonathan took out the letter and read: '*You have proved yourselves resourceful in the past. Also, being children, you can go many places where adults can't.*'

'He's right,' said Flavia.

Nubia turned to Jonathan. 'Where in Africa is he wanting us to quest? Could it be Egypt? Or Nubia, my home?'

Jonathan shook his head. 'Titus wants us to start in a town called Sabratha, on the coast. His mother, Flavia Domitilla, came from there and he's got a cousin who will help us.'

Flavia almost choked on a pistachio nut. 'Great Juno's peacock!' she said. 'Sabratha is where Gaius's ship was headed. Now I'm sure of it: this is a mission from the gods!'

'Pater!' cried Flavia, running into the tablinum. 'Pater, I have the most exciting news!'

Marcus Flavius Geminus was a clean-shaven, good-looking Roman in his early thirties, with the same light-brown hair and grey eyes as his daughter. His eyes widened in surprise.

'Great Neptune's beard!' he exclaimed looking from Flavia to Nubia and back. 'What on earth are you two wearing?'

'Good morning, sir,' said Nubia politely.

'Pater! A letter!' said Flavia. 'A letter from Rome! From someone very important. Can you guess?'

Her father's stern expression melted. 'Praise the

Twins. I thought you weren't going to tell me.'

'Of course I'd tell you!'

'I thought you'd turned him down,' said Marcus, rising to his feet and smiling. 'That would have been the biggest mistake of your life.'

'Turned him down? Of course not. But how do you know about it?' asked Flavia suddenly.

'He sent me a letter, too.'

'The Emperor sent you a letter?'

Marcus frowned. 'The Emperor? Titus? Are you telling me Titus wants to marry you?'

Flavia glanced at Nubia and giggled. 'Pater, don't be silly. Of course Titus doesn't want to marry me. He has a mission for us. A quest! The hunt is on!'

Her father sat down in his chair again. 'A quest. The Emperor has a quest. He was the one who sent you the letter.'

'Actually he sent the letter to Jonathan. He wants us to go to Africa. But, pater, I haven't told you the most exciting news: Uncle Gaius isn't dead! He's in Africa, too! A sailor saw him boarding a ship to Sabratha in December. Just after Miriam's funeral. And Sabratha is exactly were the emperor wants us to start our quest! It can't be coincidence. It must be the gods!'

Instead of praising the gods, her father looked at her coldly. 'Flavia, ships do not set sail in December. I know that and you know that. Do you have anything else to tell me?'

'But this ship *did* sail in December, and Uncle Gaius was on it. He's alive! Isn't that wonderful news? We can go look for him!'

'Flavia,' said her father quietly. 'Has anything else happened today?'

Flavia's smile faded as understanding dawned. 'Oh! Gorgias. Is he badly hurt? Did he complain?'

'What are you babbling about?'

'I accidentally shot a man—'

'You *shot* a man?'

'Yes, but only a little, and he seemed all right, unless the wound has started to fester . . . His name is Gorgias and he would like to sail with you.'

'Good gods, Flavia, you're completely out-of-control! I'm talking about marriage. Have you not just had a proposal of marriage?'

'A proposal of – oh! Oh, pater! Did Floppy,' stammered Flavia, 'did Flaccus write you a letter?'

'He did.' Her father tapped a sheet of papyrus on his desk. 'He tells me that he proposed to you this morning, but that you turned him down. Alma overheard you saying you had renounced men. Some nonsense about Diana and her virgin huntresses.'

Flavia caught Nubia's hand. 'Nubia took a vow, too, pater.'

Her father's jaw clenched. 'I am not concerned with Nubia. I'm concerned with you. The family line must continue.'

'What about Uncle Gaius's twins? Can't they continue the family line?'

'But *my* line ends with you, Flavia. You're my last burning coal.'

'And I want to stay that way! Alive, I mean. I don't want to die in childbirth like Miriam.' She paused and then added. 'Like mater.'

The blood drained from his face and he rose slowly to his feet.

Flavia realised she had gone too far. 'I'm sorry, pater!' she cried. 'But it's true. Myriads of women die in childbirth. You don't want me to die, do you?'

Her father took a breath. 'No. Of course I don't want you to die. But I do want you to stop charging about on insane quests and mad adventures. I want you to stop dressing like a character from a pantomime. I want you – good gods! – I want you to stop shooting men with arrows. I want you to show dignity and courage. Real courage! The courage to accept your responsibilities to our family and to our household gods.'

'But, pater, what about Uncle Gaius? This is our chance to find him! We can all sail to Sabratha on the *Delphina* and you can help us look for him. And after we've found him we can all do Titus's quest.'

'If Titus sent a letter to Jonathan, then let Jonathan go. Not you. As for Gaius, I do not want to hear another word about him being alive and well in Africa. That Gorgias is a drunk. His claim is ridiculous. And a cruel one to those of us who loved Gaius. You will stay in this house until you learn to behave like a proper Roman lady.'

'But, pater—'

'Enough!' He slammed his fist on the desk, making the silver inkwell and pen jump. 'I am not sailing to Sabratha on some fool's quest. I am going to Alexandria as planned. Tomorrow, at dawn. You and Nubia will remain confined to this house until my return, be that one month, two or even three! That means no walking the dogs in the graveyard. No going to the baths. No shopping. No investigating. You will not leave this house.'

'But—'

'ENOUGH!' he shouted. 'I am the paterfamilias and I have spoken. Now go to your room. Both of you!'

SCROLL IV

Outside it was raining. Nubia loved the rain, but this winter had been so miserably wet that she desperately longed for sunshine.

From the room next door came the plaintive notes of a song. Their young Greek tutor Aristo was playing his lyre again. Nubia loved Aristo, but his music had been so mournful these past two months that she sometimes longed for silence.

For the past twenty-four hours, Flavia had been in a sour mood. Nubia loved Flavia, but when her friend was in a bad temper Nubia was tempted to run away. The prospect of three more months of this was unbearable.

So when the secret signal came on their bedroom wall, Nubia was ready. She helped Flavia pull back the bed, and together they began to remove the bricks from the wall.

At last Lupus came through, brushing plaster dust from his hair. Jonathan followed. 'We tried to see you the normal way,' he explained. 'But Caudex said you weren't allowed visitors. He also said that your father had forbidden you to leave the house until May!'

Flavia nodded grimly.

'Why didn't you give us the secret signal?' asked Jonathan.

'We were afraid Aristo might hear us knocking.' whispered Flavia, 'he's right next door.'

'I know,' said Jonathan. 'I can hear his sad plinky-plonky music leaking through the walls day and night. It's driving me mad.'

'Shhh!' said Nubia, holding up her hand. 'He stops.' After a moment she said, 'Now he starts again with the wretched music.'

'By Hercules!' muttered Jonathan. 'If even Nubia thinks it's wretched, then it must be bad.'

'It is,' said Flavia. 'But we don't have to endure it much longer. We're packed and ready to go. Have you found a ship?'

'You're sure you want to come with us?' said Jonathan. 'You're happy to leave Scuto and Nipur?'

'We're not happy to leave them. But we can't very well take them to Africa.'

'Alma loves them,' said Nubia. 'She will walk them and care for them.'

'Great Juno's beard! You *are* ready to go, aren't you?'

The two girls nodded resolutely.

'And you've left your father a note?'

Flavia pointed to a piece of papyrus on her bedside table. 'He doesn't deserve it. He was horrible to me. But I don't want Aristo or Alma or Caudex to get in trouble. So I told him not to blame them.'

'Your father's going to be angry ...'

'Not if we find Uncle Gaius and bring him home. Besides, pater set sail for Alexandria this morning and he won't be back for weeks, maybe months.' She hung her head. 'He barely said goodbye to me.'

Nubia patted Flavia's back and then looked at Jonathan. 'What boat do we embark on?'

'I've booked passage on a ship called the *Isis*, bound directly for Sabratha,' said Jonathan. 'A company of beast-hunters are on their way to get animals for the arena. And your friend Mnason is one of them.'

'Mnason?' cried Nubia. 'Mnason head beast-hunter and owner of Monobaz? Mnason who gives me lion-skin cloak?'

'That's the one,' said Jonathan.

Nubia clapped her hands in delight.

'He's happy to be sailing with us. And thanks to a bag of gold from Titus, the captain is happy to take us. We're going to be the guests of honour.'

An hour later the four friends stood at the stern of the merchant ship *Isis* and watched Ostia slip away from them.

'Nobody to say goodbye to us this time,' murmured Flavia, as she gazed back at the wet, deserted docks.

'They are thinking us to be in our bedroom,' said Nubia. She was wearing her lionskin cloak.

Flavia turned to Jonathan. 'Do *your* parents know you've gone?' she asked.

Jonathan shrugged. 'My father's in a haze of poppy-tears most of the time and my mother is trying to run the household without his help. She has her hands full of wet-nurses, babies and nappies. I doubt if either of my parents will notice I'm gone. But I left a note, too,' he added.

'Behold!' cried Nubia, and they turned to see her pointing towards the horizon. The rain clouds had broken and the pearly sliver of a crescent moon hung in the pink sky of dusk.

'Oh, Nubia!' cried Flavia. 'It looks like a bow. It's a sign from Diana, goddess of the moon and of the hunt.' She felt a numinous shiver and turned to her friends. 'Let's go to front,' she said, 'and look towards Africa.'

As they made their way carefully across the rearing deck, the sailors and other passengers greeted them. A middle-aged Syrian with oiled hair and a neat pointed beard came forward with a copper tray. He was Mnason, the head beast-hunter.

'Warm spiced wine,' he said cheerfully, 'for our honoured passengers. To warm your bellies and for a libation to Neptune. Glad to see you're wearing the lionskin I gave you,' he said to Nubia. He leaned forward and lowered his voice. 'The crew are glad you're sailing with us. They've heard of your luck and they think it's a good omen.' He nodded towards the west. 'Red sky at night is a sailor's delight. Another good omen.'

Each of the four friends thanked him, took a copper beaker and made their way to the prow. Beneath their feet the deck was rising and falling, as if bowing to the setting sun. The salt breeze whipped their hair and the piercing cries of gulls filled their ears, and before they drank, each of them tipped some of their hot spiced wine into the cobalt blue water as an offering to Neptune.

If not for Flavia's dreams, the journey would have been perfect.

During the day they ploughed blue waters with the breeze filling their sails and at night they sailed beneath a sky choked with stars. They gamed with Mnason and his beast-hunters, played music and watched dolphins. Lupus acted out some of their past adventures as Flavia and Jonathan told the stories, while Nubia played her flute.

During the night they slept in empty cages down in the hold. On the *Isis*'s voyage home, these cages would be full of exotic beasts, but for now the clean sawdust formed a blissfully soft cushion beneath their cloaks.

For the first three nights of the voyage, Flavia had the same dream.

In her dream she was walking in a town she did not recognise. Then a woman's voice said: *Do not pass a beggar by without giving.* Was it Diana speaking to her? Was it a saying of Pliny's? A verse from Virgil? Every morning she woke with the words echoing in her head. But she could not decipher their meaning.

On the morning of the fourth day she went to the altar at the back of the ship and bowed her head.

'Dear Diana,' she prayed, ' – or whichever of you gods has been sending that dream – I promise I will not pass a single beggar by without giving something.'

That night she did not dream, but slept soundly, and in the late morning they sailed into the port of Sabratha, a city of apricot-coloured sandstone and lofty palm trees.

'Africa!' breathed Flavia, as she stepped off the gang-plank onto the dock. 'We're in Africa!'

The four friends had said their goodbyes to the beast-hunters and the crew, and now they stood in the port of Sabratha on a sunny March morning.

Nubia opened her arms wide and smiled up at the

sun. 'I am being warm,' she said. 'First time in three months.'

Lupus nodded happily.

But Jonathan looked around and shook his head. 'It doesn't look like Africa,' he said. 'It looks a lot like Ostia, except it's a kind of dusty pink colour rather than red brick.'

'Of course it's Africa!' cried Flavia, 'Look!' She pointed to a line of tall black Africans weaving their way through the bales of cloth and amphoras piled on the dock. 'Look at their colourful loincloths, crested hair and ostrich-skin shields. Would you see that in Ostia?'

'You might,' said Jonathan.

'Then what about that?' She pointed to a turbaned man fluting a cobra out of his basket.

'I've seen snake-charmers in Ostia.'

'Behold! Date palms!' cried Nubia, clapping her hands in delight.

Jonthan folded his arms. 'There are palm trees in Ostia.'

'How about those!' Flavia pointed triumphantly towards half a dozen camels swaying through the crowded wharves, with colourful striped blankets covering the loads on their backs.

'You might not see camels in Ostia, but there are plenty at the vivarium in Laurentum.'

'You win,' laughed Flavia. 'Where do we go now? Oil Press Street, isn't it?'

Jonathan reached into his belt pouch and took out a well-folded piece of papyrus. 'Yes. Titus said when we reach Sabratha we should contact a man called Statilius Taurus, a cousin on his mother's side. He lives on Oil

Press Street. Let's ask someone at one of those stalls,' added Jonathan.

'Wait!' said Flavia. 'Do we have everything? Do we have our travel-bags?'

'Yes,' they said, and Lupus nodded.

'Do we have our imperial passes?'

They tapped the ivory rectangles on scarlet cords round their necks.

'Then let's go,' said Flavia, and added over her shoulder, 'The first thing we need to do is thank the gods for a safe journey. Keep your eyes open for a shrine or temple.'

Jonathan sighed and followed Flavia and the others across the sunny docks past stalls selling piles of silver fish, baskets of grain and exotic birds in cages. Someone was heating pine-pitch and its pungent smell reminded him of Ostia.

When a poor beggar with a withered leg raised up his claw-like hand and pleaded for money in a foreign tongue, Jonathan was surprised to see Flavia stop and hand him a quadrans. She also made Lupus show the beggar a portrait of Gaius which he had painted on the back of his wax tablet. The beggar shook his head.

'Why did you give that beggar a coin, Flavia?' said Jonathan, as they passed beneath the arch of the town gate. 'Don't you remember what happened last September?'

Flavia nodded. 'Of course. But when we were on board the *Isis*, I kept having a dream with a woman's voice saying: *Do not pass a beggar by without giving.* I think it was the goddess Diana.'

'Really?' Jonathan raised an eyebrow. 'It doesn't sound

like something Diana would say. Isn't she a rather cruel goddess?'

'Well, whichever of the gods it was, I can't afford to offend them. I don't suppose you've had any of your prophetic dreams recently?'

'No,' said Jonathan, and murmured: 'Praise God.'

'I dream of woman and baby last night,' said Nubia.

They all turned their heads to look at her.

'Who was it?' asked Jonathan.

'I do not know,' said Nubia.

'Was she a goddess?' Flavia fished in her purse for another copper as a half-naked beggar boy extended his hand.

'Maybe,' said Nubia. 'She is very beautiful. She is holding a baby. She looks a bit like that.' Nubia pointed to a little shrine. Set into a niche in the sandstone wall of a building was a painted marble statue of a beautiful woman. She held a baby on her lap, and a bronze rattle in her right hand.

'I think that's Isis,' said Flavia 'There's a shrine to her in Ostia, too.'

Lupus nodded his agreement.

'Nubia and I have made a vow to Diana,' said Flavia, 'but that doesn't mean we can risk offending other gods and goddesses. Isis is the first deity we've met here in Africa. Let's make our thanks-offering to her. Let's buy some fruit for our offering.'

'Behold!' cried Nubia, pointing to a stall. 'Dates!'

Jonathan and the others made their way to a nearby stall selling dates, figs and melons. While Nubia helped Flavia choose the best dates and Lupus showed Gaius' portrait to the fruit seller, Jonathan went to the stall next door and picked up a bronze rattle. It jingled.

'What's this?' Jonathan asked the stallholder.

'It's a sistrum,' said the man in good Latin. 'Today is the festival of Isis.'

'That's a good omen!' cried Flavia, coming up with a papyrus cone of dates. She turned to the sistrum-seller. 'Nubia here saw Isis in a dream last night.'

'Beautiful woman with baby,' said Nubia.

Lupus picked up a smaller sistrum and gave it a rhythmic shake.

Jonathan turned to the stallholder. 'How much for that little one?'

'To those who've seen the goddess,' said the man with a wink at Nubia, 'half price. Two sesterces.'

'We'll take it,' said Jonathan. He put down a silver denarius and received two brass sesterces in return.

'Excuse me, sir,' said Flavia. 'But have you seen this man?' She pointed at the wax tablet in Lupus's hand.

'Sorry,' said the stallholder, bending forward to have a closer look. 'Haven't seen him.'

'One last thing,' said Jonathan. 'Can you tell us the way to Oil Press Street? Near the Seaward Baths?'

'That I do know. See the red roof of the temple of Liber Pater rising above the roofs there? That's the forum. Head that way. When you get to the forum, turn left and follow the back of the colonnade. Soon you'll see a statue of Aphrodite outside the Seaward Baths. Turn left at the statue – before you reach the baths – and you're there.'

They thanked him, offered their dates at the shrine of Isis, and a quarter of an hour later were knocking on the door of a house on Oil Press Street.

As they waited for a response, Jonathan looked around. It was a wealthy residential quarter, close to the sea. In the pure blue sky above, seagulls drifted and whined peevishly, just like the gulls in Ostia. Some houses had red-tile roofs in the Roman style, but others were flat-roofed with plain white walls: distincty un-Roman. Jonathan could tell from the clusters of date palms rising up here and there that many had inner gardens.

He was about to knock again when the door suddenly swung open to reveal a massive door-slave in a one-sleeved pink tunic. He glowered down at them and they stared in amazement. He was bald, and his strangely shaped head with its broad jaw and narrow cranium reminded Jonathan of an upside down egg.

Flavia and the others were staring open-mouthed so Jonathan said, 'We're looking for your master. Er ... Taurus.'

Without a word, Egghead disappeared into the gloom.

Presently a short, stocky man in a cream turban came to the door. He glanced at Jonathan's letter, then burst out laughing. 'Are you four children the agents Titus told me about?'

'Yes, sir, we are,' said Flavia.

Taurus winked at his big door slave. 'Well, drop your bags and cloaks here in the vestibule, and come with me. Pullo and I were just on our way out. Today is the most important day of the year in Sabratha. It's the festival of Isis. If we want our mission to succeed, she's one goddess we must not neglect!'

Lupus enjoyed the festival of Isis.

He liked the procession, with its strong beat of drum, castanet and sistrum. He liked the pretty girls in white linen shifts, tossing their petals onto the street. He liked seeing the three bald priests get the hems of their long white robes wet in the sea as they pushed out the gilded boat with its effigy of Isis. He liked the way they drew back the boat with a secret cord, lifted the goddess onto their shoulders and took her to the massive apricot-coloured temple by the water's edge.

But most of all, he liked the pantomime.

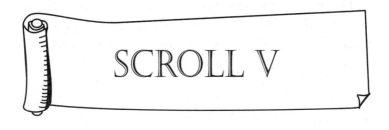

SCROLL V

Sabratha's theatre was made of the same pale apricot-coloured sandstone as the other monumental buildings in the town. Taurus had a section of the seating at the very front and he insisted that the four friends sit on cushions at his feet. He himself sat on a leather and wooden chair, brought by his egg-headed slave Pullo.

Lupus had seen mimes acting out their rude un-masked satires, and he had seen tragedies and comedies, but he had never before seen a pantomime. He studied the papyrus programme he had been handed at the entrance.

THE WORLD FAMOUS PANTOMIME NARCISSUS
and his distinguished troupe
will perform three mythic scenes
in honour of Isis, the great goddess:
Diana and Actaeon
Isis and Osiris
Venus and Mars
show sponsored by C. Flavius Pudens

When the herald announced Narcissus's name, the whole theatre broke into hearty applause.

The musicians came on first, four young men filing out into the orchestra – the circular space below the stage. As the applause died down, they launched into a jingly, buzzing tune with a strong deep beat. They wore long unbelted caftans in jewel-like colours. Aquamarine for the aulos-player, sapphire for the harp and emerald for the man banging the tambourine. The drummer was Lupus's favourite. He wore a jade tunic and provided a compelling beat with a goatskin drum and iron-soled shoe. In addition, he had laid out a small array of instruments on the lip of the stage behind him, including a gourd and a sistrum.

A slender girl with frizzy dark hair joined them a moment later and when the applause died down she began to sing in a pure sweet voice, announcing the tale of Diana and Actaeon.

Again the audience cheered as a man did half a dozen flips forward onto the stage then stopped and slowly turned to look at the audience. His masked face lifted all the tiny hairs on Lupus's neck and arms. The mouth of the mask was closed and the two sides were painted differently, giving the staring face a disturbing beauty. The man wore a short brown tunic, with flesh coloured leggings underneath, and a flowing red cloak over it.

'Euge! Narcissus!' the crowd was shouting.

'How can one person play two roles?' Lupus heard Flavia ask Taurus.

'See his mask?' said Taurus. 'It has two profiles. One is male, the other female. Watch.'

Lupus saw the dancer turn the male side of his mask to the audience, and begin to move across the stage in time to the pulsing rhythm. This was Actaeon, sang the woman. He was a handsome young hunter who had been separated from his companions while hunting deer with his hounds. The young hunter was hot, and when he heard the bubble of water he pursued the tempting sound as avidly as any prey.

Still keeping beat with his stamping foot, the drummer tipped a hollow gourd full of small pebbles to imitate the rush of flowing water. Then he made a sparkly noise by stroking tiny silver bells. To Lupus the sound perfectly evoked a forest stream.

Abruptly, the dancer turned the other side of his mask to the theatre. Now the music became exotic and sensuous as he imitated the beautiful goddess Diana, bathing in the pool of a dappled glade. How a clothed man could imitate a naked goddess, Lupus did not know. But he did.

And now the man was Actaeon again, peering through the branches, transfixed by the sight of the goddess's beauty. The music became soft and furtive, then suddenly exotic and regal as the pantomime dancer took on Diana's persona once more.

The female singer told how Actaeon's foot crunched a twig and how the goddess heard. For a heartbeat the music stopped, and the double face of the mask looked straight out from the stage. Lupus heard the intake of breath from the audience behind him, and he felt the delicious shudder of dread.

Horrified that a man should see her unclothed beauty, the virgin goddess Diana points her terrible finger at Actaeon, commanding him to change from the shape of a man into something entirely different.

Actaeon feels horns sprouting from his head and his clenched fists become hooves. And suddenly he is a deer, full of speed and terror, pursued by his own baying hounds. The hunter has become the hunted, leaping for his life.

Lupus stared open-mouthed. How did the dancer do it? How did he so perfectly imitate man, woman and beast?

Jonathan echoed Lupus's thoughts. 'Amazing,' he murmured. 'He's like an actor, dancer and rhetor mixed all together.'

Without taking his eyes from the stage, Lupus nodded.

The singer continued her tale. Now the first hound is upon Actaeon, sinking his fangs into the back of the hunter's neck, then another clamps on with sharp teeth, and another. And now Actaeon is down, and a dozen dogs crowd round their former master, burying their bloody muzzles in his bowels.

The dancer's red cloak flowed over him like blood. Beside Lupus, Flavia and Nubia squealed and covered their eyes with their hands. Lupus felt another delicious thrill of horror.

Now the dancer had writhed out from under the blood-red cloak, and he was Diana, austere and composed, gazing down at the red patch, her outrage quenched by Actaeon's blood. The goddess shrugged and turned and coldly walked away.

The music stopped and for a moment the audience was silent. Then the theatre resounded with rapturous applause.

The pantomime dancer ran back to the centre of the stage and took off his mask and bowed. As he stood again, he revealed a startlingly handsome face, sweat-glazed and smiling. In the rows behind Lupus some women screamed with delight and two seats down a magistrate's wife fainted.

Lupus could physically feel the waves of adulation rolling over him towards the stage. He groped for the programme. He wanted to know the name of the man who could inspire such adoration without speaking a word.

Narcissus.

The pantomime dancer was called Narcissus.

SCROLL VI

'The singer,' said Nubia at dinner that afternoon. 'She was most skilled.'

'Almost as good as you,' said Flavia.

'No,' said Nubia. 'She was better. She was sublime.'

'Do you sing?' asked Taurus. They were all sitting around a table in the inner garden of his house, eating a spicy mutton soup.

Nubia nodded.

'And she plays the flute, too,' added Flavia.

'Perhaps you'll play for us after dinner?' said Taurus.

'I can't believe I've never seen a pantomime before,' said Flavia. 'It was wonderful. I still don't know how one man can play so many parts.

'Where is he from?' Jonathan asked Taurus. 'Narcissus, I mean.'

'Alexandria, I believe,' said Taurus. 'My cousin Pudens paid him a handsome sum to perform for the festival.' He tore a piece of bread from a large flat loaf. 'So you live in Rome and you've never seen a pantomime?'

'Actually we live in Ostia,' said Flavia.

'They must have pantomimes there.'

'Probably,' agreed Flavia. 'But my father's never taken me.'

'Then you've never seen Paris?'

'Who?'

'Paris. They say he's the greatest pantomime dancer who ever lived. Makes Narcissus look like a galumphing oaf.'

'Nobody could make that man look like an oaf,' said Flavia. 'He was wonderful.'

'How about you, Lupus?' said Jonathan. 'You've been very quiet all evening. Did you like the pantomime?'

Nubia glanced at Lupus and was surprised to see the passion blazing in his eyes. The mute boy nodded once.

'You could be pantomime dancer, Lupus,' said Nubia softly. 'Remember how you delight the sailors on our trip? Acting out the adventures of us?'

'She's right,' said Jonathan. 'You'd be a natural.'

Lupus kept his head down, staring at a half-eaten piece of flatbread on the table. Nubia noticed that his cheeks were flushing pink and she glanced at Flavia, who understood immediately and changed the subject.

'Excuse me, sir,' Flavia said to Taurus. 'Are you going to tell us about our mission? All we know so far is that Titus wants us to steal a valuable gem.'

Taurus nodded. 'My imperial cousin is too superstitious by far. I'm afraid he's at the mercy of his soothsayers and astrologers.' He must have seen their looks of puzzlement for he continued. 'Have you heard of Nero?'

'Of course,' said Flavia. 'He was the evil emperor who murdered his mother. He died the year before I was born,' she added.

'And yet,' said Taurus, 'there have been persistent

42

rumours that Nero didn't really die.'

Jonathan raised his eyebrows. 'Nero didn't die?'

'Some people claim it was not Nero who died that night, but rather a man who looked like him. According to the theory, his look-alike was given a hasty burial while the real emperor escaped on a ship from Ostia. Over the past twelve years, there have been mutterings, but it was only a few months ago that we had firm reports of sightings of Nero in the east. Parthia, to be exact. This pretender not only looks like Nero, but he plays the lyre and sings like him, too. He already has quite a following.'

'Pretender?' echoed Flavia. 'So you don't think it's really him?'

'No. I believe Nero died twelve years ago of a self-inflicted stab-wound. I'm certain this impostor just wants power. Despite his crimes, Nero was popular with the plebs. If they thought he was really Nero, he would have massive support.'

'What does this false Nero have to do with the gem?' asked Jonathan.

'Nero used to have a large emerald,' said Taurus. 'Recently, an oracle prophesied that whoever possessed Nero's emerald would rule the world.'

'So Titus wants the emerald,' said Flavia, nodding thoughtfully. 'I can understand that.'

'Mainly to prevent someone challenging his power,' said Taurus. 'For example, imagine what would happen if a man pretending to be Nero got his hands on it.' He put down his spoon and shook his head. 'The problem is: nobody knows exactly where the emerald is.'

'It's not here in Sabratha?'

'No, but I believe it may be here in Africa. As I told

Titus in my latest letter, there are reports of an emerald among the treasures of Volubilis.'

'Volubilis!' said Flavia. 'Isn't that near the Gardens of the Hesperides?'

'Not quite,' said Taurus with a chuckle. 'Volubilis is the capital of the Roman province of Mauretania Tingitana. It's about a thousand miles west of here, in a valley surrounded by mountains. I think you should go there and see if you can find the emerald. If you can't find it, then you are free to return to Rome.'

'And if we do find it there?' said Jonathan.

'Then you must steal it and bring it to Titus. Of course, if you are caught you must not implicate the Emperor. He would disavow all knowledge of your actions.'

Nubia shyly raised her hand. 'Is it not wrong to steal?'

'Not in this case. You see, the emerald was the property of SPQR, the senate and people of Rome. So you're actually just taking back what rightfully belongs to Titus.'

Flavia frowned. 'Can't we just ask whoever has it to give it to us? Tell them the emperor wants it?'

'No. Better you quietly steal it. If people learn of the emperor's interest they might ask why.'

'How do we get there?' asked Jonathan. 'To Volubilis, I mean?'

'Caravans go there; it's on their trade route. But the easiest and quickest way is to sail west through the Pillars of Hercules and down to a port called Lixus, a Phoenician trading port. From there we will head inland to Volubilis.'

'We?' said Flavia and Jonathan together.

'Yes, of course. Titus obviously has great faith in your skill and abilities, but he doesn't expect you four children to make your way to one of the furthest outposts of the Empire unchaperoned and alone. And I can see now that he was not exaggerating when he said you were young.' Taurus shook his turbaned head. 'I will certainly come with you. I have already spoken with the captain of a merchant ship called the *Aphrodite*. He is happy to set sail as soon as we are ready. You *are* ready, I hope?'

'Not quite,' said Flavia. 'We have a quest of our own.' She nodded to Lupus and he took out his wax tablet, with the picture of Gaius painted on it. 'Have you seen this man?'

Flavia and Nubia spent most of the following morning taking the small portrait of Gaius around Sabratha. Taurus let them borrow his big door-slave Pullo as a guide and bodyguard. First they tried the basilica, but with no luck. Flavia left a written description of Gaius on a message-board in the forum which bore other notices of lost or missing persons. Then they tried the markets. The spice-sellers had not seen him. The snake-charmer had not seen him. The dealers in ivory, copper and ebony had not seen him. Finally, Pullo suggested they visit the harbourmaster.

'Yes, a ship did come in from Ostia last December,' said the harbourmaster, a tall, dark-skinned man with a gold tooth. 'It docked two days before the Kalends of January.'

'Yes!' cried Flavia. 'That would fit.'

'Well, I don't know about your man there,' the harbourmaster nodded towards the portrait of Gaius, 'but according to my notes, most of the passengers were on their way to the interior to trap wild animals for the amphitheatre.'

'The interior?'

'Inland. Away from the coast.'

'Is the ship still here?'

He checked a papyrus scroll.

'According to this,' he said, 'the ship was going on to Alexandria, then due back here on the Ides of April. That's just over a month from now. Of course, your friend might have travelled on to Alexandria.'

'He's not my friend,' Flavia hung her head. 'He's my uncle.'

'I'm sorry, but I do not recognise him.'

The gongs were clanging noon when Flavia and Nubia met Jonathan outside the Seaward Baths.

'Nobody's seen Uncle Gaius,' said Flavia. 'But at least his ship arrived safely. It didn't sink in a winter storm or get captured by pirates. It docked here and then sailed on to Alexandria. That means Uncle Gaius might be here. Or in Alexandria.'

Jonathan sighed. 'Or anywhere in between. We'll never find him now.'

'Don't be such a pessimist,' said Flavia. 'The goddess Diana brought us here for a reason. And I know we'll find him, even if we have to go to the ends of the earth!' She sighed. 'Speaking of the ends of the earth, Taurus told us to meet him on board the merchant ship *Aphrodite* at three hours after noon. That's when the easterly breeze rises.'

'I know,' said Jonathan. 'He told us, too.'

'Where is the Lupus?' asked Nubia.

'He's at the theatre. Watching the pantomime dancer again. But he promised to get to the ship in good time.'

The gong of the bathhouse had stopped clanging.

'It's noon now,' said Flavia. 'If we don't sail for three hours, that gives us time for the baths.'

'After five days at sea,' said Jonathan, 'I need a good soak.'

'I also.' Nubia looked at Flavia. 'Can we go, too?'

Flavia nodded and pointed at some veiled women going in a side entrance. 'It looks as if this bathhouse has a women's section. A long soak in the hot plunge would be sublime. And maybe even a little nap.' Flavia stifled a yawn. 'I couldn't sleep last night. All those people celebrating. I think everybody in this town owns a sistrum.' She looked at Jonathan. 'Shall we meet you here or at the docks?'

'Let's meet right here in two hours,' said Jonathan. 'That will give us plenty of time to get to the harbour before the *Aphrodite* sails.'

The tickle of a fly on her cheek woke Flavia. She was lying on a couch in a humid, warm room that smelt faintly of sweat and strongly of some unfamiliar spice. Where was she?

Africa! She was in Africa. In the solarium of the Seaward Baths of Sabratha. The golden light of late afternoon was slanting through the hexagonal holes in the wooden latticework screen. It was at least three hours past noon. And the merchant ship *Aphrodite* was due to sail at the third hour.

'Oh Pollux!' She sat up and brushed away the fly. 'Nubia? Nubia, where are you?' Nubia had been on the couch next to her. But apart from a few flies, the couch was empty.

One or two other women were dozing on couches, but most had left. A withered old woman wearing wooden clogs and a long brown tunic clumped around the solarium, stirring up dust with a twig broom.

Clutching her linen towel around her, Flavia ran barefoot through all the rooms of the bath. No Nubia. At last she went to the apodyterium and hurried to her cubicle. It was one with an octopus painted above it. But it was empty. And so was Nubia's next to it, the one with the crayfish. A frantic search showed that only two or three cubicles had clothing in them and none of it was hers. 'Oh, no!' she wailed. 'I've been robbed! And now I'm going to miss the boat!'

Half an hour later Flavia arrived at the port, her hair undone and the long-sleeved brown tunic flapping around her ankles. She had tried to use her imperial pass to buy new clothes, but nobody at the baths had ever seen such a thing. In the end, she had traded her gold and glass signet-ring for the bath attendant's long tunic and clogs.

'Pollux!' She cursed as one of the wooden clogs fell off.

She ran back, slipped it on, and lifted her eyes to see a ship sailing out of the harbour. It was already passing beyond the lighthouse.

'Excuse me, sir!' she cried, tugging the sleeve of a fishmonger packing up his few remaining sprats. 'Do you know what ship that is?'

The man squinted in the direction she was pointing. 'That's a red sail, isn't it?'

'I think so.'

The man sighed. 'Only sometimes I get red and green confused. My wife can't understand it. "How can a tree be red?" she says to me. "Or how can blood be green?" Mind you, I can't understand it either.'

'It's red!' cried Flavia. 'That ship has a red sail!'

'Then that'll be the *Aphrodite*. Bound for the Pillars of Hercules.'

SCROLL VII

'Jonathan! Nubia! Lupus!' sobbed Flavia Gemina. 'Come back! Wait for me!'

She stood on the furthest end of the pier and waved her arms at the red-sailed ship, sailing out through the curved arms of the breakwater. She thought she could see tiny figures in the rigging so she jumped up and down. 'Come back!' she cried. 'Don't leave me!'

'I don't think they ... can hear you,' wheezed a familiar voice behind her.

Flavia whirled. 'Jonathan! Nubia! Oh, praise Juno! But where have you been? And where's Lupus? Why aren't you on that ship? Why didn't you wake me up? Oh, you gave me such a fright!'

Jonathan's chest was rising and falling and he was wheezing. Running always made his asthma flare up. 'Didn't you get ... my note? Nubia left a note ... telling you we'd ... gone to look for Lupus.'

'I left it in cubicle with octopus above,' said Nubia.

'No!' cried Flavia. 'I didn't get your note. Someone must have stolen my things: my sandals and my coin purse and my best blue tunic. I had to trade my signet ring for *this*!' She looked down in disgust at the shapeless brown tunic and the too-small wooden clogs.

'Oh!' cried Nubia. 'Poor Flavia! You were sleeping

50

so deep. When bath-slave comes to tell me Jonathan wants us, I leave you for a moment and Jonathan says you can sleep.'

'That's right,' said Jonathan, breathing from his herb pouch. 'I wrote you a note ... and Nubia put it in your cubicle ... I didn't think anyone would steal it.'

'So where's Lupus?' asked Flavia, angrily brushing away the tears. 'This is his fault, isn't it?'

'We don't know,' said Jonathan, whose breathing was almost normal again. 'He was supposed to meet us on board ship. I started to worry, so I only spent an hour in the baths, then I ran to the docks to see where the *Aphrodite* was berthed. Taurus was there and he'd brought all our satchels, just as he promised to do. But Lupus wasn't on board yet, so I came back here and sent for you, so you could help me look, but only Nubia came out. She said you were fast asleep. So I scribbled a note, telling you we would come back for you. We ran all the way to the theatre but there was another troupe doing a comedy and Lupus wasn't there. So then we went back to the Seaward Baths, but you had gone. We rushed back here just in time to see the ship sailing away.'

'Why do they embark without us?' asked Nubia.

'I hate to say it,' said Jonathan. 'But I think Lupus must be on board the ship. They must all think we're on board, too. Otherwise,' added Jonathan, 'they wouldn't have sailed away.'

'Oh, no!' wailed Flavia, 'I can't believe it. We're stuck in Africa and now we don't know anybody and we have to get to Volubilis. We'll have to try to get another ship tomorrow. Do we at least have money? Tell me you have some money!'

'Not a lot,' said Jonathan. 'Most of my gold is hidden

in the bottom of my satchel. And that's on board the *Aphrodite*. I only have about twenty sesterces in my coin purse here.'

'What about you, Nubia? How much have you got?'

Nubia looked in her purse and said, 'Two silver coins, three brass ones and a tiny quadrans.'

'That's only about thirty sesterces in all,' moaned Flavia. 'And I haven't even got a copper.'

'We'd better go back to Taurus's house,' said Jonathan. 'And see if he's there, or if anyone knows what happened.'

But when they arrived at the house on Oil Press Street it was silent, with all the shutters closed, and although they knocked for a long time, nobody answered.

The harbourmaster shook his head. 'Most ships sail east to Alexandria, not west to the Pillars of Hercules,' he said. 'This time of year ships have to sail against the prevailing wind, and there are treacherous reefs. I don't know when the next one's going. You'll have to check in with me daily. But sometimes you have to wait a few weeks. A month even.' He shrugged.

Flavia looked at Jonathan and Nubia, then turned back to the harbourmaster. 'Can you recommend somewhere for us to stay?'

'Well, there's the hospitium near the forum, but it's expensive. The Sheep's Head Tavern is cheaper, but that's a bit rough. So's the Fountain Tavern. Sailors and slave-dealers and all ...'

'Slave-dealers?' said Nubia, her golden eyes wide.

The harbourmaster shrugged again. 'It's one of our main industries. You could also try the caravanserai outside of town.'

'What's a caravanserai?' asked Flavia.

'It's where the caravans stay.'

'Caravans on their way to where?'

'Through the interior, mostly,' said the harbour-master.

'And would some of them go to Volubilis?' asked Jonathan.

'They might. You'd have to ask.'

'How do we get to this caravanserai?' asked Flavia.

The harbourmaster stood and beckoned them over to the arched window of his office. To the right loomed the massive lighthouse with its rising plume of black smoke. Before them lay the blue harbour, with the town beyond, orange in the light of the setting sun.

The harbourmaster pointed. 'See that turret in the town wall? That's the Carthage Gate. And see those palm trees beyond, silhouetted against the horizon?'

'Yes.'

'If you go out through the Carthage Gate and walk for half a mile, you'll reach those date palms. That's where the caravanserai is. But you'd better hurry. They close the gates at sunset.'

Nubia smelled the caravanserai before she saw it. The scent of charcoal fires, spices and camel dung came wafting through the date palms on a warm evening breeze. It was such a familiar smell that it almost made her cry.

'Oh,' said Flavia. 'I'm famished. I hope we can buy food there.'

'No need to buy food,' said Nubia. 'Behold.' She gestured at the ground. 'Dates everywhere.'

53

'Can you just eat them right off the ground?' asked Flavia. 'Don't you have to cure them, like olives?'

'No.' Nubia picked up a handful of golden-brown dates. 'Try some.' She shared them with Flavia and Jonathan, then popped one into her own mouth. It was perfect: not too sweet and with a faint tang.

'They're delicious,' agreed Flavia, and spat out the thin stone. 'But I want some real food. Something savoury, like cold roast chicken. Or bread and salt. Oh, look!' she cried suddenly. 'Chestnuts! We can roast these.' She started to gather some of the round brown objects scattered on the path.

Nubia giggled and covered her mouth with her hand. 'No, Flavia,' she said. 'Those are not chestnuts. Those are camel droppings.'

Jonathan snorted and Flavia squealed. 'Ewww! Camel dung! I touched camel dung!'

'Behold!' said Nubia, as the road emerged from the grove of date palms. 'Caravanserai.'

The setting sun threw the long shadow of the building towards them. The caravanserai was two storeys tall and had a blank white wall pierced by a single arch. As they came closer Nubia could see the plaster was grey rather than white, and peeling. Passing through the arched entrance, they entered a straw-scattered earthen courtyard surrounded by stalls, each one filled with camels, donkeys, even horses. On an upper level above the stalls were rooms, with a wooden balcony running right the way round.

Nubia inhaled deeply and smiled; the smell of animals, hay and dung always made her irrationally happy.

In the centre of the courtyard, groups of men sat on

54

grass mats or blankets. Some had already lit fires and were cooking their evening meal.

'Oh, that one smells good,' said Flavia. As she inhaled, her stomach growled enthusiastically.

Nubia touched Flavia's arm and pointed.

A dark-skinned old man was shuffling towards them across the courtyard. He wore a brown and white striped caftan with long sleeves. On his head was a grubby white skullcap.

'Where his animals?' he said when he reached them. He spoke in heavily accented Greek.

'Whose animals?' asked Flavia in the same language.

'His. *His.*' The man jabbed his forefinger at her.

'Oh. You mean *our* animals … We don't have any. No animals.'

'No animals, no stay. Go now. You go.'

The man reminded Nubia of the old men of her clan and she said in her own language. 'Please, Grandfather, may we not spend the night? We don't need a room. We can stay in a stall.'

The old man's eyes widened. 'You speak my language!' he cried. 'What clan are you from?'

Nubia clapped softly and let her knees bend. 'I am Shepenwepet of the Leopard Clan. My father was Nastasen.'

'My name is also Nastasen!' He revealed pink toothless gums in a wide grin. 'But I am of the Hyena Clan.'

'Please, Nastasen of the Hyena Clan. May we stay here tonight?'

He beamed at her and nodded. 'I have a little room up there. For special guests.' He turned and pointed to the southeast corner of the balcony. 'The one with the green door. As you have no animals, I will only charge you one sestertius each. That includes stew for dinner and bread and dates for breakfast.'

'Thank you, Grandfather.' Nubia clapped and bowed again.

'What's he saying?' cried Flavia. 'Can we stay here?'

Nubia looked up from undoing her coin-purse and smiled. 'Yes. He is of my people. He says we may stay.'

'Oh, praise Juno!' breathed Flavia.

Nubia placed three sesterces in the old man's calloused palm. He nodded his thanks and gave her three clay beads, each the size of an olive. 'Give these balls to the cook.' He pointed at a man standing over a cauldron, serving a queue of men. 'He will give you stew. Wine is extra.'

'Thank you, Grandfather,' said Nubia.

'Nubia!' hissed Flavia. 'Ask him if any of these people are going to Volubilis.'

'Tell me, Nastasen of the Hyena Clan,' said Nubia. 'Are any caravans going to a place called Volubilis?'

The old man showed his gums again, and nodded. 'Yes, indeed.' He pointed towards a man in an indigo blue turban. 'Macargus over there has a caravan of thirty camels. They are leaving for Volubilis tomorrow.'

'I hope this one speaks Latin,' said Flavia to Jonathan and Nubia, as they approached the man in the dark blue turban. He was sitting with two other men around a small charcoal fire.

'Excuse me, sir,' said Flavia in Latin. 'Are you Macargus?'

The man turned a cheerful face towards her. 'Yes. I am being Macargus,' he replied, in fair Latin.

'Are you going to Volubilis tomorrow?'

He nodded and grinned, revealing a front tooth that overlapped the others. 'Once again, you are correct!'

'We would like to go to Volubilis, too,' said Flavia politely. 'May we come with you?'

'Yes. Please, sit! We shall discuss this.' Beneath his indigo turban and above his short, dark beard he had dark eyes in a copper-coloured face.

Flavia and her friends sat cross-legged on the striped blanket beside him. They nodded politely at the other two, a man in black from turban to toe, and a green-eyed youth in a white turban and brown caftan.

'Have sage tea,' said Macargus, and nodded to his younger companion. Green-eyes poured out three small glasses of sage tea.

'How much would it cost us to travel with you?' asked Flavia, accepting a glass.

'No, no, no.' Macargus waved his hand in front of his face as if he were brushing away a fly. 'We speaking business in a moment. First, we must drinking tea and eating tasty morsel.' He offered her a bowl of something that looked like dates.

'Thank you,' said Flavia with a sigh, and accepted one of the tasty morsels. It was both salty and sweet. Crunchy, too. Macargus offered the bowl to Jonathan and Nubia, who both accepted.

Flavia sipped her tea while Macargus nodded at them and smiled. Jonathan was the last to finish. Finally he put down his empty glass.

'For you,' said Macargus, 'The cost of caravan to Volubilis is being five hundred sesterces each.'

Flavia choked on a tasty morsel and Jonathan had to pat her back.

'This price,' said Macargus cheerfully, 'is including use of a camel and all your meals, plus your guide and protection.' He gave a little bow. 'That is being me. I am very good guide. Making this journey many times.'

Flavia glanced at Nubia and Jonathan. 'We can pay you when we get to Volubilis,' she said. 'But we don't have any money now.'

'Oh, I am most sorry,' said Macargus. 'But I am only accepting payment in advance. Here.' He held out the bowl. 'Have another tasty morsel.'

'We can pay you ten sesterces each now,' said Flavia, 'and *one thousand* when we get to Volubilis. Each,' she added, as the man smiled and shook his head.

'Our money is in our bags,' explained Jonathan. 'But they're all on board the merchant ship *Aphrodite* along with our friend Lupus. We're meeting him in Volubilis and we hope our bags will be waiting when we get there. *If* we get there.'

'We can pay you then,' said Flavia. 'Three thousand sesterces.'

'I am most sorry,' said Macargus, 'truly most sorry. But I do not believe you are having this money.'

'You don't—? Can't you tell we're highborn?'

He smiled apologetically. 'Most sorry.' He pointed at Nubia. 'But she is looking like a slave, he is looking like a Jew, and you are looking like a beggar. You are not appearing to have even one as between you.'

'Anyone can see we have three asses,' muttered Jonathan under his breath.

Green-eyes chuckled.

Flavia tried to control her temper. 'But I am freeborn!' she said. 'See my bulla?' But even as she spoke, her heart sank. The amulet proving she was freeborn had been stolen from the baths, along with her other possessions. Then she felt a surge of hope as her fingers touched the ivory rectangle on its cord. In his letter, Titus had instructed them to never take them off. 'Jonathan! Nubia!' she cried. 'We forgot all about our imperial passes! Look!' she said excitedly to Macargus. 'We have imperial passes. These mean you should take us for free.'

He smiled and nodded. 'Most sorry, but I do not understand. First you are offering me three thousand sesterces to take you. Now you are saying you won't pay anything?'

'No. Yes. I mean: the Emperor will pay you back.'

Macargus looked at Green-eyes who shrugged and said in good Latin. 'I've never heard of anything like that.'

Macargus leaned forward and squinted at the ivory tags. 'They are being small flat pieces of elephant tooth with scratchings on them.' He tapped her pass with his fingernail.

'It's not scratchings. It's writing. Can any of you read?'

They shook their heads.

'Well, it says the Emperor will reimburse you.'

'Reimburse? What is reimburse?'

'Pay you back. Cover our costs.'

'Excuse my confusion,' said Macargus. 'Do I understand you are saying Vespasian is coming to Volubilis and giving me three thousand sesterces?'

'Titus,' said Flavia in a small voice. 'The Emperor is Titus.'

'Ha ha ha,' chuckled Macargus. 'Now I know you are joking. Leader of the great Roman Empire is Vespasian.'

SCROLL VIII

'Don't cry, Flavia,' said Jonathan. 'You'll think of something.'

It was a purple evening, and the three of them were sitting cross-legged in the dusty courtyard of the caravanserai. Each of them had a wooden bowl of stew, which they had to eat with their fingers.

'Our imperial passes are useless,' sobbed Flavia. 'Nobody's seen Uncle Gaius, we've lost Lupus and we're stranded in Africa with no money!'

Nubia stroked Flavia's back. 'At least we are having a place to sleep tonight,' she said, 'with hot stew for dinner.'

Jonathan nodded. 'And also these tasty morsels,' he said. 'It was nice of Macargus to give us some. Here, Flavia: take one.'

Flavia blew her nose and took a tasty morsel. Jonathan took one, too.

'I wonder what they are,' he said, chewing thoughtfully. 'They taste slightly fishy. Like shrimp.'

'Locusts,' said Nubia. 'These are being roast locusts.'

'Locusts?' said Jonathan, gagging. 'You mean locusts, as in insects? Like grasshoppers?'

'Yes,' said Nubia. 'But bigger than grasshoppers.

They are eaten in my country. Also stew of baby camel. Like this.' She pointed at the stew in her bowl.

'Bleccch!' cried Flavia, spitting her mouthful onto the dust. 'I'm eating bugs! And poor little baby camel!'

'Hark!' said Nubia, putting down her bowl. 'I hear music. Do you hear it?'

'Oh, who cares!' cried Flavia, and she threw her bowl of stew in the dust. Immediately a mangy white dog slunk forward and began to devour it with furtive gulps.

'It is pantomime troupe of yesterday,' said Nubia. 'I recognise voice of aulos and harp.'

'She's right,' said Jonathan. 'Look. They're up there on the balcony.'

In the courtyard of the caravanserai the hubbub died away and all eyes turned to the musicians standing on the upper level. Jonathan saw two of the musicians from the previous day's pantomime, one on the double reed, the other on harp. Then a smattering of applause broke out as a masked boy in a green tunic did four somersaults onto the torchlit balcony, then leapt up onto the rail. Here he clowned and danced on the narrow railing, while the merchants and camel drivers laughed and gasped and applauded below. The musicians played a jaunty tune.

Down in the courtyard, the dark-haired singer was coming round with a tambourine that made a jingly sound each time someone dropped in a coin. She was a plain girl with a large nose and dark frizzy hair pulled back in a bun. She reminded Jonathan of someone, but he couldn't think whom.

Meanwhile, up on the balcony there was a flourish of music. With a final flip off the rail and back onto the balcony, the boy in the sea green tunic removed his mask and bowed.

'Master of the Universe,' gasped Jonathan, squinting into the gloom. 'I think that's Lupus!'

Lupus was just as surprised to see them as they were to see him. At their shouts he scrambled over the balcony rail, dangled for a moment, then dropped ten feet to the ground and ran to throw his arms around Flavia's waist.

'Lupus!' cried Flavia, not sure whether to be angry or relieved. But when she saw the tears gleaming in his eyes she knew he hadn't run away deliberately. Lupus gave Nubia and Jonathan a fierce hug, too. Now he was writing on his wax-tablet with a shaking hand.

WENT TO SHIP, he wrote, BUT YOU WEREN'T THERE. I CAME OFF TO LOOK FOR YOU. THEN IT SAILED WITHOUT ME! I THOUGHT YOU MUST HAVE GONE ON BOARD.

'Oh, poor Lupus!' cried Nubia. 'You think we are forgetting you.'

He nodded and angrily brushed tears away with his fist.

'And we thought *you* were on board!' said Flavia.

'What did you do next?' Jonathan asked Lupus. 'How did you end up here?'

I FOUND NARCISSUS AND ASKED IF I COULD TRAVEL WITH HIM TO VOLUBILIS. HE SAID YES BUT THAT I WOULD HAVE TO EARN MY WAY.

'They are going to Volubilis, with caravan of Macargus?' cried Nubia.

Lupus nodded and wrote: I THOUGHT I COULD FIND YOU WHEN I GOT THERE.

'Lupus,' said Flavia. 'All our money is on board the *Aphrodite*. We've only got a few sesterces left between us. Do you have any money?'

Lupus hung his head and wrote:

I SAW MY BAG ON BOARD SHIP NEXT TO YOURS.

'Master of the Universe,' said Jonathan. 'Maybe that ship didn't accidentally sail without us. Between us, we had nearly eight thousand sesterces in our luggage. They probably left on purpose so they could steal our things.'

'Or maybe someone knew about our secret mission for Titus,' hissed Flavia. 'And tried to sabotage us!'

'Whatever the reason,' said Jonathan, 'the four of us are stuck here with no money. We can't even get home again.'

'Wait!' cried Flavia. 'Maybe Narcissus will take all of us! Nubia plays the flute beautifully and Jonathan can play the barbiton. And I can bang a tambourine. If he took on Lupus then he might take us, too.'

Jonathan turned to Lupus. 'I don't suppose Narcissus will let us join his troupe, too?'

Lupus shrugged, then wiggled his hand as if to say: maybe, maybe not.

TWO OF HIS OTHER MUSICIANS STAYED BEHIND he wrote. ONE HELPED BACKSTAGE.

I AM THE NEW DRUMMER AND BACKSTAGE
HELPER.

'I could do that,' said Jonathan. 'I could help backstage.'

'Let's ask him,' said Flavia. 'We've got to get to
Volubilis. Even if our money isn't there when we arrive,
the magistrate will recognise our imperial passes and
honour them.'

Flavia sent up a quick prayer to Diana as she and her
friends approached Narcissus. The dancer and his
troupe were reclining on striped blankets around a
charcoal fire. It was dark now, and a million stars were
twinkling overhead.

Narcissus was shorter than he appeared on stage, with
shoulder length blond hair and a muscular body. Flavia
guessed he was about thirty years old. He did not even
look up as they approached. 'Sorry,' he said, spitting a
date stone over his shoulder. 'No locks of hair and no
pieces of clothing. And absolutely no autographs.'

'We're not fans,' said Flavia. 'We're musicians.'

'Musicians?' He turned and looked up at her with
kohl-rimmed blue eyes. He had a straight nose and
full lips, and in the soft light of the fire he was almost
beautiful. It was no wonder he was called Narcissus,
after the mythical youth so beautiful that everyone
who saw him fell in love with him.

Flavia realised her jaw was hanging open. She closed
her mouth and took a deep breath. She must not allow
herself to be affected by his good looks. After all,
she had consecrated herself to Diana and renounced
romance.

'We're musicians,' she repeated. 'I play tambourine, Jonathan plays barbiton and Nubia plays flute. We need to get to Volubilis but we have no money and we wondered if we could join your troupe? We're friends of Lupus here,' she added.

'If you're musicians, then where are your instruments?'

'Several hundred miles away by now,' muttered Jonathan under his breath.

'We don't actually have them with us,' said Flavia. 'We think we were robbed. We were going to sail on the merchant ship *Aphrodite* to Volubilis, but then it sailed without us.'

Narcissus snorted suavely. 'Volubilis is inland. You can't sail there.'

'We know. We were going to sail to Lixus, then go—'

'You were going to sail to Lixus?' He looked up sharply. 'They told me there were no ships travelling west.' He looked at the frizzy-haired girl and shook his head in disgust.

'That ship was one of the few,' said Flavia. 'But it sailed without us. Our money will be waiting for us in Volubilis. We can pay you something when we get there.'

'I'm sorry,' he said. 'It's true: I could use another couple of musicians, but you don't even have your instruments and you look very young to me ...'

'Nubia has her flute,' said Flavia, and to Nubia: 'Play something!'

Nubia nodded and pulled out the flute from beneath her tunic. She wore it on a golden chain around her neck.

'What's that?' said Narcissus. Nubia's ivory pass was tangled in the chain of her flute.

'Imperial pass,' said Nubia.

He narrowed his blue eyes at them, then shrugged and looked away.

'See?' muttered Flavia. 'I told you nobody knows what these are. They don't even know who's Emperor. Play a song, Nubia.'

Nubia began to play. She played 'Slave Song', a song she had written while still a slave. It was a song about travelling through the desert in a caravan, and as she played, silence fell over the caravanserai. Even the animals in their stalls grew quiet. Lupus disappeared into the darkness, came back and handed Flavia his sistrum. She jingled it in time to the music while he pattered the beat on an upturned wooden bowl. Jonathan pointed at the harp, lying besides one of Narcissus's musicians. After a pause the man shrugged and handed it up to him. Jonathan began to strum its strings.

Presently the song ended and everyone in the caravanserai broke into applause.

Flavia saw that a smile had transformed the female singer's plain face; she almost looked pretty. She was clapping as enthusiastically as the others.

'Casina obviously likes your music.' Narcissus stretched languorously and slowly rose from his blanket. 'All right,' he said. 'You may come with us to Volubilis. I've already paid for our food and drink and camels. My tambourine player and percussionist had to stay behind, so I have two spare camels. That means if all four of you come, you'll have to ride two per camel.'

Flavia nodded, not trusting her voice.

'You'll also have to learn all our songs, and you must agree to perform with us in Volubilis, whether your money is waiting there or not.'

'Yes,' said Flavia. 'Thank you. Oh, thank you, sir.'

He tossed his long hair. 'I haven't quite finished. If your money *is* waiting for you, then I want a thousand sesterces each.'

Flavia glanced at her friends and they nodded. 'Done!' She spread her arms and bowed: 'Behold your new musicians!'

SCROLL IX

The caravan set out at mid-morning. On either side of each camel's hump was a large, soft basket filled with provisions and luggage. A mattress and bolsters lay over these twin baskets – making a soft platform – and the whole lot was secured with hemp cords.

Flavia and Nubia were assigned a young, cream-coloured female camel. Her thick eyelashes and heavy lids made her look sleepy and smug.

The first time Flavia mounted this creature, she almost fell off. She had climbed up onto the mattress easily enough, for the camel was kneeling, but when Nubia gave the command 'Tsa! Tsa!' Flavia was pitched violently forward, then violently back as the camel rose to its feet.

'Oh!' cried Flavia, as they began to move forward. 'We're so high. I can barely see the ground from here.'

Behind her, Nubia giggled. 'Do not worry,' she said. 'You will not fall. I will catch you. Lean back. Rest against sausage pillow. Take off clogs and put your bare feet on neck of camel. See? Is that not pleasant?'

'No,' groaned Flavia. 'I feel seasick. This thing is swaying so much.'

'You will become used to it. Camels are much smoother than horse or ass. And they are going many miles with no water. I used to have my own camel: Siwa,' she said, and added, 'I love camels.'

'Well, you should be happy then,' called Jonathan from the camel in front. 'There are plenty of them in this caravan.'

'These are not so many,' laughed Nubia. 'I once am seeing caravan with maybe a thousand camels. Here we are just having thirty. Twenty-one for riders, nine for packs. Merchants are carrying senna leaf, cotton, spices, salt and elephant tooth.'

'How do you know all that?' asked Flavia.

'I was speaking to merchants this morning. Two speak my language. They say Macargus is good leader. They have travelled with him before. They say he will guide us and make sure no harm comes to us from bandits or wild animals.'

'Bandits? Wild animals? Are there wild animals in the desert?'

'Yes, very many. Lion. Rhino. Scorpion. Snakes, too.' She shuddered. 'We must be careful at night. But do you know the most dangerous part of the desert? It is the sun. It waxes unbearably bright. Even with parasol up, you must put turban over your head and face and sometimes even over your eyes.'

'But I don't have a turban.'

'Yes, you do.' Nubia passed a folded bundle of cloth to Flavia. 'Here. It is matching caftan and turban of pale blue cotton. I get brown robe and turban for Jonathan, dark green for Lupus and yellow for me. These will protect from sun.'

'Oh! The material is so light and soft! But where did you get these? We don't have any money.'

'I trade my gold chain to cloth merchants. Merchants

also give me cola-nuts.' In the palm of her hand were several objects the size and shape of cloves of garlic, but red, like radishes. 'These are very good for when you are hungry or tired. You chew them. But we must save them for necessary time.'

'You traded your gold chain for coloured cotton and red nuts?'

'And also for camel-skin slippers and matching belt pouch. And papyrus parasol. They are for you.'

'Nubia! They're wonderful! The slippers are so soft, and so beautifully embroidered. Oh, thank you!'

'No! Do not try to embrace me or you will fall off. And it is long way down.'

'I know. And I feel sick. I think I'd feel less nauseous if I was at sea.'

Nubia giggled. 'Some people call camel "ship of the desert". I have named our camel Selene, because she is pale like the moon. She is very good. You will become used to her soon.'

On the first day they travelled for nearly eight hours across a barren undulating plain of thin grey soil and the occasional low shrub. Sometimes they walked and sometimes they rode, and always the camels maintained their steady pace. Lunch was taken on the move: a handful of dates from the saddle bags and warm water squirted from the goatskin. There were no latrines, and sometimes not even any bushes to crouch behind. So when either Flavia or Nubia had to go, one would shield the other from view.

Finally, as the stars began to prick the lavender sky in the east, Macargus called a halt to the caravan and announced the end of their first day's travelling.

They ate dinner that night in the shelter of some flat-topped acacia trees. It was a simple meal: camel cheese and sand-baked millet-bread, this last prepared by Assan. The twelve merchants sat around their own fire, but Flavia and her friends – plus Narcissus and his troupe – ate with Macargus and his two camel-drivers.

As they ate, Flavia studied the camel-driver's two helpers.

Assan Cilo was a short energetic youth with a small, fluffy mustache. All day long he had been singing tunelessly as he moved up and down the caravan, steadying a load here, retying a hemp rope there, breaking up a squabble between camels. Beneath his white turban, his eyes were a startling green. He explained in good Latin that this was because his grandmother had been from Italia.

Iddibal was a sinister man in black robes and turban who took up the rear. He seemed to be the caravan's lookout, for even here his dark eyes were always scanning the horizon. Flavia had not yet heard him say a single word.

At the end of the meal, Assan brewed fragrant mint tea and poured out some for all around their campfire. The merchants were brewing their own.

'There won't be tea every night,' said Assan with a gap-toothed smile. 'Only while the honey lasts.'

'Mint tea,' murmured Flavia, taking a sip from a small thick glass. 'It reminds me of Ostia.'

'Oh, yes,' said Jonathan, lying back on the sandy ground with his hands behind his head. 'Sky blazing with a million stars, camels groaning, flat-topped acacia trees. It's just like Ostia.'

'Are you homesick for Ostia?' asked Nubia.

'No,' said Jonathan and Lupus grunted his agreement.

'I don't miss Ostia,' murmured Flavia, 'but I wish I hadn't argued with pater. Just thinking about it makes my stomach hurt.' She sighed. 'If we could just find Uncle Gaius and bring him home, it would make everything right. Oh, Uncle Gaius, why did you go away? Why didn't you leave a note? Did you want us to think you were dead?'

'Who's dead?' asked Narcissus from the other side of the fire. He and Casina and the two musicians had been chatting in Greek during the meal, but now they were all looking at her.

'My uncle,' said Flavia. 'Only he's not dead. He disappeared from Ostia in December and we think he might be here in Africa.'

'Ah. So that's why you're here. Four Roman children in the middle of Africa with no money. And I suppose you hope to find him in Volubilis?'

'Yes,' Flavia lied, and then thought of something. 'I don't suppose you've seen him?'

Lupus had been lying on his back beside Jonathan. Now he rolled over and fished among his things and brought out a wax tablet with Gaius's portrait on it. He handed it to Narcissus

'Nice-looking man.' The pantomime dancer showed the tablet to his three companions, who all shook their heads. 'But, no, I'm afraid we've never seen him.'

'Our camel hates us,' announced Jonathan the next morning.

Nubia was putting on Flavia's turban. She looked up

at Jonathan. 'Why do you think this?'

'He spat a disgusting green wad at me and he groans all the time.'

Lupus imitated the camel's groan.

'Groaning is normal,' said Nubia. 'This is how camels are talking with each other. But your camel should not spit or bite. You must make friends with your camel.'

'How do we make friends with a camel?' asked Jonathan. 'Does it involve playing a flute or singing a camel-song? Because I'm not very good at that.'

Nubia giggled. 'You must name him.' She finished tying off Flavia's turban and went to help Jonathan with his.

'How about Grumpy?' said Jonathan. 'Or Nasty?'

Lupus guffawed. He was wearing his green caftan and attempting to wrap his own turban by imitating Nubia as she put on Jonathan's.

'No,' said Nubia. 'You must give camel good name, to show respect.'

Without letting go of his turban, Lupus used the toe of his sandal to draw in the sand: HELIOS

Jonathan craned to see.

'Stand still,' said Nubia. 'I am tying your turban.'

'Helios,' read Flavia. 'What a good idea! Our camel Selene is white like the moon. But yours is a boy, and golden, so naming him Helios after the sun is perfect.'

'Yes,' said Nubia. 'That is good name. Second thing to make friends is give him dates. Camels love dates. You give him dates and he will be following you like dog.'

'Is that it?' said Jonathan, as Nubia finished off his turban.

'That is it,' said Nubia. 'Very simple. To make friends

with the camel, give to him nice name and give to him dates.'

She turned to Lupus and examined his turban. 'Very good, but make it tighter next time, lest it come loose while walking.' She made a few adjustments and then draped the tail of the turban over his front. 'You must be able to reach this easily, to put over mouth or eyes in sandstorm. Now come,' she turned toward the camels being hitched in a long line. 'We must go. Caravan departs.'

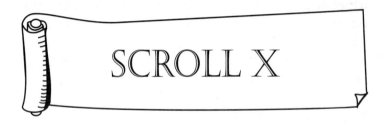

SCROLL X

The days soon took on a steady rhythm.

The twelve merchants rose before dawn, lighting a fire and brewing their tea. They were experts at packing and unpacking camels and were ready to go as soon as the sky grew pale.

Macargus and his men packed their own camels, then those of Narcissus and his troupe. Everyone helped, and within a few days everyone could pack their own camel.

After a hasty breakfast of camel's milk and dates, they rode or walked throughout the day, for at least ten hours, and sometimes fourteen. Usually they would stop at around the fifth hour after noon. Everyone would unpack and hobble their camels, and give them fodder if there were no weeds or acacia bushes nearby. Then Assan would make a fire and cook dinner, while Macargus and Iddibal checked the camels' health: a thorn in the foot or bite from another camel could easily become infected if not treated at once.

The merchants rested quietly before dinner, but Narcissus made his troupe practise whenever possible. Flavia, Jonathan, Nubia and Lupus had to learn the music for four dances. Sometimes Narcissus took Lupus to a flat open space and taught him the basic dance steps used by a pantomime dancer. Within a few days he had Lupus doing back flips and walking on his hands.

'This boy's a natural,' said Narcissus one evening, as he and Lupus came to sit beside the musicians in the long shadow of a lofty palm tree. Casina handed him a goatskin of water and he took a long drink, then handed it to Lupus. Flavia saw that Lupus was glowing with pleasure.

'These three are making good progress, too,' said Casina. 'Nubia is an extraordinary musician. She tells me she has only played the aulos once or twice before and yet she has almost mastered it.'

'She's good,' admitted Hanno, the aulos player. 'Almost as good as I am.' He had a round, brown face and eyes made slits by a permanent smile. Flavia liked him. She liked Barbarus, too. He was a quiet young man in his early twenties who played the harp beautifully. He reminded her a little of her tutor Aristo.

The thought of Aristo sent an unpleasant pang of guilt through Flavia. She knew that he and Alma and Caudex must be sick with worry, despite the reassuring letter she had left on her beside table. She must write to them again and tell them they were well and on the trail of Uncle Gaius. She wouldn't mention that the trail had gone cold. Flavia pushed her unease away and turned to Casina, 'what was that song you were singing earlier today? I haven't heard it before.'

'I'm writing a new pantomime for the governor of Volubilis,' said Narcissus, tossing his tawny locks. 'It's called The Death of Antonius and Cleopatra, based on an account of Antonius's life I recently came across in Alexandria.'

'I know about Cleopatra,' said Flavia. 'She was the beautiful and powerful young queen of Egypt in the time of Julius Caesar.'

'It's a myth that Cleopatra was beautiful.' Narcissus gave Casina a wink. 'But she was charismatic and attractive.'

Casina looked at Flavia. 'Did you know that Cleopatra and Marcus Antonius had three children?'

'I know she bore Julius Caesar a son called Caesarion,' said Flavia. 'But their enemies killed him.'

'Yes,' said Casina. 'Caesarion died when he was only seventeen. But Cleopatra had other children with Marcus Antonius: twins called Cleopatra Selene and Alexander Helios, and later a boy.'

'Twins!' said Flavia, and looked at her friends. 'Sun and Moon. Did they survive? Or were they murdered like Caesarion?'

'They survived.' Casina's plain face was animated with excitement. 'Cleopatra's daughter grew up to marry a Numidian king called Juba II, who had been educated in Rome. He was a wise and good king, and very handsome.' She glanced at Narcissus.

He gave her another wink. 'Cleopatra Selene and Juba II ruled the kingdom of Mauretania from their royal palace in Volubilis,' he said. 'Their descendants are no longer in power, but their memory is still greatly revered. That's why I'm writing about Antonius and Cleopatra. Come!' He stood up. 'We still have about half an hour of light. Let's practise the song.'

Jonathan followed Narcissus and the others to a flat sandy space beneath some towering palm trees. The sun had almost set and the trees threw their long slender shadows across the sandy ground. A little pack of black and white birds fluttered away, alarmed by the arrival of so many strangers in their private oasis.

Narcissus glanced at Hanno. 'We'll sing this to the tune of White Peacock.' To the others, he said. 'Join in when you feel ready.'

Jonathan nodded and gave his harp a strum; it was one of Barbarus's spares. Beside him Nubia held her flute, and Flavia jingled a small tambourine. Lupus was ready, too, with a homemade drum slung over one shoulder and a sistrum stuck in his belt.

Round-faced Hanno nodded the beat, then began to play his buzzy aulos. After a moment the four friends looked at each other in delight; it was a popular tune from Alexandria that Aristo had taught them a few months before, in happier times. He had called it 'Song of Isis'.

Narcissus raised his eyebrows in surprise as the four friends easily joined in with the song, then he grinned and nodded his approval.

Casina held a sheet of papyrus and Jonathan could see where some of the lines had been crossed over and rewritten.

'*Cleopatra was twenty-nine,*' sang Casina. '*when she met the handsome Roman commander Marcus Antonius. And though her blood was Greek, she dressed as Egyptian Isis, in lapis lazuli and tissue of gold.*'

Narcissus moved forward in a slinky, seductive walk: his imitation of Cleopatra. Jonathan allowed himself a smile; Narcissus was really very good.

'*Marcus Antonius looked like Hercules,*' sang Casina. '*Or so they said.*'

Narcissus swivelled as she sang this, turning his masculine profile to the audience. *'And he was the bravest commander,'* sang Casina, *'in the history of Rome, nay the World!'*

Beside Jonathan, Flavia stopped banging her tambourine. 'Wait a moment!' she cried.

Narcissus sighed and rolled his kohl-rimmed eyes at her. 'What?'

'Excuse me for interrupting, but didn't Cleopatra's ships flee at some battle? And didn't Antonius panic and run after her? Our tutor Aristo said he practically handed the victory to Octavian. And isn't that why all his men deserted and went over to the other side? Because they thought Marcus Antonius was a big coward?'

Narcissus was glaring at Flavia, his hands on his hips.

'Actually,' said Jonathan, 'I think she's right. We studied the battle of Actium with our tutor.'

'Have you never heard of poetic licence?' scowled Narcissus. 'Everybody knows writers stretch the truth sometimes. I want this performance to stress the noble qualities of Antonius and Cleopatra.' He turned back to Casina and Hanno. 'Carry on.'

Hanno started up again and the others joined in as Casina sang: *'He was the bravest commander in the history of Rome, nay the World. They say Fortuna favours the Brave. But Fortuna favoured not him. Fortuna favoured Octavian, adopted son and great-nephew of Julius Caesar. Antonius could never beat young Octavian, destined to be Augustus. At their final conflict, it took no prophet to predict that Antonius would not profit.'*

Jonathan watched Narcissus twist and turn as he

moved forward through an invisible mass of enemies, thrusting, parrying, deflecting a blow with his imaginary shield.

'*Finally,*' sang Casina, '*abandoned by his men, his armies, and Fortuna, the cruellest blow came. Antonius heard that his life's true love – Cleopatra – had taken her own life. Or so they said. And so brave Antonius did not hesitate. He plunged the sharpened blade into his belly.*'

As Narcissus thrust the invisible sword into his stomach, a flow of bright red poured out. Beside Jonathan, Flavia and Nubia stiffened.

'Relax,' he whispered to them. 'It's just a piece of red silk. He did the same trick with the cloak in Sabratha.'

'*But his life's true love – Cleopatra – was not dead,*' sang Casina. '*She had only loosed a rumour, lest Antonius be angry at her flight from battle. She had taken refuge in a tower, a tomb, a mausoleum. When she heard that Antonius lay dying and crying out her name, she sent her servants to bring him to her.*'

Narcissus writhed convincingly on the sandy ground.

'*Looking down from her lofty vantage,*' sang Casina, '*Cleopatra pitied her Antonius, and lowered a rope to lift him up. For she feared to open the lower doors, lest her enemies come upon her. There never was such a pitiful sight. Or so they say. Poor Antonius rising into the air, his hands uplifted, as if to some goddess.*'

'How cruel!' cried Flavia. 'What a cowardess!'

Jonathan and the others stopped playing as Narcissus sat up and twisted angrily towards her. 'Now what?'

'Well, that poor man was dying from a wound in his stomach. They're the most painful, aren't they, Jonathan?'

'Yes,' he muttered, 'but this might not be the best time—'

'And Cleopatra wouldn't even let poor Antonius in the front door. She hauled him up on a rope, like ... like a piece of furniture! That's so cowardly and cruel!'

Narcissus stood up, brushed himself off and stalked angrily towards Flavia.

'Are all girls from Rome as bossy as you?' he said from between gritted teeth.

Jonathan quickly stepped forward to distract the dancer: 'Sir, why don't we lift you to an upper floor of the scaena?'

Narcissus turned his handsome, angry face from Flavia to Jonathan. 'What?'

'I was thinking,' said Jonathan. 'You know how the actor is sometimes lowered to the stage on a rope hanging from a crane?'

'Of course I do! It's called *deus ex machina*. What of it?'

'Why not have *homo ad caelum*? Lift a man to the top of the scaena?'

Narcissus snorted and tossed his hair. 'I'm a pantomime dancer, not an acrobat.'

'I know. But think how impressive it would be if Antonius ascends, writhing in pain and with his arms uplifted.'

Narcissus cocked his head to one side. 'Go on.'

'I could wait at the top in a Cleopatra mask,' said Jonathan, 'waving my arms as if in distress. I think the crowd will love it,' he added.

Narcissus nodded slowly, then opened his mouth to say something.

'But is it true?' persisted Flavia, her hands on her

hips. 'Did Cleopatra really—'

'Be quiet!' said Jonathan and Narcissus together.

They looked at each other in surprise. Then Narcissus chuckled and slung his muscular arm around Jonathan's shoulders. 'That's one of the craziest ideas I've ever heard,' he said, 'but when we get to Volubilis, I think we should do it.'

That night after dinner, the three girls went behind some date palms to improvise a latrine. Nubia was carrying the torch and on their way back to the camp she saw the glint of metal on the ground.

She bent to pick it up.

'Behold!' she said. 'Silver coin.'

'What have you found?' asked Flavia, stopping and coming back.

'Coin on chain. It is necklace.' Nubia's golden eyes grew wide in surprise. 'Behold it is Casina. Casina looking angry.'

'Casina on a coin? Impossible. Let me see!' Flavia snatched the coin from Nubia's hand. 'Great Juno's peacock!' she exclaimed. 'It does look like Casina. Only uglier and in a bad mood. It's a silver denarius,' she said, examining it in the flickering light of Nubia's torch. 'It looks old. What does this inscription say? Something about ... Cleopatra. Great Juno's peacock! It's not Casina. It's Cleopatra!'

'Oh, you found it!' cried Casina, running up to them. 'Praise Isis! You found my necklace.'

Flavia looked up at her. 'This is yours?'

'Yes,' she said breathlessly. 'It must have fallen off.'

'It's Cleopatra, isn't it?' Flavia handed her the coin-on-a-chain.

Casina did not answer. She was fumbling with the clasp. Flavia stepped behind her to help and Nubia held the torch a little closer.

'Cleopatra is obviously special to you,' said Flavia.

'It's just a trinket,' said Casina. 'It doesn't mean anything. A friend gave it to me.'

Flavia finished doing the clasp and patted Casina on the back. 'You know,' she said, with a glance at Nubia, 'you could almost have posed for that portrait of her.'

'She's not very pretty, is she?' said Casina, pulling the coin away from her neck so she could look at the profile of Cleopatra. 'Hooked nose, jutting chin, beetling brows ... The first time I saw a picture of her I couldn't believe it.' Casina tucked the coin back under the neck of her tunic, and turned away. 'But they say she was charming and witty, and that she had a lovely voice.'

'You have a lovely voice,' said Nubia softly.

Casina gave a bitter laugh. 'Ironic, isn't it? I have her plain looks, but not her charm or wit.'

'I'm sure Nubia didn't mean that,' said Flavia. 'She just meant that—'

Casina rounded on them, her wet eyes gleaming in the golden torchlight. 'Is it a crime to admire a woman who was ugly, and yet won the love of the greatest man in Rome?'

'We didn't mean—'

'It's all right for you. You're both pretty. But I—' Casina burst into tears. 'Oh why don't you just leave me alone?'

With that, she turned and ran towards the camp.

Nubia and Flavia stared at each other in amazement.

'I only said she looked like Cleopatra,' protested Flavia.

'I think she is hiding secret,' said Nubia quietly.

'That she's in love with Narcissus?' said Flavia.

'Of course,' said Nubia softly. 'But I am thinking there is something else.'

SCROLL XI

On the seventh day out of Sabratha, Flavia almost fell off the camel and broke her neck.

It was mid-morning of an overcast day. They had walked for two hours first thing, to warm themselves after the cold night. But now it was getting hot and the ground was littered with strange grey rocks, so they were riding. Flavia had grown so used to the rocking motion of the camel that it sometimes put her to sleep. She had been nodding off when Selene stumbled on something and lurched forward, nearly pitching Flavia onto sharp stones and sunbaked earth.

'Oh!' she cried, and felt Nubia's arms around her waist.

'Here,' said Nubia. 'Come back to middle of mattress. Do not worry. I hold you.'

'Thank you, Nubia. Oh! I dropped the parasol. It's our only one!' She leaned out to look for it on the stony ground behind her. And she screamed.

Assan uttered a high 'loo-loo-loo-loo-loo!' and as the camels slowed their pace he rode up beside the girls.

'What is it?' he cried, reining in his camel. 'What happened?'

'There are skeletons down there,' said Flavia. 'Human skeletons!'

By now the caravan had stopped and Macargus was making his way back to see what the problem was. Nubia gave Selene a gentle hiss and the camel sank to her knees.

'Look!' cried Flavia, scrambling off the camel. 'That's what the camel tripped on.' She pointed to a human skull a few paces away.

'Behold,' said Nubia softly. 'There are myriads.'

Flavia saw that the strangely-shaped grey rocks along the trail were not rocks, but human bones.

'They are from slaves,' said Assan, sinking down to their level as his camel knelt. 'From slave-caravan leading to Sabratha, Oea or Leptis Magna.' He dismounted.

'What is wrong?' said Macargus, coming up on camelback. 'Why do you stop?'

'Skeletons. Everywhere,' said Flavia with a shudder. 'Oh, it's horrible. I don't even want to touch them. Assan, will you fetch my parasol?' Assan nodded and stepped over some bones to retrieve her parasol. 'They're so small,' murmured Flavia, staring at one of the skeletons. 'Does the sun shrink them?'

Assan shook his head. 'No. These are the bones of children. Look there!' He pointed to a small scrubby bush. Beside it lay two-medium sized skeletons with their arms around each other. The bones were clean and white, all except for the hands, where some sinews still remained.

'They were sisters,' said Macargus, 'or maybe friends.' He made the sign against evil.

'How can you tell they're girls?' said Flavia, horrified.

'Hip bones. And their teeth show they were young. About your age.'

'How did they die?' asked Jonathan. He and Lupus had also dismounted.

'Thirst, probably,' said Assan. 'The slave-drivers tell them there is water just ahead. Just over the next ridge, they say: the well is just ahead. They say that to make them keep going. But they are usually lying. They only give them one or two squirts of water per day.'

Macargus shook his head sadly. 'Slave-drivers can afford to losing many slaves. They are still making good profit. Now come. We must continue. It is eight more hours to the next well and we do not want to be suffering their fate.'

As they turned to get back onto their camels, Flavia saw the sinister black-robed figure of Iddibal standing alone at the end of the caravan. As usual, he was staring out towards the horizon.

The following morning was overcast and grey, but like the previous day, it soon grew hot. They stopped briefly around noon for a latrine break, and as the three girls returned to join the others, Nubia pointed to the south.

'Behold!' she said. 'Caravan this way comes.'

Flavia turned and shaded her eyes. Tiny dark pips seemed to wobble in the shimmering heat haze above the horizon.

'They look like they're floating,' said Flavia. 'Are they coming toward us?'

'Are you sure it's a caravan?' said Casina.

'Nubia is correct,' said Assan. 'It is a caravan coming. Come, we will walk the camels.' He gave his special cry of 'Bokka, bokka! Bok! Bok!' to the camels, and the caravan groaned into motion.

Half an hour later the approaching caravan could

be clearly seen: four riders and more than a hundred people on foot.

At first Flavia thought they were old men and women, but as they came closer she saw that they were little black-skinned children.

'Oh, Nubia!' she cried. 'They're almost all children. They look like walking skeletons.'

'Behold,' said Nubia softly. 'It is slave-caravan.'

Assan walked up abreast of them, his camel on its lead behind him.

'Is it true, Assan?' asked Flavia. 'Are they slaves?'

'It is true.'

'Can't we do something? Can't we help them?'

'What could you do?' said Assan. 'There are more than one hundred. They are not our property.'

'We could buy them and then set them free!' said Flavia, and then her shoulders slumped. 'But we don't have any money.'

'Even if you did have money to buy them all, you cannot just set them all free here in the desert. They will die. That is why they wear no chains. There is nowhere for them to go. You would also need to feed them, clothe them, take care of them—'

'Yes! We could do that. And when they're better then we could take them back to their families.'

'Their families are probably dead. Murdered by the slave-traders. If they are not dead, they are hiding in the bush. We would never find them. These slaves come from hundreds of miles. Perhaps,' he added, 'some of their own parents even sell them for money, if they are very poor.'

Nubia was trembling, and Flavia began to cry. 'What can we do? We can't just watch them pass by.'

'I know what we can do,' said Jonathan, coming up from behind. 'We can show them mercy. Assan, please ask Macargus to stop our caravan. Just for a short time.'

Assan nodded and gave his high 'loo-loo'. The caravan slowed to a halt.

'Lupus,' said Jonathan. 'Bring those two skins of water. Flavia and Nubia, bring that basket of dates we collected at the last oasis.'

Lupus and the girls went to get the water and dates, then followed Jonathan. When the little slave-children saw the boys with their water-skins they ran eagerly and let Jonathan or Lupus direct jets of water into their mouths.

Flavia and Nubia gave each child a single date. Flavia knew that was all they could spare. Tears were running down Nubia's cheeks as the children kissed their hands and feet. Many of the children were holding out their hands to them, pleading in their own language. But now one of the slave-drivers was looming up on his camel. He wore a black caftan and a black turban, and only his angry eyes were visible. He cracked his whip and shouted at the children in some strange glottal language.

Suddenly another figure in black robes was standing beside them. It was Iddibal, and for the first time Flavia heard him speak. She could not understand his words, for he spoke the same harsh language as the slave-driver, but the gist was clear. The man on the camel spat onto the ground, but he did not use his whip again. He merely kicked his camel forward. The children turned to follow him, throwing many yearning glances behind them.

'*If anyone gives even a cup of cold water to one of these little ones because of me, he will not lose his reward,*' quoted Jonathan softly.

'What?' said Flavia.

Jonathan's eyes were fixed on the retreating column. 'It's something our Messiah said: *I was hungry, and you gave me food. I was thirsty, and you gave me water. I was naked, and you gave me clothes.*'

'But we didn't give them clothes. Or enough food and water. Some of them will die. Do you really think your Messiah will reward us for giving them a single date and a mouthful of water?' She put an arm around Nubia, who was sobbing silently. 'Don't you think he wants us to do something more?'

'Yes,' said Jonathan. 'I know he does.'

SCROLL XII

They remounted their camels and the caravan rode on, silent and subdued.

Late in the afternoon of the following day they caught sight of a town on the horizon. Date palms and curious men lined the road as they approached the town walls, which were built of doughy grey mud baked hard by the desert sun.

'Behold!' said Nubia. 'City of Bread.'

'It does look like it's made of bread,' agreed Flavia and turned eagerly to Assan, riding beside them. 'Is this it? Is this Volubilis?'

Assan laughed. 'Volubilis is another thousand miles further west,' he said. 'That is Cydamus.'

The roadside was becoming crowded with men and boys who stared at them with open mouths. Some of the boys ran after the camels and cheered.

'Where are all the women, Assan?' asked Flavia.

He pointed straight ahead and Flavia saw dark, veiled shapes lining the crenellated ramparts above. As she looked the women began to ululate their greetings.

The caravan did not enter Cydamus, but veered right at the town gate and followed the wall round to a shady grove of palms. They came to a halt outside the walls of a caravanserai, and led the camels to a nearby well.

Flavia climbed off Selene, but she did not forget to pat the camel's head and feed her a date, as Nubia had taught her to do.

Narcissus and Casina came up to them. 'Assan tells me there's a Roman-style bath-house over there,' said Narcissus. 'Through the grove.'

'Did you say a bath-house?' said Jonathan, coming up to them. 'I would kill for a long soak and a massage.'

Lupus grinned, then narrowed his eyes at a group of grubby boys who were approaching them. The boys scattered and regrouped a short distance away. Flavia noticed their tunics were no more than rags, and that some of them had pink and swollen eyes.

'I doubt if the baths here will be up to Roman or Alexandrian standards,' said Narcissus, 'but Assan says the water is naturally hot and there are separate sections for men and women. I want you all to bathe, because we've just been invited to spend the night with one of the local dignitaries. He wants us to perform and in return he's giving us dinner and a bed.'

'Of course we'll go to the baths,' cried Flavia. 'You won't be able to keep me away.' She caught Nubia's hand. 'Are you coming, Casina!'

'Put on your best clothes after,' called Narcissus after them. 'And it wouldn't hurt to wear a little make-up, either. I'll meet you back here in an hour and a half.'

Two hours later, a small black boy guided them into Cydamus.

Flavia and her friends looked round in wonder as they passed through the arched gate of the town. Everything seemed to be made of dough: houses, courtyards, arches, deep square windows – some appearing so soft that she was tempted to touch it. When her fingertips encountered stuccoed mud brick, rough and hard, she was almost disappointed.

Everything was connected in this doughy town. This arch merged into that house and the walls bulged out into benches at ground level. Here was a long covered street, like a zebra-striped square tunnel with a bright section beneath a light well and then a dark patch where the sun did not reach, then bright, then dark, and so on. And there was another covered side street, dark except for the bright arch at the end and the silhouette of a turbaned man who stood framed for a moment, and then was gone.

Palm trees rose up from hidden courtyards. The doors of the houses were made of palm wood. Even the roofs of the street were made by laying palm fronds over date-palm trunk beams, then covering this with mud. It was almost chilly on this March evening, but Flavia knew these tunnel streets would be deliciously cool in the blazing heat of July and August.

Presently they reached a house with double doors and the boy led them inside. Like the rest of the town, it was made of dough-coloured brick, but its plan was almost Roman: rooms off a large central courtyard, and in the centre of this courtyard, a well.

It was in this courtyard that they were to perform the pantomime. The elder was a jolly fat man named Ipalacen. He greeted them, then he and his sons and other village men happily crowded the courtyard to watch. Women and children lined the balustrade of the flat roof above.

On a raised wooden platform which seemed made for the purpose, Narcissus danced the story of Diana and Actaeon. For the first time, Flavia and her friends played the music. The performance went well, and was enthusiastically applauded with shouts from the men and ululation from the women.

Afterwards, they filed into a high-vaulted dining room for dinner. Flavia had borrowed one of Casina's long tunics, of a blue so pale it was almost white. She had lined her eyes with black kohl and shaded her eyelids with blue stibium. She felt clean and refreshed. And ravenous.

Feeling eyes on her, she glanced up to see the village elder smiling at her. She smiled back politely. Ipalacen was a fat, cheerful man in his fifties, with dark brown skin and a grizzled beard. He wore a pink turban and matching gown, and had thrust a curved dagger into his emerald-coloured sash. He raised his plucked eyebrows at her and gestured towards a large bowl in the centre of the carpeted earth floor.

'Please,' said a brown-skinned Phoenician with a small goatee. 'Our esteemed elder asks you to sit and eat. I am Bodmelqart, your translator,' he added.

Flavia nodded her understanding and sat between Nubia and Jonathan. Lupus, Narcissus, Casina and the two musicians sat on her left. Ipalacen took up a position on the floor to her right, beside Jonathan. Instantly a small black boy ran to stand behind the elder, and began to wave a goat-hair fly-flap. Bodmelqart joined them too, and three of Ipalacen's sons completed the party. They were swarthy young men in their mid-twenties with narrow eyes and bad teeth.

Flavia frowned at the large bowl before her. It was full of a glutinous, slightly translucent porridge of some kind, studded with chunks of pink meat. Flies were crawling on it. Ipalacen and his sons dug into it with their right hands, and used three fingers to form it into balls. They then dipped these balls into little bowls of sauce.

Flavia was not sure she liked the grainy, glutinous texture of the porridge, but she was hungry, and knew it would be impolite to refuse. So she awkwardly used the fingers of her right hand to form a clumsy ball and tasted it. Barley? No: millet. It was flavourless so she dipped her second ball in some sauce. It tasted like some sort of date paste mixed with olive oil and pepper. That made it a little more palatable. She tentatively tried one of the pink chunks of meat. It was slightly acrid and greasy. She could not identify it.

Beside her, Ipalacen used the tablecloth to wipe his greasy mouth. He said something to Bodmelqart, who turned to Narcissus.

'The esteemed elder says he greatly enjoyed your show.'

'Please thank your esteemed elder,' replied Narcissus.

'The esteemed elder asks if you enjoy the lizard.'

'The lizard?' said Narcissus.

'Our food. Is great delicacy.'

On Flavia's right Jonathan gagged and she had to pat him hard on the back.

'Yes,' said Narcissus. 'Delicious.'

'He wonders,' continued Bodmelqart, 'how much you would ask for the tambourine player?'

Flavia looked up sharply from trying to form a ball of millet.

'Excuse me?' said Narcissus.

Bodmelqart nodded and smiled, revealing a gap

where his front teeth should have been. 'The esteemed elder would like to buy from you the blonde one.'

Narcissus glanced at Flavia and laughed. 'Oh, she's not a slave.'

'Ha ha ha,' said Bodmelqart after a brief exchange. 'He says you are very clever at bargain. He says he will offer you one hundred thousand sesterces.'

'What?' gasped Narcissus and stared in wonder at Ipalacen. Then he composed himself. 'I am sorry but I cannot sell the tambourine-player. Flavia Gemina is a freeborn Roman girl. Also, she is extremely bossy and would give your esteemed elder a headache.'

Bodmelqart explained this to Ipalacen, who smiled at Flavia as he crammed a crumbly ball of porridge into his mouth. A fly was crawling on his rubbery lips, and as he pushed in some stray crumbs, the fly went in too. Flavia stared in horror as he chewed and swallowed. Without taking his eyes from her, Ipalacen said something in his glottal language.

This time Bodmelqart addressed Flavia directly. 'He says he has never seen a girl with grey eyes and hair the colour of camel fur. He says you are very desirable. He says if he cannot buy you, then he would like to marry you.'

Flavia tried not to choke on her millet porridge. 'What did he say?' she said.

Bodmelqart beamed. 'Our esteemed leader would like to marry you.'

Beside him, Ipalacen dabbed his greasy chin and nodded enthusiastically.

Flavia resisted the impulse to run screaming from the room. Instead, she took a deep breath and turned to the fat man in the pink turban. 'I'm sorry,' she spoke slowly and clearly, 'but I'm too young to marry.'

Bodmelqart translated this and Ipalacen roared with laughter, spraying bits of food back into the communal bowl. He said something to Bodmelqart, who translated: 'Oh, no. Our esteemed leader says you are not too young. You are just right.'

Flavia tried to keep her features composed. 'Please tell him I'm sorry,' she said, 'but I have taken a vow of chastity. A solemn vow to the goddess Diana.'

From a nearby room came the piercing scream of a little girl. Narcissus, Lupus and Jonathan all leapt to their feet.

'Do not be alarmed,' said Bodmelqart. 'A member of the esteemed elder's family is merely unwell.'

'May I help?' asked Jonathan. 'My father is a doctor.'

'Yes, please,' replied Bodmelqart a moment later. 'Our esteemed leader would be most grateful if you could look at his little one.'

A second piercing scream came from the room next door, then the sound of a girl crying.

Jonathan looked at the translator. 'Please take me to her?'

'Now?' said Bodmelqart. He looked around and opened his palms to the ceiling. 'But we are in the middle of a banquet.'

'If you don't mind,' said Jonathan. 'Flavia? Would you like to ... assist me?'

'Oh, yes!' said Flavia and shot him a grateful look. 'Yes, please.'

Bodmelqart rose and explained the situation to

Ipalacen, who scowled and pushed out his fat lower lip like a petulant child.

Flavia followed Jonathan and Bodmelqart into the next room. There were half a dozen brown-skinned young women and girls sitting on a divan around the wall. Three of them held babies. In the centre of the room an old man with a tattered white beard sat on a threadbare carpet. A girl of about nine or ten sat facing him. She was crying.

Bodmelqart gestured towards the girl. 'Her eyes are infected. It is common ailment here. Our medicine-elder applies special salve. But she does not work very well.'

Jonathan squatted beside the girl and brushed away the flies. Gently, he examined her eyes. Flavia saw that her left eyelid had brown paste on it. Her right eyelid was red, and swollen almost shut. The medicine-elder reached out and dipped his calloused thumb in a small bowl of brown paste on a goatskin beside him. Other medicinal items were arranged on the skin: a monkey's head, dried lizards, fragments of ostrich egg and what appeared to be the eyeballs of goats or sheep.

Jonathan quickly examined the doctor's supplies, then said to Bodmelqart: 'Please ask him which of these ingredients your medicine-elder puts in the salve.'

'The usual,' said Bodmelqart, after a brief exchange with the bearded man. 'Powdered ostrich egg and antelope horn mixed with lizard blood and salt, all bound together with goat fat.'

As he spoke the medicine-elder thumbed some of the gritty brown paste onto the girl's right eyelid. He was not gentle and the girl screamed again, though she remained perfectly still, submitting to his treatment.

'Oh, the poor thing!' Flavia turned to Jonathan. 'Doesn't your father have something better than that for eyes?'

'Yes,' said Jonathan grimly. He turned to Bodmelqart. 'Tell him to try some saffron with ground copper flakes in a solution of acacia gum and vinegar.'

Bodmelqart related this to the medicine-elder, who grumbled a reply, gesturing angrily at his goatskin of potions.

'He says saffron is very expensive. Even for our esteemed and wealthy elder.'

Jonathan turned and marched back into the vaulted dining room. Flavia and Bodmelqart hurried after him.

Jonathan halted in front of the fat man and looked down at him. 'Sir,' he said. 'You must give her proper salve. I know it's expensive, but you must use saffron. Otherwise your daughter could lose her sight.'

Instead of translating, Bodmelqart laughed. 'No, no, no, young man,' he said, brushing away a fly. 'She is not the daughter of our esteemed elder. She is his wife number four.'

SCROLL XIII

Flavia pleaded stomach-ache and asked if she could spend the night in the caravanserai, but they told her the gates were already closed for the night.

'Marauders, you understand,' explained Bodmelqart. 'But your sleeping quarters are only a little way from here. If you are tired then I will ask a boy to take you.'

Narcissus glanced at Flavia and then at their host. He rose to his feet. 'I think we should all be going now,' he said. 'We've had a long day. Thank you, sir, for your hospitality.' He nodded politely to Ipalacen.

They all left shortly after, another little black boy leading. By torchlight the streets were ominous and frightening, the black tunnels leading off them like paths to the underworld.

'That poor little girl,' said Flavia to Nubia, who was walking beside her. They were at the front of the group, close behind the boy with the torch. 'Can you imagine being married to that horrible fat man?' Flavia shuddered, then jumped with fright as a hand patted her back. It was Narcissus, giving her his most charming smile.

'Flavia,' he said, slipping an arm around her shoulder. 'How would you like to pay for your trip without performing for us, and earn a few thousand sesterces as well?'

Flavia stared at him. He was very handsome, but his breath smelt of rancid lizard-meat. 'I don't know,' she said. 'What do I have to do?'

'That fat elder was willing to give me a hundred thousand sesterces for you,' he whispered. 'What if I were to pretend to sell you to him, collect the money, and then later you could come and join us at a pre-arranged spot and we could make a hasty escape? I'll split the money with you,' he added.

'No,' hissed Flavia. 'That's a terrible, awful, repulsive idea. No pre-arranged spot and no hasty escapes!'

Narcissus sighed and released her shoulder. 'I suppose it's not such a good idea. Too bad. A hundred thousand would have been useful.'

The next morning the four friends hurried to the cara-vanserai as soon as the town gates opened. There they found Macargus and Assan loading the camels' baskets with fresh supplies of dates, millet, and skins of olive-oil. Jonathan and Lupus were about to help the camel-drivers fill the water-skins when Narcissus hurried up.

'Let's go,' he said to Macargus. 'I don't like this place.'

'Do not be in such a hurry,' said the leader. 'We must replenish our water.'

'Now,' said Narcissus. 'I have a bad feeling about this place.'

'Very well,' sighed Macargus. 'There is another oasis two days from here. We can take on water there.' He signalled to his drivers.

Within a quarter of an hour, the caravan was on the move and by mid-morning the town of Cydamus was only a memory. Once again, the barren desert landscape stretched from horizon to horizon.

The ground was split with frequent shallow gullies, but it was not too stony, and the camels made good progress. Once Macargus shouted a warning and held up his hand. He led the caravan off to the right and Jonathan saw what he had avoided: a deadly cleft in the desert, like a grinning mouth a yard or two wide and twice as deep, but so narrow that you could not see it until you were almost upon it.

As the day grew brighter, Jonathan pulled a fold of his brown cotton turban right over his eyes. He looked around with interest. The fierce desert sun illuminated everything with such brilliance that even through the cloth of his turban he could still see everything clearly. He could see the shrubs below him and a few flat-topped acacias on the northern horizon. He could see the camels up ahead, and the camels behind. He could even see a distant line of black riders approaching from the east.

'What's that?' he called out to Macargus, who was riding at the front of the caravan as usual. 'Another caravan?'

Macargus turned to look back and his cheerful expression turned to one of alarm.

'I don't know,' shouted the caravan leader. 'They're coming from the direction of the town.' He called to Assan and pointed them out.

'Run!' bellowed Narcissus, when he saw the dots on the horizon. 'They're slave-traders! Someone warned me about them last night. He said if they caught us they'd kill us men and take the girls and children as slaves.'

On the camel ahead Flavia and Nubia clutched each other in terror.

'Run!' repeated Narcissus. He closed his papyrus parasol and used it to strike his camel hard on the rear.

At the head of the caravan, Macargus wheeled his camel and began moving back along the line, whipping camels and uttering a shrill ululation. The creatures sensed his urgency and began to speed up. Jonathan and Lupus were almost pitched off their mattress-seat as their camel lurched forward into a bouncing trot.

Jonathan glanced back to see Flavia and Nubia clutching one another. Behind them, the merchants of the caravan were crying out to their various gods; he was surprised to hear one of the cloth merchants calling out to the God of Israel.

Now Macargus was galloping back up along the line of trotting camels. 'We cannot outrunning them!' cried Macargus, his voice jolted by the motion of his camel. 'We just taken on full load of provision. And all camels are bloat with water.'

'If they catch us, we're dead!' cried Narcissus over his shoulder. 'They're armed and we're not.'

'I am having armed,' said Macargus, and he pulled his sword from his scabbard. It was curved, with a wickedly sharp edge. 'And so is Iddibal.'

'There are only two of you,' shouted back Narcissus, 'and at least half a dozen of them.'

'How long ... until they catch up ... with us?' wheezed Jonathan as Macargus came abreast of them. Excitement always made his asthma flare up.

'Quarter of the hour,' said Macargus, glancing back at the approaching riders. 'Maybe little bit more.'

'Then I have an idea,' said Jonathan. 'But we'll need ... a large sheet of beige or brown cloth ...' His chest was growing tighter but he managed to add: 'And we'll all have to work quickly.'

Jonathan crouched in the sand behind a small bush and tried to relieve the tightness in his lungs by breathing from his herb pouch. He looked at his camel trap with satisfaction. One of the cloth merchants had supplied him with a canvas awning. They had stretched this over a narrow gully, then weighted it with rocks and sprinkled it with grey sand to make it look like the desert floor.

He glanced over his shoulder and grunted in satisfaction. The merchants and his friends were riding northwest as if for their lives. The trap lay directly between them and the approaching riders. If the slave-traders kept on in the same direction they would fall into the natural pit. If the trap failed, it was up to them.

Jonathan had collected a little pile of sharp rocks to share with Lupus, who lay on the hot earth beside him. He and Lupus each wore a belt made from a leather sling, so they were ready. Narcissus lay in the dust on the other side of Lupus. He clutched a bejewelled ceremonial sword that he had borrowed from one of the merchants.

Jonathan raised himself up on his elbows. On the other side of the covered gully crouched Macargus and his wicked curved sword. Iddibal was supposed to be with him, but Jonathan could not see him. Perhaps he had gone forward for a better view.

The pursuers were closer now, and he could see there were only four of them, not a dozen as Narcissus had said. The leader seemed to be a heavy man in a pink turban and caftan. Behind him rode three slimmer men in black. All four rode dark camels.

Suddenly Lupus grunted and pointed at the riders.

'What?' said Jonathan, squinting.

In the dust Lupus wrote the name: IPALACEN

'Great Juno's beard!' exclaimed Jonathan. 'You're right. Narcissus! It's our host from last night. And his three sons. He's not a slave-trader!'

Jonathan and Lupus looked at each other in wide-eyed alarm for a moment.

Then Jonathan leapt to his feet and waved his arms. 'Stop!' he cried. 'You'll be killed! Stop!'

'No, Jonathan,' cried Narcissus, 'get down!'

But instead of causing Ipalacen and his sons to slow down, his action made them spur their camels towards Jonathan and the pit.

'Stop!' cried Jonathan.

But it was too late. The riders were onto the tarpaulin now, and he saw the terrible effect of his trap. The camels were pitching forward, their riders crying out in surprise. And now the groans of camels and the screams of men rose up with a cloud of grey dust. Jonathan wheezed and coughed and wrapped the tail of his turban over the lower half of his face.

Suddenly a huge dark shape emerged from the dust-cloud and charged directly towards him. Jonathan felt someone pull him down and it was only by some miracle they weren't trampled by the terrified camel. Jonathan glanced over his shoulder to see the riderless creature running northwest, its saddle dragging behind.

Narcissus released his grip, and Jonathan stood up, his knees trembling violently.

Three camels writhed in the pit, and two men were struggling to their feet. Two others lay silent and still: one crushed beneath a camel and the other with his neck at an unnatural angle. Jonathan shuddered. His plan had been horribly effective. A heavy man in a dirty pink robe was staggering out of the pit, his right arm dangling uselessly by his side. He was uttering curses and heading straight for Narcissus.

Without a word Narcissus ran forward and his blade flashed in the bright sun.

Ipalacen slumped to his knees and something like a dirty pink ball tumbled down and bounced back into the pit.

Jonathan cried out in horror. It was Ipalacen's head.

SCROLL XIV

'What's happening?' cried Flavia from the jouncing back of her fleeing camel. She glanced over her shoulder at the cloud of dust rising into the air on the horizon. 'Oh, Nubia! What if they catch us?'

Flavia was holding tight to Nubia and she could feel her friend's whole body trembling. She remembered that most of Nubia's family had been killed by slave-traders.

Flavia risked another glance behind and her heart nearly stopped as she saw a black camel racing towards them. 'Look, Nubia! They're catching up!' she cried.

Flavia felt Nubia's body tense as she twisted to look, then relax. 'No,' said Nubia. 'Behold, that camel has no rider.'

Assan peeled off from the trotting line of camels to intercept the runaway camel. He managed to slow it down and catch the dangling reins. Then he shouted something and pointed towards a clump of date palms further north.

'He wants us to go there,' said Nubia. She made Selene veer right, along with the other camels, and they soon reached the palms.

'We'll wait here!' cried Assan, coming up beside them on camelback. He turned to the merchants. 'We men will hide among the palms, in case the marauders are still coming. You girls wait behind us.' He turned frightened green eyes on Flavia. 'If we must fight, and if you see we are losing, then you must flee to those mountains. Understand?'

Flavia and Nubia nodded, and Casina on her camel beside them.

Presently they saw some dark dots approaching in the shimmering heat haze. Gradually these dots became six camels, three of them riderless. As the shapes grew bigger and clearer, Nubia could see that one of the camels had two riders on its back.

'Behold!' cried Nubia happily. 'The Jonathan and the Lupus!'

'And I see Narcissus,' cried Casina.

'Praise Juno!' cried Flavia. 'That means they've vanquished the slave-traders.'

Flavia and Nubia hugged each other and smiled at Casina.

Among the palms, Assan and the merchants were rising and moving forward, so Nubia urged her camel forward too. Casina's camel followed, and when they reached the others in the shady grove they all three dismounted.

Narcissus was the first to ride into the palm grove and his camel was the first to kneel. He dismounted and strode forward, like Achilles returning from battle. He gave Casina a quick hug, then slapped Hanno and Barbarus manfully on their backs.

'We got them!' he laughed. 'Killed them all and captured two camels. I see you got the runaway.' He gestured towards the black camel.

'Who were they?' cried Casina.

'Slave-traders, all right,' said Narcissus. 'They were bent on evil.' He glanced over his shoulder at Macargus and the boys. They did not seem to share his elation, but climbed off their camels dejectedly.

'Jonathan! Lupus!' Flavia and Nubia ran forward. 'Are you all right?'

Jonathan glanced back at Lupus, then nodded. 'We're all right,' he said, and added under his breath. 'We'll tell you about it later.'

Flavia looked past him to see Iddibal approaching. The sinister black figure was wiping his sword.

'Behold!' said Nubia. She pointed to the southeast and they all looked to see vultures spiralling down from the blue sky.

Macargus nodded, his eyes inscrutable beneath his indigo turban. 'We have no time for burying them,' he said. 'And we have no time for talking now. Their friends are perhaps soon coming after us. We must leave caravan trail. If you need to do latrine, now is the time. We must leaving as soon as possible.'

As Macargus led the caravan south, they rode into a different kind of desert. The hard-baked grey earth gave way to yellow dirt with stony hillocks, a few acacia trees and many stunted shrubs. The sun grew bigger and redder as it sank to the horizon and soon it sent the long distorted shadows of camels stretching out to their left.

Macargus called a halt as they reached a dry river-bed. Nubia nodded to herself as the camels carefully picked their way down into the wadi. It was bone dry down here, but full of low scrubby brush for the animals to graze on. It was also sheltered. Perhaps most importantly, they would be invisible to anyone in pursuit.

There was no summons from Narcissus to practise a pantomime, and she saw Jonathan walk up to the top of the opposite bank. His footsteps sent pebbles scuttling back down. She and Flavia followed and sat beside him at top of the bank. He was staring west, towards the setting sun, with his back towards the camp.

'We made a terrible mistake,' he said, without turning his head. 'It wasn't slave-traders. It was our host from last night.'

'That fat man in the pink turban?' said Flavia with a shudder. 'The one who wanted to marry me?'

'Ipalacen?' whispered Nubia.

Jonathan nodded. 'Him and his three sons.'

A figure joined them on the crest of the dune. Lupus. He sat silently on the other side of Jonathan.

'One of the sons was crushed by his camel,' continued Jonathan in a flat voice. 'The other broke his neck when he fell. But two were still alive. Ipalacen came charging up out of the gully and before any of us could do anything . . .' Here Jonathan broke off and rested his turbaned head on the tops of his knees.

'What?' whispered Flavia.

Lupus used the side of his hand to make a slicing motion across his throat.

'Someone kills him?' asked Nubia.

'Narcissus.' Jonathan was still staring down and his voice was muffled. 'He chopped off his head and it bounced like a ball.'

'Oh!' cried Nubia and Flavia together.

Jonathan lifted his head and stared west. The sun hovered above the horizon like a huge blood-bloated tick, squashed by the invisible thumb of a giant.

'The third son was still down in the gully,' said Jonathan. 'One of our men, the one in black—'

'Iddibal,' said Nubia.

'Yes. Iddibal cut the son's throat. Without one word. Just cut his throat.'

Lupus grunted wrote in the dust with his finger: THEY WERE SLAVE-TRADERS. NARCISSUS SAID SO.

'I don't think they were, Lupus,' said Jonathan. 'They weren't even armed. Ipalacen had that jewelled dagger stuck in his sash, but that was all.'

Flavia frowned at Jonathan. 'But if they weren't slave-traders, why were they chasing us?' Suddenly she gasped. 'Great Juno's peacock!'

Jonathan turned his head to look at her and Nubia saw that his eyes were red-rimmed beneath his black turban.

'You think you know why?' he asked.

Flavia nodded. 'Last night, when the fat man offered Narcissus a fortune for me, Narcissus whispered that I should pretend to agree so that he could get the money and then later he would help me escape. I said no, of course. It's a terrible idea.'

'In so many different ways,' said Jonathan.

Lupus scribbled in the dust: HE WAS PROBABLY JOKING

'I thought so too,' said Flavia. 'But what if Narcissus *did* agree to sell me after all, and then took the money. Maybe that's why Narcissus was in a such a hurry to leave this morning. Maybe that's why they were pursuing us. Ipalacen paid Narcissus and he wanted his goods: me!'

All four were silent for a while. The setting sun had burst and was bleeding into the horizon, shrinking by the moment.

'What do we do?' asked Nubia.

'There's nothing we can do,' said Jonathan. 'We have to get our money and luggage back, and that means we have to get to Volubilis. This caravan is the only way. Especially now that we're in the middle of the desert. Also, Ipalacen's family might be after us and they'll assume we were all in on the scheme.'

'That is why we camp in wadi,' murmured Nubia.

'In what?'

'Wadi is what we call dry riverbed. From ground level nobody can see us.'

The sun was a shrinking pool of blood on the horizon. The sky above it a livid purple.

'Come,' said Nubia, rising to her feet and brushing off her robe. 'It is becoming dark soon.'

'You're right,' said Jonathan. 'There's nothing we can do about it now. Let's go and eat.'

'But how can we just go and sit and eat with Narcissus?' cried Flavia. 'If my theory is right, then he's a cheat, a liar and a murderer.'

Lupus angrily shook his head at her. He used his sandalled foot to scuff out the previous messages he had written in the dust. Then he squatted and wrote a new one with his finger: I TRUST NARCISSUS. I THINK THOSE MEN WERE BENT ON EVIL.

'Nubia's good at sensing what people are like,' said Flavia, and turned to her friend. 'What do you think about Narcissus? Is he good or evil?'

Nubia considered. 'I do not think he is evil, but I think he hides something,' she said at last.

'Hmmph!' said Flavia, and turned back to the livid horizon.

'Listen, everyone,' said Jonathan, 'If Lupus is right, then we have nothing to fear from Narcissus. But if Flavia is right about Narcissus, and if he suspects we might betray him, then he could murder us, too. Either way, we've got to behave as if everything is normal and treat him exactly as we have in the past.'

In spite of Jonathan's warning to treat Narcissus normally, Flavia could not bear the thought of eating dinner with him. So she decided to sit with the merchants. She had been travelling with them for over a week but had not yet exchanged more than a polite greeting. They were chattering away in a foreign language but when she approached them with her wooden bowl of barley porridge, they all smiled up at her. One of them had a jolly, light-brown face beneath a white turban, and he moved over to make space in their circle. Flavia sat beside him.

'Salvete!' she said.

'Hello, Roman girl,' they replied.

'Flavia,' she said. 'My name is Flavia Gemina, daughter of Marcus Flavius Geminus, sea captain.'

'I am Zabda,' said the jolly one in the white turban. He smiled – showing bad teeth – and introduced her to the others.

They all spoke either good Greek or fair Latin, and she discovered that they had set out from Alexandria and hoped to reach Volubilis. They had been travelling for nearly two months, selling and buying along the way. They took turns telling her about their adventures and warning her about the evil spirits of the desert.

'Are there really evil spirits in the desert?' asked Flavia, putting down her empty bowl.

'Oh, yes,' said Zabda. 'We have all encountered them. Some call them ghuls. Others call them jinns. But I call them demons.'

'What do they look like?'

'They are invisible!' cried a long-nosed merchant in a black turban. 'Sometimes they will mount a camel, and the poor creature – feeling a rider but seeing nobody behind – will run for days and days in pure terror until finally it drops dead. I have seen it happen.'

Several of the other merchants nodded their agreement.

'Some of them look like beautiful girls,' said Baricha, who had bushy black eyebrows beneath an orange turban. 'Once I was wandering in the desert, separated from my comrades, when I saw an oasis. I could see it all! The bright pool of water. The lush palm-grove. And dusky maidens with jars of water on their heads. But just as I reached it: pouf! It disappeared! It was a mirage, caused by succubae: demons who take the form of lovely women.'

'A mirage?' said Flavia.

'Yes. A trick of demons in the desert. You see something that is not there.'

'I saw a demon once,' said Zabda. 'And heard it, too. It was a ghul, a shadow of the night. It had glowing orange eyes and pointed ears. And it made an eerie, whooping noise. They say whenever you hear that sound, someone will soon die.'

Flavia shuddered.

'Oh, look, now you've gone and frightened Miss Roman girl,' said Baricha. 'Senna tea?' He held up a long-spouted brass teapot that had been sitting in the coals of the fire.

'Thank you,' said Flavia. He handed her a small thick glass and continued pouring for the others.

'Oh, it's delicious!' cried Flavia a moment later.

'Sweetened with syrup of figs,' explained Zabda as he accepted his.

'More?' said Baricha to Flavia, at the sight of her already-empty glass.

'Oh, yes please!' said Flavia.

Baricha raised his caterpillar-like eyebrows, but said nothing as he topped her up.

The merchant in the black turban asked Flavia about life in Italia, and soon Flavia was telling them about Titus's massive new arena in Rome, how she and her friends had witnessed the games, and how she had escaped from hippos and crocodiles.

Presently she held out her cup for a fifth helping of tea.

'Are you sure?' said Baricha.

'If you don't mind,' said Flavia, and launched back into her tale.

Finally she noticed that her friends were rising from the other fire to prepare for bed, so she excused herself to join them.

The next morning at dawn Flavia discovered the effects of too much senna tea.

SCROLL XV

All that day almost on the hour, the whole caravan had to stop while Flavia dismounted and ran to squat in the riverbed. Nubia always offered to come with her but each time Flavia refused: it was too horrible and embarrassing.

'Oh, Juno!' she groaned, as she lifted the hem of her blue caftan for the tenth time that day. 'Why me?' She swatted away a buzzing fly.

'We're stopping here for the day, Flavia!' called a voice. Flavia looked up in horror to see Jonathan standing on the bank of the wadi. It ran east to west and they had been following it all day.

'Jonathan!' She angrily stood and pulled down her caftan. 'Don't spy on me!'

'I'm not spying,' he snapped. 'I just wanted to warn you that we're all about to come down here to camp, like last night.'

Flavia glared at him, then turned and marched across the riverbed, up the opposite slope and towards the north. The sun was still fairly high, about three handbreadths above the horizon, and she finally found a shallow dip behind a stunted bush.

Her bowels cramped painfully, but nothing came.

She was as empty as the water-skin hanging from her shoulder.

She knew everyone was annoyed with her because the caravan's water was almost finished. Macargus had been hoping to reach a well today, but her frequent stops had slowed the whole caravan. She knew they would blame her for having to ration their water. There would be no brewing of senna tea tonight.

'It's not my fault,' she muttered to herself. 'Nobody told me senna tea was a laxative. Why are those merchants carrying it anyway? Why would anybody want to buy senna leaf?'

Finally she rose and sighed. She was just about to turn around and set back to the camp when she saw a clump of date palms and a pool of water only a few hundred yards away in the opposite direction of the wadi. Was it a mirage?

She rubbed her eyes, but she could clearly see the pool of water glinting in the sun. She could even make out something like white foam on its surface, and little islands rising up from it. An entire lake! She turned to run back to camp, then hesitated. Better to make absolutely certain it was real. She didn't want people to be even more annoyed with her than they already were.

Flavia had crested half a dozen hillocks, but the lake seemed no nearer.

But now the sun was only a handbreadth from the horizon and she knew she must go back to camp, lake or not. She sighed and turned and began to retrace her footprints, quite clear in the sandy earth.

A moment later she stopped with a cry of delight. Before her, a herd of tiny gazelle swarmed past, heading west. There must have been two hundred of them flowing past in an undulating wave. Every so often one of them would spring up high above the rest, his hooves and horns gleaming in the setting sun.

Flavia was enchanted and watched them out of sight. At last they were gone and now the sun was almost touching the horizon. She hurried on towards camp.

The hoof prints of two hundred gazelle had obliterated her own tracks, but it didn't matter. She knew the camp lay just over the next hillock beyond that little acacia tree.

For the first time all day her bowels felt settled, and her stomach growled. She was ravenous and her mouth watered at the thought of food, even the same old goat and barley stew. She topped the rise, expecting to see friends and camels and campfires in the riverbed below, but there was nothing. Only more scrubby hillocks. It must be the next one.

She reached the crest of the next rise, and just before the sun set she had time to see there was no riverbed here either. Where was it? She was sure it had been here.

Flavia looked frantically around. Nothing but hillocks and a few stunted acacias or tamarisks. No smoke. No sound but the wind.

'Jonathan!' cried Flavia. 'Nubia! Lupus! Where are you?'

Silence. The colour drained from the sky as she ran. It was mauve now with a star or two sparking up high, and trees and bushes flat and black on the horizon. There! That acacia tree. She had passed it earlier.

Presently she stopped running and stood on the top of a rise breathing hard. This was ridiculous. Her friends must be very near. She called out their names, again and again, until her voice was hoarse.

She mustn't despair. She could still find them. They must be just over the next ridge.

'Oh please, Juno,' she prayed. 'Please, Castor and Pollux. Please, God of Jonathan. Let them be there.'

But although it was now quite dark, starlight showed the next dip between hillocks was empty, just like all the others.

She could no longer avoid the truth: she was hopelessly lost.

On Flavia's left, a full moon detached itself from the horizon and floated up, as large and yellow as the yolk of an ostrich egg. And with its rising came the wind. Now she imagined she heard voices calling her. She called back, her voice a hoarse croak. But there was no reply. Only the moaning wind.

She stood on the crest of a hillock, looking around for something familiar. Now that the sun had set, she was cold. But all she had was her long-sleeved cotton caftan and her turban. She unwrapped the turban and folded it double and draped it around her shoulders. It helped a little.

Keeping the rising moon on her left, she headed south. She must reach the wadi soon. Had she passed it somehow?

In the moonlight, the sparse desert vegetation was deceptive. What she took for a distant tree was a little stunted bush, only a few paces away. And what she believed to be a shrub turned out to be a full-grown acacia, its trunk hidden by a rise in the terrain.

Once she saw her three friends standing in a row.

'Here!' she cried, sobbing with relief. 'Here I am!'

But as she ran towards the shapes, they resolved themselves into three tamarisk bushes.

At last she saw what she was sure was the silhouette of a kneeling camel, black against the star-choked sky. She ran towards it and had almost reached it when its outlines shifted to show yet another bush.

But this one had something hiding among its branches. Flavia gasped as a dark shape within the foliage stirred and she found herself staring into the glowing orange eyes of a ghul. 'Bhooo!' it cried, in a deep terrible voice. 'Bhooo!'

With terrible slow deliberation, the ghul raised up its dark arms and floated silently towards her.

All the other apparitions had been her imagination.

But this one was real.

Flavia heard her own scream, strangely remote, and now the star-choked sky was below her, and she was falling down into it.

Flavia woke up sometime after midnight. She lifted herself onto her elbows, then sat up. She had seen Zabda's ghul, and lived!

She rose to her feet, shivering. The cold had taken away her thirst, but not her fear. The wind was still moaning and the full moon stood small and cold at the top of the sky. She scanned the moonlit desert, hoping for the glow of a golden fire among the silver and black.

Nothing.

If she walked, the movement would warm her. But her steps might take her further from the morning's search party.

Suddenly she had an idea. With her teeth she ripped

several strips from the end of her blue cotton turban, each about as long and wide as her forearm. Then she went to the ghul bush. Up close, she saw it was not very tall – only about half her height – and she was able to tie one of the strips to the highest branch. If she left cloth strips on every shrub or bush she passed, they might guide a search-party to her.

And now she needed to walk west. The moon at its zenith was not a reliable marker, so she looked for the brightest star in the constellation of Ursa Minor, the little bear. This was the star her father used on clear nights at sea. She stretched out both her arms, in the position of a crucified man, then turned her whole body, and lifted her right arm to point at the North Star. The North Star on her right should keep her heading west, the direction she knew the caravan was travelling. That way, even if she had wandered too far south or north, at least she would be travelling parallel to her friends.

The moon had started its descent, and once again it cast strange black shadows, making even the smallest shrub appear to be a crouching leopard or a desert demon.

Suddenly she saw something that made her heart sink: a strip of cloth tied to one of the thorny branches.

For the last few hours she had been walking in a giant circle.

Flavia sank onto the sandy ground, too parched to cry. She closed her eyes and prayed to Diana. 'Please help me, goddess Diana.' She spoke in her mind, because her tongue was too dry to form the words. 'You brought me on this quest. Please don't abandon me.'

A moment later, her head was suddenly filled with a sweet, heady scent: myrrh. She opened her eyes and looked at the thorny shrub. She had not tied any pieces of cloth to a myrrh bush.

She crawled closer and sniffed. Sure enough, the stunted tree was the source of the scent. And now that she was closer to it, she saw it wasn't a scrap of her turban. It was someone else's turban, half unwound. Hers was pale blue. This one was indigo blue, or perhaps black.

She hadn't been going in a circle after all.

The much bigger strip of cloth was caught on the sharp thorns of the branches and she carefully pulled it free and wrapped it around her shoulders. It was thicker and warmer than her remnant of cotton turban, and it comforted her. She lay down beneath the myrrh tree's thorny branches and looked up at the moon, sinking down towards the west.

She might not have been walking in circles, but she was still hopelessly lost. She would never see her friends again. Or her dog Scuto or her uncle or Alma. Or her adored father. Of all her regrets, this was the worst: that she had parted from him in anger.

The sweet scent of myrrh enveloped her, heavy as a drug, and she thought that if she had to die, it might as well be here beneath this perfumed tree.

In Flavia's dream, Diana the huntress was running in the moonlit desert.

In one hand she held her bow, and the arrows rattled in her quiver. The joy of the hunt filled her heart and the wind tugged her hair. Presently Diana stopped and looked around, puzzled. She was alone. No hunting dogs. No virgin companions. The desert suddenly seemed an empty, sterile place.

Then the wind brought the distant sound of flutes and tambourines to her ears and she turned.

Coming across the desert was a procession led by a woman. The woman walked sedately, and hundreds of people of all ages followed her. Her head was modestly covered, and as she came closer, Diana saw that the woman held a baby in her arms.

Diana the huntress was alone and in darkness. But this woman had two thousand attendants and their faces showed quiet joy. Who were they?

Diana's chest tightened and she felt a strange unwelcome emotion: a softness that was repulsive to her. Angrily plucking an arrow from her quiver, she notched it to the string and with a single fluid motion she drew the bow and brought the arrow to her cheek. She aimed at the baby, but just as she was about to loose the arrow, the woman stopped and turned and looked directly at her.

The woman's gaze held such tenderness and love, that it was like an arrow in Diana's heart.

'No!' she cried. Her arrow flew off harmlessly into the darkness and her bow fell to the barren desert terrain.

The woman smiled and extended her hand towards Diana. But the huntress's pride would not let her follow.

So the procession moved on. And when it finally passed, Diana was alone.

The first thing Flavia saw the next morning were two vultures hopping in the dust no more than twelve feet away from her.

She tried to scream, but her mouth was too parched to make a sound. She pushed herself up on her elbows, then gasped as three vicious thorns stabbed her scalp. Blinking away tears, she crawled out from underneath the myrrh bush and ran at the macabre birds. They flapped up into the air, then rose higher as she flung stones at them.

They remained circling in the air above her. Nothing she could do would make them go away.

Flavia gazed around in despair. Apart from a few scattered acacia trees, the rolling savannah was as featureless as the sea. No approaching camels. No smudge of campfire smoke. She felt like an ant in the middle of the arena.

The scent of the myrrh bush was making her dizzy so she moved away from it and breathed in the pure desert air. It was still cool but soon it would grow warm. Her head hurt and she pressed her right palm against it. When she brought her hand away she saw blood from the thorns. Taking the indigo strip of cotton from around her shoulders, she tied it as a turban around her head. Then she began to walk west, away from the rising sun. Her shadow stretched out before her, thin and lonely with an elongated turban on its head.

She knew without looking up that the vultures were still circling above her. There was something indescribably evil about their constant presence. A sudden nausea made her stop and rest her hands on her knees and take deep breaths. When the dizziness passed, she lifted her water-skin and directed the spout towards her mouth. Still dry. On an impulse, she opened her little camel leather belt-pouch and searched inside. Right at the bottom was a garlic-shaped, radish-coloured cola-nut. What was it Nubia had said? *These are very good for when you are hungry or tired.*

She put it in her mouth and began to chew. A bitter taste flooded her mouth, so intense that she was tempted to spit it out, but it had made her saliva flow, and that must be good. So she continued to chew, and presently found the taste almost pleasant.

It was a fine pure day, without a breath of wind.

Her step quickened and a tiny seed of hope blossomed in her heart. A low violet smudge lay on the western horizon. Those must be the mountains Macargus had mentioned. Between her and the mountains lay Assan's oasis. She might reach it after all and find her friends waiting, with dates and bread and salt. And cold, sweet water.

Her shadow had shrunk to only twice her height when she came face to face with the ghul.

The creature was perched in an acacia tree. He was golden brown and his ears – sharp as clay shards – pointed straight up. The ghul's back was to her but when her foot scuffed a pebble, he slowly swivelled his entire head to face her. Then he opened huge orange eyes and blinked.

The ghul blinked orange eyes at Flavia, then slowly raised his wings. Silent as a cinder, he drifted up and out of the tree.

Flavia smiled weakly and shaded her eyes with her hand. 'You're only an owl!' she thought. 'A very big desert owl.' She watched him diminish against the blue sky and land in an acacia much further away. Then her eyes focused on something just beyond the place where the owl had settled: something like a black pip wobbling on the heat haze of the horizon. It seemed to be a rider on a lone camel.

Was it another mirage? Or could it really be a rider? And if it was a rider, was he friend or foe?

SCROLL XVI

It was Iddibal, the black-robed camel-driver.

He reached Flavia within a quarter of an hour and leapt off his camel and ran to her and let her drink squirts of water from his goatskin.

'Not too much,' he said presently. He spoke Greek, in a deep growl. 'Not too fast.' Flavia nodded and waited, then sipped a little more. It was so good! She felt tears of gratitude and relief waiting to squeeze out, but they would have to wait. She was still too dehydrated.

'How did you find me?' she croaked at last.

'Your two friends.' He pointed up.

Flavia tipped back her head and saw the two vultures circling overhead in the hot blue sky.

'They guide me straight to you,' Iddibal continued in his deep-voiced Greek, and he helped her mount his black camel. She felt the familiar forward surge as the camel straightened his hind legs, and as the camel extended its forelegs she rocked back against Iddibal's chest, as comforting as her father's. Iddibal turned the camel and as they started east, towards the sun, Flavia took regular little sips from the waterskin.

She was exhausted physically and emotionally and the comforting swaying of the camel soon caused her to doze off. Then something jerked her awake and she saw her friends waving from the shade of an acacia tree. She felt Iddibal's chest expand and then he uttered a huge ululation and waved his right arm.

'All this time the caravan was behind me,' whispered Flavia in amazement. 'I was ahead of you.'

'Yes. We spend night and day search for you.'

'Oh,' said Flavia in a small voice. 'I'm sorry.'

'I must tell you something else,' he said.

'Yes?'

'The men who were pursuing us. Ipalacen and sons. They were bad. They have knife hidden in clothes. They mean to steal you for slaves and kill us.'

'They did?'

'Yes. So do not be angry with the pretty dancer. He helps to save your life.'

Her friends greeted her and gave her dates and bread, but they did not have time to linger, for they had now been two days without water. Iddibal's goatskin had contained the last of it.

Flavia slept on her camel, in Nubia's arms, but presently stinging sand and the howl of wind woke her.

The camels had been walking beside the wadi – the dry riverbed – and now Macargus indicated that they should go down into it and make camp, even though it was not yet noon.

'Shouldn't we keep going?' Flavia asked Nubia, pulling the tail of her indigo turban across her mouth and nose.

'No,' said Nubia, and her expression was grim. 'In sandstorm you should always be taking shelter. They sometimes last three days,' she murmured.

Macargus and his two camel-drivers arranged the kneeling camels as a windbreak, then struggled to erect low tents to keep out the worst of the storm.

Finally they all rested in the grey half-light of the black goatskin shelter. Outside the wind howled and groaned. The camels closed their double-lashed eyes and chewed their cuds stoically; they had drunk deeply three days previously and were unperturbed. It was their riders who needed water.

Nobody accused her, but Flavia knew it was all her fault. If she had not drunk five glasses of senna tea and held up the caravan with her latrine-breaks, they would have reached Assan's oasis by now.

Nobody said so, but she also knew that if this howling sandstorm blew for more than a day, they might end up as bleached bones in the wadi.

Mercifully, the sandstorm abated the following day and they slowly packed the camels and continued west. Now there was sand everywhere: in their mouths, in their hair, in their clothes.

In silence they swayed towards the violet hills, now clear and jagged on the horizon. They travelled all that afternoon, right through the moonlit night and into the morning. Nubia had never been so thirsty.

As the sun rose she saw they had almost reached foothills, and that there was a gully up ahead with a promising fringe of something dark: date-palms.

Around noon that day the camels broke into an eager trot. Unlike their riders, they were not desperate for water, but they could smell the oasis and they sensed it meant rest.

At last they were there, by a blue pool of water. The

camels knelt without being told. Flavia was still weak, so Nubia helped her dismount. Then the two of them followed the others to the pool.

Nubia dipped her hands in the water, and splashed her face. 'Do not drink too much, Flavia,' she croaked, when she was able to speak. 'After so long, too much water is deadly. Just take little sips.' The water was slightly stagnant, but she could tell it was not bad.

'Oh!' cried Flavia. 'It's the most delicious thing I've ever tasted.'

The others were beside them, splashing and laughing and drinking.

'Don't drink too much!' cried Macargus hoarsely. 'It's dangerous to drink too much.'

Lupus waded out into the middle of the pool and fell backwards with a splash. When he rose up his wet tunic clung to his body and Flavia could see how skinny he had become.

'Dates!' cried Nubia, pointing up. They looked up and saw the tree laden with massive clusters of dates, some green, some yellow, some orange and some brown.

Lupus whooped and came splashing out of the pool. Then he tossed a stone up into the branches. This sent a shower of ripe dates raining down on their heads.

Assan ascended one of the palm-trunks as nimbly as a monkey and cut down more clusters. Man and beast devoured the sweet brown fruit.

'They're ambrosia!' laughed Flavia. 'The best thing I've ever tasted!'

Nubia nodded. 'Now you are knowing why I love dates!'

★

That night Assan slaughtered their last goat and they all feasted together on goat stew and sour camel-milk pancakes. For dessert they had more dates washed down with date-sweetened mint tea. Because they intended to spend the next day resting in the oasis, they stayed up until almost midnight, singing and playing the happiest songs they knew.

Lupus woke sometime in the early hours, bloated and needing to use the latrine. Not wanting to awaken the others, he tiptoed around the moonlit forms of sleeping people and camels and went into the palm grove.

On his way back to camp, his sharp ears caught the murmur of voices. Following the sound, he discovered Narcissus and Casina standing in a clearing among lofty date palms. The moon shed a silver light on them, making their shadows – and those of the palms – ink-black.

Casina was weeping and Narcissus was patting her back in a brotherly manner.

'Oh, I wish we were home in Alexandria!' sobbed Casina. 'I hate the desert. I hate the sand and the wind and the flies and the heat and the cold.'

'Shhh. Be brave. We'll be in Volubilis soon,' said Narcissus. 'Just a few more weeks.'

Lupus crept a little closer and peeped out from behind a palm tree.

'And then what?' hissed Casina. 'What happens if the procurator won't pay you to perform for his festival? You've been telling everyone he invited you, when he didn't. For all we know, he might hate pantomime.'

'Shhh!' said Narcissus. He glanced around to make sure they were alone, and Lupus pulled his head back behind the palm trunk.

'He won't hate pantomime,' Lupus heard Narcissus say. 'Nobody hates pantomime. If he won't pay us, we'll offer to do it for free. After all, we'll be rich soon enough.'

'What?' whispered Casina. 'You think the procurator will just hand over Cleopatra's treasures? They probably don't even belong to him. They probably belong to the SPQR.'

'So we'll have to prepare the citizens a little,' came Narcissus's voice. 'That's why we're doing the Death of Antonius and Cleopatra.'

Lupus edged his head out from behind the palm trunk. Narcissus was holding Casina by her shoulders, at arms' length. She was staring miserably at the ground.

'As soon as the performance ends,' continued Narcissus, 'everyone will be full of pity and admiration for Antonius and Cleopatra. That's when I'll tell them who you are. They'll demand the governor give you compensation and he'll hardly be able to refuse. After all, the whole point of his festival is to gain the admiration of his subjects.'

'I don't care about riches,' pouted Casina, and lifted her homely face towards his. In the silver light of the moon, Lupus could see her eyes were swollen with weeping. She sniffed. 'All I want is you.'

'And you have me.' Narcissus pulled her into his arms and kissed her.

Lupus's eyebrows went up in surprise. Everyone knew Casina loved Narcissus, but nobody had suspected he liked her in return. He was so handsome and she was so plain. Now, with a little moan of pleasure, she melted into his arms. Lupus wrinkled his nose in distaste and turned to go, but Casina's next words stopped him cold.

'Would you love me,' she said, 'if I wasn't the great-granddaughter of Cleopatra Selene and King Juba? If I was just an ordinary girl, without royal blood, would you still love me?'

'Of course, my little gazelle,' said Narcissus. 'But you *are* Cleopatra's descendant and you *do* have royal blood, and when you claim your heritage we will become powerful as well as rich.'

SCROLL XVII

The next morning Lupus woke to the sound of music and the smell of camel-milk pancakes. He stared up at the infinite blue sky. Had he been dreaming last night? Was Casina really a descendant of the famous Cleopatra? Was Narcissus really planning to gain power by revealing her identity? But how? He had to tell the others.

He sat up and pushed away his blanket.

It was a glorious fresh morning in the oasis, with the tall palms throwing cool blue shadows across the sandy ground. Not far away, Flavia, Jonathan and Nubia were practising 'Cleopatra's Theme' with Casina and the two musicians. Over by the well, Assan and Iddibal checked the camels' feet for thorns and wounds. And further beyond, in a clearing among the palms he saw the merchants examining their goods and chatting together happily. They must all have been up for hours.

'Good morning, Lupus!' came a voice from behind him.

Lupus turned to see Narcissus squatting by the coals of last night's fire with Assan's iron pan.

'I told them to let you sleep,' said Narcissus. He was bathed and clean, wearing his sleeveless practice tunic. His long tawny hair was damp and his muscular body lightly oiled. 'I've made you some breakfast.' Narcissus flipped a pancake onto a mat of woven palm leaves and passed it to Lupus. 'I told them you were the best pupil I've ever had and that I wanted you all to myself today.' He gave Lupus his dazzling smile.

Lupus dropped his head to hide the flush of pleasure, and pretended to examine his pancakes.

'Enjoy your breakfast,' said Narcissus, giving Lupus's hair an affectionate tousle. 'I'll be waiting over there when you're ready to practise.'

As Lupus watched the dancer walk away, he decided he would investigate further before telling the others about Narcissus and Casina.

'Narcissus isn't my real name, you know,' said Narcissus to Lupus later that day. 'When I was young, my father claimed I was always looking at myself in the mirror. That's why he gave me the nickname.'

Lupus nodded. He knew the myth of Narcissus, the youth who fell in love with his own beauty and lingered by the reflecting pond for so long that he took root and became a flower.

Narcissus turned and looked over his shoulder. 'Scrape harder,' he said. 'You won't hurt me.'

Lupus was standing on a fallen palm trunk, helping Narcissus scrape off. He pulled the strigil firmly down the dancer's muscular back. It was satisfying to see the sweat and oil and dust come off, leaving a clean strip of smooth, tanned flesh. Lupus flicked away the residue and scraped again.

'That's better,' said Narcissus. 'Of course, good looks aren't enough. Skill is the most important thing. Skill and talent.' He glanced over his shoulder again. 'And you, Lupus, have talent. I don't plan to be a pantomime dancer much longer,' he added. 'But if I did, I'd take you on as my apprentice.'

Lupus gave his questioning grunt.

'No,' said Narcissus. 'I won't be a pantomime dancer for ever. There is only one thing that matters in this life. Power. Being a pantomime dancer brings you fame and public adulation. But it can't bring power. I'm not Roman. My mother was from Germania and my father was an Alexandrian Greek. But I admire the Romans. They understand that power is good. They aren't ashamed to crave it. Marcus Antonius, for example. He bet everything on one throw of the dice. He lost the throw – and his life – but if he'd won he would probably have become Emperor. What a glorious gamble! What incredible stakes! Imagine the world if Antonius had become Emperor instead of Augustus, and Cleopatra his empress rather than Livia.' He paused and then said, 'You heard us talking last night, didn't you?'

Lupus stopped scraping.

Narcissus turned and fixed Lupus with his beautiful blue eyes. 'I'm not angry. I'm glad you know, because I want you to throw in your lot with me. You have great skill, intelligence and daring. I could use you.' He glanced around and lowered his voice. 'I can't tell you any more at the moment. Just this. I intend to go all the way to the top.'

Lupus felt his eyes grow wide.

'That's right,' said Narcissus. 'Emperor of the Roman Empire. There is no more powerful position in the world. And power is all that matters. I know it. Antonius knew it. Now you know it, too. The most important thing in life is not fame or adulation. It's not land or money or jewels. It's power. Because if you have power, all those other things will fall into your lap.'

Later, looking back on the journey, it seemed to Nubia that after all their bad luck the gods must have decided to grant them good fortune. The next month passed almost in a dream. Each day was very like the others; only the scenery changed. Nubia sometimes felt like a bug on an endless unrolling papyrus scroll. But she knew she would never forget the beautiful barren mountains or the acacia-studded savannah or the mystical Sand Sea.

In the course of their thousand-mile trek, Nubia learned to love camels even more. With their long-lashed, half-closed eyes and sedate rhythm, they were a constant reassuring presence. Their yawning groans became as comforting and familiar as Nipur's whines and barks.

The caravan was usually up at dawn. Fuelled by little more than a handful of dates and diluted camel milk they were often on the move for eight or ten hours a day. In the evening Narcissus and Lupus practised their dancing while the others did the little chores of the caravan. Jonathan often helped Assan skin a goat bought in a village, and the girls sat stiff-legged to plait cords of palm fibre, having looped one end around their bare toes.

Best of all was the time after dinner, when they sat around the fire eating dates and sipping sweet syrupy mint tea. This was when they practised their songs. Soon they knew a dozen different melodies by heart, and the words to as many songs.

Sometimes Hanno and Barbarus would play a duet,

mixing the buzzy aulos and honey-sweet chords of the harp. Sometimes Casina would sing solo, her voice pure and haunting in the twilight. And sometimes Nubia and her friends would play their own music. Nubia had written three new songs, one for each of her friends: 'Lost in the Desert' for Flavia, 'Sunset in the Sand Sea' for Jonathan and a song called 'Leaps and Tumbles' for Lupus.

The Kalends of April came and went, and at last they reached the cedar-covered slopes of the Middle Atlas Mountains.

Finally, on the Ides, they stopped in a line on a ridge and gazed down over a vast green valley with a river running through it. The valley plain looked like a vast patchwork blanket, with yellow-green squares of winter wheat next to expanses of silver-green olive groves. In the centre of this fertile plain was a city of coloured marble and red-tiled roofs.

Even as Nubia looked, a stork flew by on their right, clacking his beak in greeting. They all watched the black and white bird become a speck as it sailed down and down towards the marble city. At last it disappeared.

'A good omen,' said Macargus, turning his beaming face back towards them. 'For that city is our goal. That is Volubilis.'

As they began their descent towards Volubilis, Nubia thought she heard the distant cough of a lion.

'Yes, there are many wild animals in these hills,' said Assan. 'That is why beast-hunters love this place.'

But later she heard the trumpet of an elephant. Like the lion's cough, she could have sworn it came from the town rather than the slopes around them.

When they reached the outskirts of Volubilis, she discovered why. A large tent had been erected not far from a caravanserai outside the town gate. There were caged wild animals near the tent and an enclosure full of zebra.

'Mnason!' Nubia turned to look over her shoulder at Flavia. 'I am thinking Mnason is here, having caught many beasts.'

'I think you're right, Nubia. He must have brought them for the governor's games!'

'No,' said Jonathan, twisting on the camel ahead of them. He pointed. 'Look at the banner flying over the tent. Mnason's sign is an elephant. That banner has another symbol on it.'

'Crown of five points with fish in centre,' said Nubia, whose vision was the sharpest.

'Five points!' cried Flavia suddenly. 'It's the Pentasii!' 'The corporation of beast-hunters who set sail last December. The ones Uncle Gaius sailed with!' She clapped her hands. 'Our hunt is on again!'

But when she showed Gaius's portrait to the young Numidian standing guard at the beast-hunters' tent, he crushed her hopes with a single shake of his head.

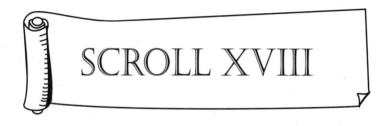

SCROLL XVIII

At the caravanserai near the beast-hunters' encampment, Flavia and her friends took their leave of Assan, Macargus and Iddibal, and of the twelve merchants. Nubia spent a long time saying goodbye to her dear camel Selene and when she finally rejoined the others, Flavia saw her friend's eyes were brimming.

She caught hold of Nubia's hand and together they followed Narcissus and the others through the Eastern Gate and straight into a covered market. After the peace and tranquillity of the caravan, the world was suddenly crowded, confused and noisy.

Someone was beating a drum somewhere, playing a strange urgent beat, and the sound assaulted Flavia's senses, along with the whine of a grindstone and the shouts of stallholders. She smelled cumin, urine, singed hair and charcoal smoke. She saw tan-skinned Numidians, brown-skinned Arabs and ebony Africans crowding the narrow streets. She pulled the tail of her turban across her face to protect her from this sandstorm of the senses.

Even Narcissus, the sophisticated Alexandrian, was gawping like a goatherd on his first visit to the city. He led his little flock: Casina, Hanno and Barbarus. Flavia and her friends took up the rear.

They wove through the metallic cacophony of the Coppersmiths' Market, the rainbow-coloured cones in the Spice Market and the pungent, tannic scent of the Leather Market. Presently they found themselves on the street of glassmakers. While Narcissus stopped to ask directions, Flavia looked around. One table had nothing but signet rings and Flavia realised the gems were made of glass rather than amethyst, sardonyx or ruby. Suddenly she had an idea.

'Jonathan!' she whispered, tugging his sleeve. 'Look how realistic these glass gems are. If we can't find Nero's emerald, we could always get one of these glassblowers to make a replica.'

'Not a bad idea,' said Jonathan, 'except for one small detail. We don't know what it looks like.' He turned back to examine the glass on display.

But Narcissus was commanding them to 'Come this instant!' so they hurried on, continuing through the covered markets of Volubilis.

As they finally emerged into the bright open space of the forum, Flavia ran to catch up with Narcissus.

'Sir!' she cried. 'Remember I told you we were supposed to come on a merchant ship via Lixus? But it sailed without us?'

'Yes?'

'Our friend Taurus probably arrived weeks ago. With our luggage and money! Maybe he's left a note asking us to contact him. May I go look at the notice board?'

'Of course,' he said. 'Especially if it means I get the money you promised me.'

He and the others followed Flavia to a board in the middle of the forum. Presently she turned away dejectedly. The notice board held no mention of Taurus, of anyone trying to contact them.

'Come on,' said Narcissus, consulting a piece of papyrus. 'I think the Triton Tavern is that way.' He pointed north.

Flavia sighed and followed him through a forum like Ostia's, with the Capitolium on one side and the basilica on the other. Had the goddess abandoned them? Would they ever recover their possessions? More importantly, would they ever find her Uncle Gaius?

Flavia smelled the beggar before she saw him. The reek of urine filled her nostrils. Then a pile of clothes at the foot of a green column stirred. It lifted a hooded head and raised a copper begging-cup.

Flavia gasped, took an involuntary step back, then stared in horrified fascination at one of the most repulsive beggars she had ever seen. Beneath the greasy hood of his grey woollen cloak was hair so filthy and matted that it had separated into ropelike clumps the colour of chalk. His bloodshot blue eyes bulged with madness, and his sallow skin was stretched as tight as parchment.

'Come on, Flavia!' called Narcissus, already several paces ahead.

'Wait!' she cried back. 'Can you wait a moment, please?'

Narcissus threw up his hands in a dramatic gesture of frustration as she turned back to the beggar.

Flavia breathed through her mouth to avoid the smell. 'Nubia,' she said. 'Can you loan me a coin? An as or a quadrans will do.'

Nubia dutifully searched in her belt-pouch. A

moment later she fished out a large coin. 'I only have sestertius,' she said. 'It is my very last coin.'

Before Flavia could accept the coin, Jonathan had snatched it from Nubia's grasp.

'Flavia!' he cried. 'This is Nubia's last coin. This is *our* last coin.'

Lupus nodded his agreement.

At the foot of his column, the beggar stared up at them and rattled his beaker hopefully. Inside was the tiniest coin Flavia had ever seen, even smaller than a quadrans. It was hardly bigger than her little finger-nail.

'But my dream,' said Flavia.

From several paces ahead, Narcissus called: 'Come on, you lot! I want to find the Triton Tavern.'

Jonathan ignored him. 'Flavia,' he said, holding up the sestertius. 'If you give this away, all our money will be gone. Here, Nubia, take back your coin.'

'Jonathan!' cried Flavia, 'I thought your god tells you to give to the poor.'

Jonathan looked sheepish. 'He does,' he admitted. 'But look at him. You can see the lice crawling in his beard. Like beasts in a thicket ...'

'Oh!' cried Flavia, looking closer and then recoiling. 'Oh! He's seething with them.'

'Why don't we come back later?' suggested Jonathan. 'Bring him some food. Or a louse-comb.'

Flavia hesitated, then shook her head. 'No. I've got to give him something now. The voice in my dream told me not to pass a beggar by.'

'For the last time, are you lot coming?' bellowed Narcissus.

'Yes!' cried Flavia. 'We're coming!' She snatched the

coin from Jonathan's fingers, leant gingerly forward and dropped it into the beggar's beaker. It gave a satisfying clang.

'Thank you so much,' rasped the beggar, in cultured Latin. 'As your reward I will answer one question for each of you.'

They all stared down at him in amazement.

He grinned up at them, revealing a toothless mouth. 'A humble beggar learns many things sitting in the forum all day.'

Flavia continued to gape. His voice was husky but his accent was that of a patrician. She turned to Jonathan. 'He speaks cultured Latin!' she gasped.

But Jonathan was not impressed. He folded his arms. 'All right, Thicket-beard,' he said. 'If you know everything then why don't you tell us the name of the current Emperor?'

'Vespasianus,' rasped the beggar.

'Wrong!' said Jonathan, and turned to go.

'Full name: Imperator Titus Caesar Vespasianus Augustus. Better known as Titus.'

'He's right!' gasped Flavia.

Jonathan shrugged. 'That doesn't prove anything,' he said. 'Just means they get the news here.'

'I used to live on the Palatine Hill,' said the beggar. 'I was Nero's freedman and secretary. Was with him until the very end.'

The friends glanced at each other.

'What is your name, sir?' asked Nubia politely.

'Mendicus,' said the beggar in his husky voice. 'They call me Mendicus.' He smiled at her and said. 'That pantomime dancer is leading you astray. The Triton Tavern is that way.' He pointed a yellow talon to the south. 'First right turning past the Capitolium.'

Flavia gasped. 'How do you know he's a pantomime dancer?'

'Pantomime dancers always shave their foreheads. Makes the mask fit easily. Everyone knows that.'

They all stared at him for a moment, then Lupus took out his wax tablet, scribbled something on it and held it before the man's bleary eyes.

The beggar squinted at it, then cackled. 'Of course I can read. Both Greek and Latin. Told you: I was Nero's secretary.' The beggar's toothless grin widened and a gleaming string of saliva dripped onto his seething beard.

'I have a question I'll bet you can't answer!' cried Flavia suddenly. She snatched the tablet from Lupus and showed the portrait painted on the back. 'That's my Uncle Gaius,' she said. 'He's been missing for three months. Can you tell me where he is?'

The beggar peered at the tablet. Then he looked up at Flavia and nodded. 'The last time I saw that man,' he rasped, 'he and his friends were passing by on their way to Calypso's Caupona. Two doors down from the Triton Tavern.'

Half an hour later, Flavia parted the bead curtain and peered into Calypso's Caupona. They had left their few things at the Triton Tavern and hurried straight here.

A low buzz of conversation filled the room, punctuated by the rattle of dice and the off-key plinking of a cithara.

Sawdust covered the floor and smoke from cheap oil-lamps hung in the air, along with the scent of sour wine and sweat. Beams of light slanted in through latticework windows and illuminated a rude fresco of satyrs pursuing nymphs. Flavia averted her eyes from the fresco and stepped inside. She heard the bead curtain clatter as her friends followed her in.

Flavia glanced around: 'Not one toga to be seen,' she murmured to herself. 'I don't think this is a very respectable establishment.'

Lupus grunted and pointed. In one corner of the tavern sat half a dozen turbaned men. One of the men wore a leopard-skin cloak and another had a monkey on his shoulder. Tethered to a leg of their table was a miniature antelope with tiny horns and large brown eyes.

'Behold!' cried Nubia. 'A dik-dik.'

'I think Lupus is pointing at the beast-hunters,' said Jonathan. 'Not that baby antelope.'

Lupus nodded, grunted again, and pointed urgently towards the men.

'What?' asked Flavia.

'Behold! It is the Uncle Gaius,' said Nubia, her golden eyes wide.

Lupus nodded and mimed stroking a beard.

'Great Juno's peacock!' muttered Flavia, and squinted through the smoky gloom. 'Is that him? That man with the scruffy beard? Wearing that greasy blue turban?'

'Master of the universe,' said Jonathan. 'It *is* him!' He looked at Flavia. 'I don't believe it! We've found your uncle. And it's all thanks to that disgusting beggar.'

'Uncle Gaius?' cried Flavia, weaving through the tables and ignoring the raised eyebrows and open mouths of the drinkers. 'Uncle Gaius, is that you?' In the dim light of the tavern, it was difficult to see his features.

147

The bearded man in the blue turban looked up from his dice, then turned his face towards her. He had her father's features, and Flavia felt an irrational stab of guilt mixed with love. But she knew this was not her father. It was his twin brother.

'Oh, Uncle Gaius!' Flavia ran forward and threw her arms around his neck. 'It *is* you!'

'Great Jupiter's eyebrows!' he exclaimed stiffly. 'What are you doing here?'

He made no move to return her embrace. Instead he remarked to his friends. 'It's my bossy little niece Flavia.' When he spoke, she could smell sour wine on his breath.

She pulled back, hurt and confused. 'Uncle Gaius, aren't you going to say hello?'

'Hello, Bossy-boots,' he said cheerfully.

Flavia glanced back in consternation at her friends. 'Aren't you going to say hello to my friends?'

'Hello, Bossy-bootlets.' He giggled.

'Uncle Gaius, what are you doing here?'

'I'm having a good time,' he said, shaking the dice-cup. 'That's what I'm doing here. What are you doing here?'

'We've come to find you! To take you home to Ostia.'

Six dice clattered onto the wooden table. He examined them and took another sip of wine. 'Don't want to go. Like it here.'

The other beast-hunters chuckled.

For the first time, she noticed his voice was slurred and her hurt became anger. 'Are you drunk?'

'None of your business,' he said, and the man with the monkey said. 'You tell her, Gaius.'

148

With an angry gesture Flavia swept the dice to the floor. 'Uncle Gaius!' she cried. 'How can you just sit here and gamble? Don't you realise how worried we've been about you? We thought you were dead!'

He grinned at her, his gaze unfocused. 'Well, as you can see,' he said. 'I am perfectly fine. I am now a beast-hunter.' He plunked down his glass beaker of wine.

'A beast-hunter?' Tears stung her eyes. 'We all thought you were mad with grief but instead you're playing at being a beast-hunter? I can't believe it. You abandoned your baby boys. You let us think you were dead! You're a coward, Uncle Gaius. A coward!'

He tipped his head back defiantly. 'I am not a coward,' he slurred. 'I am a brave beast-hunter as my friends here will testify. Now go away, Bossy-boots. Go away and leave me alone.'

SCROLL XIX

They found Narcissus pacing the small courtyard of the Triton Tavern. 'There you are!' he cried, and tossed his hair importantly. 'I have good news. I sent the governor a message telling him I was here and he wants me – us, I mean – to perform at his festival. Also, he's invited us to dinner.'

'When?' asked Flavia numbly. She was still reeling from the encounter with her uncle.

'Today! This afternoon! Casina is just about to go to the baths. Look! Here she comes now. I suggest you two girls go with her.' He frowned at Flavia. 'What's the matter? Don't tell me you don't want a decent bath after a month on camelback?'

'Of course,' murmured Flavia. 'Of course we do.'

'Then go with Casina,' he said. 'And you boys come with us.' Here he beckoned to Hanno and Barbarus, waiting on a bench with their bath-sets. 'We'll meet back here in an hour and then go straight on to the governor's.'

Bathed and refreshed, and wearing coloured silk caftans, Lupus and his friends followed Narcissus into the atrium of the procurator's villa.

The layout was that of an opulent Roman townhouse, but the door-slave who held open one of the double doors did not look at all Roman. He wore only a red loincloth and matching red turban. His muscular, oiled body was as smooth and black as jet. Lupus gazed at him in open-mouthed admiration.

'The illustrious procurator Gnaeus Aufidius Chius bids you welcome to his humble abode!' announced the African door-slave, in perfect Latin.

A moment later a middle-aged man in a toga strode into the atrium. He had silver-grey hair, an eagle's-beak nose and a scribe in attendance. He went straight to Narcissus and grasped the dancer's hand in both of his.

'My dear boy. I'm a huge fan. Huge. Saw you in Alexandria last year. Superb.'

Narcissus flushed with pleasure. 'Thank you, your eminence,' he said. 'And thank you for agreeing to let us celebrate your appointment as procurator.'

'The honour is mine. All mine. I would love you to perform during the festival. And it would be an even greater honour if you would stay here with me. For a week. Two weeks. As long as you like.'

'Thank you,' stuttered Narcissus. Lupus knew this was more than he had dared to hope for.

'Where is your luggage?'

'At the Triton Tavern.'

'Ah, yes.' The governor turned his body slightly towards his secretary. 'Philo. Send two or three porters to bring their things here. Install them in the guest-wing.' He turned back to Narcissus and his troupe. 'Now who do we have here?' He gave Casina a puzzled smile. 'Have we met before? You look very familiar.'

'No, sir,' said Casina shyly. 'We have never met.'

'This is Casina,' said Narcissus, 'my singer. My musicians are Hanno, Barbarus, Nubia, Flavia, Jonathan and Lupus.'

'Charming.' Aufidius smiled at each one in turn. He gave Casina another searching look, then said over his shoulder: 'Philo. Give Narcissus and Casina a room each. The two men can share, and the two younger girls and the two boys. You don't mind sharing, do you?' He smiled and raised his bushy grey eyebrows. 'I can assure you. My rooms are much better than those at the Triton Tavern. Now, come. Before we eat. Let me give you a little tour of the villa.'

The governor led the way out of the atrium and into the peristyle of a large inner garden with a shallow swimming pool as its central feature.

'It's beautiful,' breathed Casina, her homely face full of wonder.

'Yes.' Aufidius stopped, clasped his hands behind his back and looked around, as if seeing the villa for the first time. 'It's really a palace, of course. It used to belong to King Juba the second. A Numidian from these parts who was raised in Rome. Come! I'll introduce you to him. Through here.' Aufidius led them through an arched corridor into a tiny, fragrant herb garden.

Among the pots of thyme, rosemary and dill, on a column of red porphyry, was a bust of a handsome, curly-haired youth gazing pensively into the distance. The polished bronze was the exact colour of Numidian skin, and the eyes were of white alabaster inlaid with glass paste, giving the bust a startlingly realistic look.

'Oh!' cried Flavia. 'He's beautiful.'

Lupus saw that some of the colour had returned to her cheeks.

'Young Juba here was raised in Rome,' said Aufidius, 'and he became a scholar of great repute. It was in Rome that he met the daughter of Marcus Antonius and Cleopatra, whom he later married.'

'Cleopatra Selene,' whispered Casina, reaching out to stroke Juba's smooth bronze cheek.

'She had a twin brother, didn't she?' asked Flavia.

'Yes,' said the governor. 'Alexander Helios.'

'Selene means "moon" and Helios means "sun",' said Flavia.

'Like our camels,' added Nubia.

The governor raised an eyebrow.

'What ever happened to Alexander Helios?' asked Jonathan.

'He died of a fever at the age of about fifteen. His sister was devastated. But she found companionship and love with this young man. They became king and queen of Mauretania and divided their time between Caesarea, up on the coast, and this place. I believe they were happiest here.'

Lupus wrote on his wax tablet and showed it to Jonathan.

'Did they have any children?' asked Jonathan.

'A son called Ptolemy,' said the governor. 'Sadly, he was executed by the Emperor Caligula forty years ago. That's when Mauretania ceased being a kingdom and became an imperial province, governed by procurators like myself.' He gave a little bow.

Lupus nudged Jonathan again and showed him his tablet.

'Did Ptolemy have children?' asked Jonathan, and Lupus saw Narcissus and Casina exchange a look.

'Not entirely sure,' said Aufidius, 'If he did, I doubt

whether Caligula let them live. But come! Let's not dwell on that. I have devoted a whole room to Antonius and Cleopatra.' He led them down a painted corridor, through another garden courtyard and into a bright, airy room with marble tables around three walls. 'See?' He stood aside and swept his arm out. 'Some of Cleopatra's jewels, toiletries, et cetera. Her daughter inherited them and here they are!'

Casina ran forward with a little cry of pleasure. The others followed.

Lupus eagerly scanned the jewellery displayed on the table, then his shoulders slumped: there was no giant emerald there.

'Oh!' cried Casina. 'Oh! Oh! Look at this ivy wreath made of pure gold.' She glanced at Narcissus. 'It must be worth a fortune.'

Aufidius nodded. 'That belonged to Marcus Antonius. He often dressed as Dionysus. God of wine. That jeweled goblet is his, too. And that ceremonial dagger. Also the ruby signet ring. And of course this onyx cameo of Cleo –' He stopped mid-sentence and stared at Casina. 'By Jove!' he cried, holding the cameo beside her. 'That's who you remind me of. You look just like Cleopatra!'

'Do I?' Casina flushed and dropped her head.

'Of course!' said Jonathan. 'I knew you looked familiar.'

'We thought that too,' said Flavia. 'Didn't we Nubia?'

Casina's face was bright red and Lupus could see she was embarrassed.

Nubia must have noticed, too, for she said to the governor, 'We are hearing you have a big emerald.'

Lupus nodded and gestured around as if to say: Is it here?

'A what?' said Aufidius. 'An emerald? No. Cleopatra never had a particularly big emerald, as far as I know. Valuable pearl. Yes. But no emerald.'

'The emerald didn't belong to Cleopatra,' said Jonathan. 'It belonged to Nero.'

'Ah!' Aufidius nodded and smiled. 'You mean "Nero's Eye".'

'Nero's eye?' they echoed.

'Yes. Nero's Eye. It's a huge emerald. Biggest I've ever seen. Worth a fortune. They say it was brought to Volubilis about twelve years ago. Someone – nobody knows who – dedicated it at the Temple of Apollo.'

Lupus heard Flavia mutter, 'The hunt is on!' Then she turned to the governor: 'Could you tell us where the Temple of Apollo is? We'd love to see the emerald.'

The procurator shook his head sadly. 'I'm afraid the emerald is no longer there. It caught someone's eye.'

'Someone stole it?' said Jonathan.

Aufidius chuckled. 'Not exactly,' he said.

'Hello, everyone!' came a woman's voice. Lupus and his friends turned to see a dusky and curvaceous beauty coming through the doorway. She was about twenty and she wore a sleeveless, scoop-necked white stola belted under her breasts. Her sable hair was oiled and plaited into dozens of strands with gilded beads woven in. These beads made soft clicking noises and a dozen golden bangles tinkled on her bare arms.

'Ah. My dear,' said Aufidius, moving forward to take her hands. 'You're back from the baths.'

She tilted her lovely face and allowed him to kiss her perfumed cheek.

'This is my wife, Glycera,' said Aufidius, turning to the others. 'Glycera, this is the pantomime dancer I was telling you about. Narcissus. And his musicians.'

Glycera went straight to Narcissus and took his hands. 'Charmed,' she said, dimpling.

Narcissus did not reply. He was staring at Glycera's neckline in wide-eyed amazement. So were Lupus and his friends. For in addition to her bangles and earrings, Glycera was wearing a necklace: a large, lentil-shaped emerald.

'Behold!' cried Nubia. 'It is Eye of Nero!'

SCROLL XX

When they all gathered in the large triclinium for dinner half an hour later, Flavia saw that Glycera had slipped a filmy green palla over her diaphanous white stola. The dusky beauty reclined on the central couch between Casina and Narcissus, who had the place of honour. Governor Aufidius reclined in the host's traditional place, on the end of the left-hand couch, so that he was close to Narcissus, too.

Also on the left hand couch were Hanno and Barbarus. Flavia and her three friends had crowded onto the right-hand couch.

Ebony slaves in red loin-cloths and turbans had washed their feet and hands with saffron-scented water. Now these same slaves were bringing in the gustatio on silver trays. There were olives, cubes of camels'-milk cheese, hard-boiled quails' eggs and little birds roasted whole on the spit.

Aufidius gave thanks for the food, spattered a small libation of wine onto the marble floor and they began to eat.

Flavia reclined between Lupus and Jonathan. Her encounter with her uncle had destroyed her appetite, so while everyone was busy reaching for starters, she slipped out her wax tablet and secretly wrote:

We've found the gem! Then she tipped it so her friends could see what she had written.

Lupus nodded and wrote on his own tablet: WE CAN STEAL IT TONIGHT

Nubia took Flavia's tablet and wrote: *They are kind. Must we steal it?*

Before Flavia could reclaim her tablet, Jonathan took it and wrote: *It doesn't officially belong to them.*

Flavia nodded her agreement and took back her tablet. *We just have to find out*, she wrote, *where she keeps it when it's not around her neck.*

On the other couches, the adults were busy discussing Antonius and Cleopatra. Narcissus was telling them about the new pantomime he had been preparing: The Death of Antonius and Cleopatra.

'It sounds wonderful,' said Governor Aufidius, but Flavia noticed Glycera rolling her eyes and stifling a tiny yawn.

Aufidius glanced at his wife, then back at Narcissus. 'Will you perform it for us?' he asked.

'Of course,' said Narcissus. 'I've composed it in your honour.'

'Personally, I despise Cleopatra,' said Glycera, nibbling daintily at a roast bird.

Casina gasped and Narcissus stiffened.

'My dear,' admonished Aufidius gently. 'You mustn't speak ill of the dead. Not in her daughter's palace.'

'Why do you dislike Cleopatra so much?' asked Flavia.

Glycera shrugged prettily. 'I prefer Antonius's other wife,' she said. 'She's my idol.'

Flavia gave her friends a significant glance and wrote on her wax tablet: *Fulvia. She was the one who took Cicero's severed head on her lap and stabbed his lifeless tongue with a hairpin.*

When Lupus read what Flavia had written, he began to choke on a quail's egg. Flavia had to slap him hard on the back.

On the couch opposite Aufidius pushed himself up on his elbow. 'What's wrong with the boy? Will he be all right?'

Lupus hacked and coughed, then looked up with wet eyes and nodded.

Flavia explained: 'Sometimes food just goes down the wrong way.' She looked at Glycera. 'Tell me, domina,' she asked brightly. 'Where did you get the Eye of Nero? It's wonderful.'

Glycera fished out the emerald and looked down at it. 'It is wonderful, isn't it? I found it in the Temple of Apollo a few months ago, just after we arrived here.'

Aufidius gazed at his young wife affectionately. 'I really shouldn't have allowed it. The plebs loved to admire it. I've recently had several clients requesting that I put it back on public display.'

Casina stretched out her arm. 'May I try it on, domina?' she asked.

Glycera's pretty smile faded. 'Oh, my dear, I'm sorry. But I never take it off. Never.'

Casina's smile faded, too, and she let her arm drop back onto the couch. 'You never take it off?'

'Never.'

'Not even in the baths?' Flavia couldn't help asking.

'Not even when I go to the baths,' said Glycera, fondling the gem. 'Not even when I go to sleep at night. I never, ever take off Nero's Eye.'

★

'Well, that's going to make stealing the emerald more difficult,' said Flavia later that night. 'If Glycera sleeps with it on.'

The four friends had all congregated in the girls' lamplit bedroom to discuss their plans for acquiring the emerald.

A slow grin spread across Lupus's face and he began to write on his wax tablet. They all bent closer to watch:

I VOLUNTEER TO TRY TO GET IT, wrote Lupus. I COULD SNEAK INTO HER BEDROOM TONIGHT AND—

'Lupus!' gasped Flavia, and gave his hand a mock slap. 'You naughty boy!'

Lupus nodded and they laughed.

Then Jonathan grew serious. 'Even with your sneaky skills, Lupus, I think this will be difficult. We've got to come up with another plan.'

'I have plan,' said Nubia shyly.

Flavia turned eagerly to Nubia. 'Yes?'

'Now we know what it looks like.'

Flavia frowned at Nubia. 'What do you mean? I don't understand.'

'Remember this morning when we enter city? We see glass emeralds? You say we could not make pretend emerald because we do not know what it looks like—'

'And now we do!' cried Flavia. 'So we can have a replica made!'

'Yes,' said Nubia. 'Then we take away real emerald and put glass one looking exactly like Nero's Eye in its place.'

Lupus touched the tip of his forefinger to the tip of his thumb, an orator's gesture meaning 'excellent!'

'That's brilliant,' agreed Jonathan.

'That way,' said Flavia. 'We only need the real emerald in our possession for a few moments, just long enough to replace it with the duplicate. A jeweller might be able to tell the difference, but I'll bet Glycera won't be able to. And when she eventually does, by then it will be too late.'

Lupus held up his wax tablet.

I CAN MAKE DRAWING TO SHOW JEWELLER
EXACT SHAPE AND SIZE.

'Excellent,' said Flavia. 'All we need to do now is find someone who can make a replica. That means we'll need to come up with enough money to pay for the gold chain and clasp.'

'Where will we get that much money?' asked Jonathan.

'If I have to,' said Flavia grimly, 'I'll make Uncle Gaius loan us some. Then, once we've got the replica, all we need to do is find a way to make Glycera give us Nero's Eye for an hour or so.'

Jonathan shook his head. 'That's going to be difficult,' he sighed. 'She said herself: she never takes it off.'

'Difficult,' said Flavia, 'but not impossible.' She thoughtfully tapped her ivory stylus against her bottom teeth. Abruptly she stopped tapping and looked at them with bright grey eyes. 'Eureka!' she cried. 'I've got it!'

After a sumptuous breakfast the next day, Narcissus and his troupe spent the morning rehearsing at the theatre where they would perform in five days time.

Finally, as the gongs clanged noon, Narcissus clapped his hands. 'Well done, everyone,' he said. 'Be back at the Governor's by the eighth hour; we're invited to dinner again.' He smiled around at them all. 'In the meantime, I think we deserve an afternoon at the baths. I hear the Forum Baths are the best. They have a women's section, as well as a men's, and apparently they serve good snacks there, too.'

Flavia turned to Jonathan and said under her breath. 'You and Nubia hurry to the glassmakers' quarter. See if you can find someone to make a replica. Say it's for a friend.'

Then Flavia turned to the youngest of them: 'Lupus, give Jonathan your drawing of the emerald, then go back to the procurator's house. If anyone asks, say you want to take a nap. But nose around and see what you can find out. And if Glycera's there, you can spy on her.'

Lupus nodded happily.

'What are you going to do?' whispered Jonathan.

'I'm going to see if I can get Narcissus to add a new dance to our programme,' said Flavia. 'One in which we need the emerald for a prop!'

Flavia ran to catch up to Narcissus.

'Oh, it's you,' he said. 'Where are the others? Aren't they coming to the baths with us?'

Flavia shook her head. 'They're going back to the procurator's villa for a little nap. They're still very tired from the desert journey.' She took a breath. 'May I ask you something?'

He narrowed his kohl-rimmed eyes at her. 'What?'

'You know we only have four plays and you were saying it might be nice to have a fifth.'

'It's a little late for that now,' he said, tossing his tawny mane.

'Wouldn't it be nice to perform a dance which has something to do with one of the procurator's ancestors? Now who was it he mentioned at dinner last night?' Flavia bit her lower lip and stared up at the pure blue sky and pretended to think. 'His uncle was in the court of ... Now who was it?'

'Nero,' said Narcissus drily. 'It was Nero.'

'What a brilliant idea!' cried Flavia. 'Why don't you do a dance portraying the Death of Nero?'

Narcissus raised one eyebrow. 'Did I just have an idea?'

'Yes, I think you did! You told me the plebs like to watch famous people die. Who better than Nero? Also, he was cruel to the procurator's ancestor. You could draw out Nero's death. Make it very horrible and dramatic.'

'We already have the Death of Antonius and Cleopatra.'

'And of Actaeon,' said Flavia. 'It could be a theme.'

'No. I don't think so.' He turned to say something to Casina, walking on his other side, and they laughed.

'I think you'd be a wonderful Nero,' said Flavia, pressing on. 'You have blond hair, like him, and you're about the same age as he was when he died. Thirty.'

Narcissus tossed his long hair again. 'I'm only twenty-eight,' he said, then added: 'Of course, I could play a person of any age: from a teenager to an old man.'

'Of course you could,' said Flavia. They were approaching the Forum and would soon be at the baths.

She needed to convince him as quickly as possible if they were to write and rehearse an entire pantomime in four days.

'The emerald!' she cried, as if the idea had just come to her.

He stopped and turned to her in annoyance.

'What about the emerald?'

'Glycera's necklace used to belong to Nero. We could use it as a prop in the pantomime.'

'What pantomime?'

'The Death of Nero! You could wear the emerald during the dance. The governor was saying the people wanted to see it. Well, this will give them a chance.'

Narcissus glanced at Casina and Flavia thought she saw him lift his eyebrows in a quick, small movement.

'Actually,' he said. 'That might not be such a bad idea. The Death of Nero.' He seemed to weigh the words as he spoke them. Then he gave his head a little shake. 'There's only one problem. I don't know anything about the death of Nero. Only his last words.'

'That doesn't matter,' said Flavia. 'I could do the research for you. I'll bet the procurator has some books about Nero somewhere. I could even write it!' she cried. 'Nubia could compose the tune and I could write the words.'

'His last words were very good,' murmured Narcissus: '*What an artist dies in me!*'

Flavia could see he had almost taken the bait. What more could she offer? The emerald had been her most tempting worm.

They were passing the basilica and her nose caught the faint whiff of urine. The beggar was sitting in the same place he had been the day before: at the foot of one of the columns. Suddenly she had a flash of pure inspiration.

She caught Narcissus's arm and when he turned to look at her she said, 'We might not know much about Nero's death.' She turned and pointed toward the beggar. 'But he does. He was an eyewitness!'

SCROLL XXI

'Salve!' said Flavia politely to the beggar. Narcissus and his troupe stood behind her. 'Are you well?'

The beggar rattled his copper beaker. It had the same tiny coin in it as the previous day.

'Do you remember me?' asked Flavia. 'I was here yesterday. I gave you our last sestertius and you told me where my Uncle Gaius would be. You were right. Thank you!'

The beggar gave her his toothless grin, and rattled his beaker.

Flavia turned to Narcissus. 'May I have a coin?'

Narcissus rolled his eyes and folded his arms, but Hanno fished in his pouch and gave her a quadrans.

'Thank you, Hanno,' said Flavia. She dropped the coin in the beggar's cup and crouched before him. 'Remember yesterday? You told us you were with Nero when he died?'

The beggar's smile faded. But he gave a small nod.

'Can you tell Narcissus here about it? We want to do a pantomime.'

The beggar looked up at Narcissus and smiled again. 'I like pantomime,' he said in his hoarse, cultured Latin. 'I like you.'

'By Apollo!' breathed Narcissus, and glanced at

Flavia. 'His accent is as good as the Governor's.'

Flavia nodded at him. 'Told you,' she said, and smiled at the beggar. 'I'm sorry,' she said. 'But I've forgotten your name.'

'Mendicus. They call me Mendicus.'

'Please, Mendicus,' said Flavia. 'Tell us about Nero's death.'

'No, no,' muttered the beggar, shaking his head. 'Mustn't think about that. Mustn't talk about that.'

'Why not? Tell us.'

'Too much blood. That nice man died. I tried to stop him, but he cut me.' Mendicus stretched out his scrawny left arm and they all saw the raised pink scar of a knife wound. 'See? See where they cut me? Here. And here.' He thrust his forefinger through his beard towards his throat.

'By Hercules!' Narcissus squatted beside Flavia and rested his elbows on his knees. 'Were you really with Nero when he died?'

The beggar nodded and rolled his bloodshot eyes.

'What were his last words?' said Narcissus. 'Nero's last words before he died ...'

'It hurts,' said Mendicus. 'Ow, it hurts.'

Narcissus laughed, 'You're probably right.'

'Mendicus,' said Flavia, 'do you remember Nero's emerald? It was—'

Narcissus stopped Flavia with a hand on her shoulder. 'Let him describe it,' he said, and turned to Mendicus. 'If you really knew Nero, you'll know what his emerald looked like. Describe it.'

Mendicus shook his hooded head. 'Blood, blood, blood. Everywhere blood. It hurt. He asked me to try it, to see if it hurt. I wouldn't, so he cut me. I cried.

Couldn't help it. Wanted to be brave. But it hurt. It did.'

Narcissus rose to his feet. 'He's mad. Anyone could have cut his arm. He could have done it to himself. Come on. Let's get to the baths.'

Flavia turned desperately back to the beggar. 'Mendicus! Tell Narcissus. If you were Nero's secretary you must have seen the emerald. Tell us what it looked like.'

The beggar pursed his lips and drew his eyebrows forward in an expression of extreme concentration. 'Green,' he said at last. 'It was green.'

'Everybody knows emeralds are green,' snorted Narcissus. 'I want more.'

'Seeing-thing,' rasped Mendicus. 'For the gladiators.'

'Seeing-thing?' echoed Narcissus.

'Yes! Seeing-thing for the gladiators! Big, green, smooth. So smooth.' The beggar made a jabbing motion towards his right eye. 'Put it here. Sharp. To make sharp. Sharp as a knife. It hurt. I cried. Blood everywhere. Red not green, red not green, red not green. Ow, it hurts.'

'Wool fluff! He's talking utter wool fluff.' Narcissus scowled at Flavia. 'You might have mentioned he was madder than Orestes.'

Nubia and Jonathan were walking along a narrow street in the multi-coloured light of the dyers' quarter. Overhead, the African sun shone through billowing sheets of red, blue, yellow and green cloth, tinting everything beneath them in jewel-like colours. Skeins of coloured wool hung in rainbow rows, more shades and tints than she had ever dreamed of.

'Amazing, isn't it?' said Jonathan, then sniffed: 'Nubia, come over here.'

She went to where he stood by a low wall and looked down to see dozens of circular clay pits in the ground, each big enough for up to six men standing waist deep. The pits were filled with liquid: brown, mustard yellow, white and red.

'Those are the tanners,' said Jonathan, resting his forearms on the low wall. He pointed with his chin. 'Look! That's where they wash the skins before they treat them. And there! That's where they leave them to dry.'

Nubia inhaled, and then coughed. 'Alas!' she said. 'The odour.'

'Terrible, isn't it?' said Jonathan. 'That's because they use urine and bird droppings and who knows what else. This is bigger than the tannery in Rome, where I used to ...' His words died away and Nubia glanced at him. She was astounded to see him weeping. He hid his face in his hands and as his shoulders shook, she patted his back.

Presently he pulled a handkerchief from his belt pouch and blew his nose. 'I'm sorry,' he said. 'It reminds me of Miriam.'

'Smell of urine and bird droppings?' said Nubia with a little smile.

He laughed through his tears. 'No. Not that. When I was younger, we lived in Rome. Sometimes she let me come shopping with her. On sunny days, she always made a detour through the dyers' quarter. She loved to walk under the dyed pieces of cloth hanging out to dry and look up at the sun shining through and watch our tunics change colour.'

He blew his nose again and for a moment they watched the tanners at work. Presently he turned and continued down the multi-coloured street. Nubia hurried after him.

They passed quickly through half a dozen markets. The spring afternoon was deliciously warm and the cane-awnings overhead tiger-striped the narrow streets with golden sunshine. Soon they heard the tapping and banging of the coppersmiths from up ahead.

'We're getting close,' said Jonathan over his shoulder. 'The man said the street of the glassblowers was just past the street of the coppersmiths.'

'It should be near city gate,' said Nubia. 'We pass through on first day.'

'That's right,' said Jonathan. 'Look! There they are.'

They emerged from beneath the striped shade of the cane awning and approached the familiar tables of glassware in front of their workshops. Glass beakers and cups sparkled in the sun: amber, brown, red, dark blue, and the most common colour: a pale, watery blue-green. They passed a dark doorway just as a man opened the furnace doors and Nubia felt a huge wave of heat. Another open door showed her a glassblower with an orange blob of molten glass at the end of his tube.

'We need to find one that does green glass,' said Jonathan.

Nubia nodded and scanned the stalls. Then she pointed to a table outside a corner workshop. 'Behold! That glass is being colour of emerald.'

'You're right,' said Jonathan, picking up a mould-blown beaker of emerald glass. He held it up to the sun. 'It's exactly the colour of an emerald.'

'Yes, please,' said a short, clean-shaven man in good Latin. 'May I help?'

'Good afternoon,' said Jonathan politely, 'Are you a glassmaker?'

He nodded. 'Yes. I am Vitrarius.'

'Can you make glass which looks like an emerald?'

'Right before you.' The man indicated signet rings with what appeared to be an emerald gem in a gold setting.

'Very impressive,' said Jonathan, 'but I need a specially-made piece.' He paused. 'Have you ever heard of an emerald called the Eye of Nero?'

'Of course,' said Vitrarius. His heavy-lidded eyes gave him a sleepy look.

Jonathan took a deep breath. 'We were wondering if you could make a duplicate? It's for a friend's birthday,' he lied.

'Everyone has heard of this emerald,' said Vitrarius, and he gave an apologetic shrug. 'But I have never seen it. And now it is too late. It has been removed from public view.'

'That doesn't matter,' said Jonathan. 'I've seen it. And we have a drawing.' He extended Lupus's wax-tablet, which showed both a life-sized front and side view.

'Ah!' The glassmaker's eyes were no longer sleepy. 'Ah!'

'What is it?' said Jonathan.

'This!' cried the glassmaker. 'It is in the shape of a lentil, or "lens". This shape is very exciting. Tell me, is this the actual size of the emerald?'

'Yes, that's exact. But why is the lentil-shape exciting?'

'Wait.' He made a patting motion with his hands. 'Wait here. I will show you.'

Nubia and Jonathan exchanged a puzzled look as Vitrarius hurried into his inferno of a workshop. A few moments later he emerged and handed Jonathan a piece of pale blue-green glass shaped like a large lentil. It almost filled the palm of Jonathan's hand.

'Great Juno's beard!' exclaimed Jonathan. 'It's almost exactly the same size and shape as the Eye of Nero! Why do you have this?'

'Look,' said the man. 'Look through it.'

Jonathan brought the glass lentil to his eye and gasped. 'It makes everything bigger!' he cried. 'That's amazing!' He turned to look at Nubia, his right eye hugely magnified.

'Behold!' she giggled. 'It makes your eye overweening.'

Jonathan handed the lentil to Nubia. 'Here. You have a look.'

'Look at my signet ring.' Vitrarius laid his hand palm down on the table.

Nubia bent forward and brought the clear lentil close. 'Behold!' she cried again. 'It is little Perseus with shield of Athena and head of Medusa shown inside.'

'Let me see!' cried Jonathan. A moment later he looked up in amazement.

'I've never seen or heard of anything like this. I know people who can't see things close up. This could help them.'

'That is exactly why I make them,' said Vitrarius. 'To help people see. Both close-up and far away. That is why I was excited to see your drawing of Nero's Eye. It is concave, for seeing far. These ones I have just shown you are convex, for seeing near. I have heard of such

172

gems but have never seen them. They are what first gave my grandfather the idea.'

'Oh!' cried Nubia suddenly. 'That is why they are calling it Nero's Eye!'

Jonathan and the glassmaker frowned at her.

'Do you not understand?' said Nubia. She raised the glass lentil to her eye and said: 'The emerald was not being colour of Nero's eye. It was for helping him to see.'

Lupus crept through the rooms of the governor's villa. As a houseguest, he had every right to be there, but he liked spying. He liked being invisible. And he loved the excitement of the hunt.

He glimpsed one of the procurator's Ethiopian slaves approaching, so he pressed himself against a pillar. His ears were sharp as a rabbit's and when he heard the slave's bare feet crunching on the gravel path he moved slowly around the pillar, keeping it between him and the slave. Presently all was silent, except for his thumping heart. It was the time of siesta and he knew most of the household would be asleep. He had left his sandals in his bedroom so that he could move on silent bare feet. He padded forward now, and each time he came to a doorway he stopped and cocked his head to listen.

Presently he heard a woman's low voice coming from an inner courtyard somewhere nearby and followed the sound to a wing he had not previously visited. Rooms were grouped around a small shady courtyard with marble benches and a rainwater pool. At the centre of the pool stood a bronze statue of Diana, her image perfectly reflected in the still water.

Lupus heard the woman's voice again. There! It was coming from that room in the corner of the courtyard. Lupus crouched low and ran behind a low green hedge of some pungent-smelling herb. He quickly popped up his head, like a rabbit peering from its hole, then crouched down again. A gauzy white curtain covered the door of the room. Occasionally the breeze made the fabric billow up and out. If he could get closer he might be able to see in.

He moved along behind the hedge, then quickly ran to one of the columns of the peristyle. It was dark red Egyptian porphyry: cool and smooth.

A woman's laugh – low and sweet– came from the room. Lupus was certain it was Glycera, the procurator's voluptuous young wife.

Then he heard a man's voice. He could not distinguish the words, but he knew it was not the procurator. This was the voice of a much younger man.

Lupus ran forward to the next column, and then the next. And now he was close enough to hear Glycera say. 'You must go now.'

'No, not yet,' pleaded the man's voice.

'Yes, my sweet,' came Glycera's voice. 'Now.'

There were sounds of movement and presently Lupus heard the slap of sandals on the marble floor. He pressed himself against the column and held his breath. A moment later he heard the footsteps going along the peristyle in the opposite direction.

He peeked round the column to see the back of a slender young man with fair hair wearing a simple blue tunic with a black meander pattern at the hem. Abruptly the young man stopped and turned his head, as if to listen.

Quickly Lupus pressed his back against the column, then breathed a sigh of relief as the footsteps continued to retreat.

Then he felt a slow smile spread across his face: his brief glimpse of the man's profile had confirmed his suspicions.

Glycera's afternoon visitor was very good-looking.

SCROLL XXII

'Which do you want to hear first?' asked Flavia. 'The good news or the bad news?' It was the third hour after noon. The four friends had gathered in the boys' bedroom to discuss their progress. A large fresco of a beast-hunt dominated the room, with life-sized lions and leopards

'Better tell us the bad news first,' said Jonathan.

'Good news,' said Nubia.

'Lupus?' said Flavia. 'Your vote decides it.'

Lupus grinned and pointed to Nubia.

'All right,' said Flavia. 'The good news first. After I went to the baths, I stopped by the Capitolium and showed the priest my imperial pass. He gave me one hundred gold pieces, ten thousand sesterces! Even after paying Narcissus we'll have six thousand left over. At last we can afford to do things. I wish I'd thought of that earlier.'

'Me too,' said Jonathan. 'We could have given the glassmaker a down payment. What's your bad news?'

Flavia sighed and began counting out coins. 'Narcissus doesn't want to do a pantomime of the death of Nero. We'll have to think of another way to get the emerald off Glycera for a few moments.'

Lupus held up his wax tablet with excitement.

GLYCERA WAS ENTERTAINING A MAN IN
HER BEDROOM THIS AFTERNOON. IT WAS
NOT HER HUSBAND.

'Oh!' Flavia stopped counting long enough to exchange a glance with Nubia. 'Was he handsome?'

Lupus nodded and grinned: VERY. ALSO TALL,
SLIM AND FAIR

'Are any of us surprised?' said Flavia, handing out the
gold.

'I suppose her husband *is* rather old,' said Jonathan,
slipping his coins into his belt pouch. He looked at
Flavia. 'Why didn't Narcissus take your bait?'

'I made the mistake of introducing him to that lice-
ridden creature who begs in the forum.'

Jonathan frowned. 'Why in Hades did you do that?'

'Well, he claimed he was with Nero when he died
and I thought that might intrigue Narcissus. If he could
get an eyewitness account ...' She sighed. 'That beggar
didn't know Nero. I doubt he's even been to Rome. Do
you know what he said Nero's last words were?'

'What an artist dies in me?' suggested Jonathan.

'No,' said Flavia. 'He claims Nero said: *Ow it hurts.*'

Jonathan grinned and Lupus guffawed.

Flavia sighed. 'How about you?' She looked at
Jonathan and Nubia. 'Did you find someone to make
a replica?'

'We did,' said Jonathan. 'A glassmaker named
Vitrarius. He told us why it's called Nero's Eye.'

'Why?'

'Nero probably used to look through it,' said
Jonathan. 'Gems or pieces of glass shaped like lentils
can improve your vision.'

Nubia nodded. 'Nero's Eye is for helping to see.'

'Great Juno's peacock!' cried Flavia, leaping to her feet. 'That means he's not mad. He *did* know Nero. And I'll bet he knows all about Nero's death.'

'Who?' asked Jonathan with a frown. 'What are you babbling about?'

'That beggar,' she cried. 'He called the emerald a "seeing-thing". He knew exactly what it was used for. I'll wager he really was with Nero when he died.' She looked at them with bright eyes. 'Now that we have some gold, I'm betting he'll tell us all about it.'

An hour later Flavia and Nubia were woken from a nap by one of the governor's female slaves.

'Your friends Jonathan and Lupus request that you meet them,' she said without lifting her eyes. 'They await you in the street outside.'

When the girls emerged from the cool villa into the hot street, they saw Jonathan and Lupus standing in the shady porch of a house on the other side of the street. With them was a bald old man in a cream tunic.

'Behold!' breathed Nubia. 'It is Mendicus.'

'Great Juno's peacock,' muttered Flavia. 'I don't believe it. You took him to the baths!'

She crossed the street and stared at the beggar wide-eyed.

Instead of the stink of urine, he smelt of lavender. In place of his filthy cloak he wore a clean tunic. His face was clean-shaven and pink, his ropey clumps of white hair shaved off, and his skin colour at least three shades lighter.

His bulging blue eyes were still the same, however: bloodshot and with a gleam of madness.

'Salve, Mendicus,' she said politely.

'Ask him if he enjoyed his bath,' said Jonathan.

Flavia smiled. 'Did you enjoy your bath?'

'Very much indeed,' he rasped, and smiled to show a fine set of ivory false teeth. 'It was wonderful.'

'Great Juno's peacock!' cried Flavia, and stared in amazement, 'where did you get those teeth?'

'Someone left them behind in the baths,' said Jonathan. 'I got them for five sesterces. Now our friend here can eat meat.'

'Then let's buy you a nice roast chicken at the Triton Tavern,' said Flavia. 'And while you're eating, you can tell us all about the death of Nero.'

Another hour later, Flavia found a quiet spot on a shady bench by a pool in one of the inner gardens of the procurator's villa. The bench faced a bronze statue of Diana, so this seemed a propitious place to sit. Her mind was dizzy with all the beggar had told them. She wanted to write it down while it was still fresh.

Flavia gazed up at the goddess, shown with her bow and arrow, and her tunic tucked up to expose her knees. 'Oh Diana,' she whispered. 'You sent me on this quest to find Uncle Gaius. And you granted me success. Please help me now to write the words for the pantomime of Nero's Death so that we can get the emerald, too.' She thought for a moment and added, 'And you, too, Polyhymnia, muse of song and dance.'

Then Flavia began to write, pushing the bronze stylus through the yellow beeswax: 'Help me, Polyhymnia. Inspire me to sing, and these to play, and him to dance—'

'Hello, Flavia,' said a woman's voice.

Flavia looked up to see Glycera in her white stola and gilded sandals.

'Hello, domina,' said Flavia politely. 'Is it all right for me to be here? It's so cool and peaceful.'

'Of course,' said Glycera, dimpling. 'And please don't call me "domina". It makes me feel old. I'm only twenty-two, you know. Just.' The golden bangles on her arms tinkled as she sat beside Flavia. 'What are you writing?'

'A new pantomime for Narcissus.'

'What's the subject?'

Flavia almost told the truth, then decided to play safe. 'Um. Diana. The Virgin Huntress.'

Glycera smiled and closed her eyes. 'Don't let me disturb you,' she said.

Flavia looked down at her wax tablet, then at Glycera, sitting less than a foot away.

'I can't think what to write,' lied Flavia.

Glycera opened her eyes, and Flavia noticed they were as green as the emerald around her neck. 'That's because Diana is selfish and vain.'

'Domina!' cried Flavia, making the sign against evil and glancing nervously at the statue. 'You shouldn't speak about the goddess that way!' After a pause, Flavia asked: 'What do you mean: selfish and vain?'

'She's selfish because she only cares about herself. She's vain because she doesn't want to grow old and fat through having children.'

'I don't think that's selfish or vain,' said Flavia. 'I'm going to be like Diana and have adventures all my life. I'm never going to have children, so I'll never grow fat. Besides,' she added, 'giving birth is dangerous. It can kill you.'

Glycera gave Flavia a searching look and then asked softly, 'Did someone close to you recently die in childbirth?'

Flavia looked at Glycera in surprise, then nodded. 'My friend Miriam,' she said. 'She was the most beautiful girl I have ever known. She was only fifteen.'

'I'm sorry,' said Glycera. 'My older sister died in childbirth. Her baby died, too.'

They gazed at the statue of Diana for a moment. The sculptor had depicted the goddess in bronze: wearing a short fluttering tunic, with her bow half drawn and her eyes on the distant prey. She seemed carefree and happy.

'Tell me, Flavia, do you plan to live for ever?' asked Glycera.

'What do you mean?'

Glycera gestured at the statue of Diana. 'She'll never die. She's a goddess. Immortal. She hunts in the woods and runs free with her friends and has adventures. But if Diana were mortal, and if one day she died, do you know what people would say about her?'

'That she ran free with her friends and had lots of adventures?'

'No. They would say that her legacy was death. Diana did not just kill animals. She also killed men. Like that poor young hunter who accidentally saw her bathing.'

'Actaeon,' said Flavia. 'Narcissus does a brilliant Actaeon.'

'And she was cruel to her nymphs,' said Glycera. 'If any of them became pregnant or wanted to have children she killed them or drove them away. No. Diana may be a great goddess, but she is not a good person.

That's why you can't write about her.' The gilded beads in Glycera's plaited hair clicked softly as she turned to look at Flavia. 'Do you know who you should write about?'

'Who?'

'Octavia. Wife of Marcus Antonius. Elder sister of the Emperor Augustus.'

Flavia frowned. 'I thought Marcus Antonius's wife was Fulvia. The one who took Cicero's severed head onto her lap and stabbed his lifeless tongue with her hairpin.'

Glycera laughed. 'Marcus Antonius had at least four wives during his lifetime. Octavia was his last and best wife. I don't count Cleopatra!'

'Why do you admire Octavia so much?'

'Because she was a loving mother. She nurtured life. She raised Antonius's children by his first wives, and she loved them as if they were her own. Even after she bore Antonius two daughters, she never showed preference. And she also took in other orphans, like young Juba, after Julius Caesar murdered his father.'

'Juba who lived here after he grew up? The one whose bust you have in the garden?'

'Yes. Juba the Second. But Flavia, do you know the most amazing thing?'

Flavia shook her head.

'You know that Antonius fell in love with Cleopatra, the Macedonian ruler of Egypt?'

'Yes. Everybody knows that.'

'Can you imagine how Octavia felt when Antonius left Rome to be with Cleopatra? How hurt and humiliated she must have been?'

'It must have been awful for her.'

'It was. He left Octavia and her children – *his* children – so he could be with that enchantress. And yet Octavia remained in his house in Rome, raising his children, receiving his clients, entertaining his friends. She sent him aid and armies in his fight against the Parthians. She continued to call herself his wife, and to act accordingly.'

Glycera rose from the bench. Her long fingers twisted each other in obvious consternation. 'Later, Antonius wrote Octavia a letter, demanding that she leave his house – her home. She obeyed him. But instead of leaving his children behind in anger, she took them with her to her brother's house. She never stopped behaving as a loving mother and dignified wife.'

Glycera went to the statue of Diana. 'Finally, Antonius was defeated in battle. He killed himself. Soon after, Cleopatra killed herself, too. Some say she had a snake – an asp – brought to her in a basket of figs.' Glycera reached out and touched the sharp bronze point of the huntress' arrow, then turned to look at Flavia. 'Cleopatra chose to die. Chose to abandon her four children: one by Julius Caesar, three by Antonius. And do you know who raised Cleopatra's children? Loved them? Protected them?'

Again, Flavia shook her head.

'Octavia,' said Glycera. 'The humiliated wife of Antonius. She took the children of Cleopatra – her enemy – into her own home. And she loved them. She loved them as if they were her own. Oh, Flavia! That is courage. That is virtue.'

Glycera returned to the bench and showed Flavia one of the rings on her left hand. 'My signet ring bears Octavia's profile. Doesn't she look kind?'

'Yes,' agreed Flavia.

'You should write about Octavia. Not about *her.*' Here Glycera looked up at the bronze statue of Diana. Flavia followed her gaze, and for the first time she saw that the goddess's eyes were cold.

'Mummy! Mummy!' A little boy of about three or four was running up the path towards Glycera. He had tawny skin, a mop of dark curly hair and a toy lyre in one hand. He threw himself onto her lap and began to cover her face with kisses.

Glycera laughed and Flavia saw two other boys approaching, one of about five, the other perhaps fifteen or sixteen. The five-year-old was also dark, with curly hair, but the older boy had light brown hair and blue eyes. He wore a blue tunic with a black meander pattern on the hem. Flavia felt her eyes grow wide: he must be the youth Lupus had seen coming out of Glycera's bedroom.

'Mater!' said the five-year-old. 'Postumus took us to a big tent to see the beasts in their cages. There was an elephant and monkeys, and a man-eating leopard!'

'Flavia,' said Glycera with a laugh, 'these are my sons. Marcus.' Here she kissed the little one on his chubby cheek. 'Gaius.' She patted the five-year-old. 'And Postumus.' She caught the hand of the fifteen-year-old and gave him a smile. The boy smiled back.

'You're her son?' blurted out Flavia.

Postumus nodded and sat on the other end of the bench, beside Glycera. 'Actually,' he said, 'Glycera is my step-mother. My own mother died when I was born. But no son,' he added, 'could ask for a better mother.'

SCROLL XXIII

Flavia put the next part of her plan into effect a short time later, during dinner.

Glycera was not dining with them – she had decided to eat with her children – but Aufidius gave Flavia the perfect opening when he said: 'My wife tells me that you are writing a pantomime.'

Narcissus looked up at Flavia in surprise.

'Yes,' said Flavia. 'I'm writing about the Life and Death of Nero.' She watched the governor carefully to see what his reaction would be.

'Ah,' Aufidius smiled politely and signalled the slave to serve him more lamb. 'My wife thought you might want to write about Octavia. A great heroine of hers, you know.'

'Yes, Octavia is very interesting, but, sir,' Flavia paused to give her words a more dramatic effect, 'I've found a man who witnessed Nero's death. Right here in Volubilis.'

'By the gods!' cried Aufidius, looking up sharply. 'An eyewitness to Nero's suicide? Tell me who.'

'His name is Mendicus. Or that's what he calls himself. He used to be one of Nero's scribes.'

'And what is he doing here in Volubilis?' asked Aufidius.

Flavia hesitated and Jonathan said, 'He's a beggar.'

Aufidius stared at Jonathan open-mouthed.

Lupus slipped off the dining couch, grabbed a silver wine-cup and sat at the foot of a column framed by the wide door of the triclinium. He pulled the back of his tunic over his head and adopted the exact pose of Mendicus.

'By Jove!' cried Aufidius. 'He's not that wretch in the hooded cape who sits outside the basilica?'

They all nodded.

'Extraordinary,' breathed Aufidius. 'I occasionally drop him a copper.' He looked up at them in wonder. 'And you discovered his identity on your second day here?'

'On the first actually,' said Flavia, flushing with pleasure.

'You wouldn't recognise him now,' said Jonathan.

'Why not? What's happened?'

Jonathan grinned. 'Lupus and I took him to the baths this morning. Got the barber to shave him and de-louse him and treated him to a half-hour massage.'

Lupus rose from the foot of the column and pointed to his tunic and sandals.

'We bought him a brand-new tunic, as well,' explained Jonathan. 'And sandals.'

'And we've rented him a room at Triton Tavern,' added Flavia. 'All meals included.'

'Edepol!' exclaimed the governor. He turned to Narcissus. 'And you knew about this?'

'Oh yes!' cried Flavia quickly. 'Narcissus remembered that your uncle served in the court of Nero and he thought Nero's death would amuse you.'

'Capital!' cried Aufidius. 'What a wonderful idea.

I should love to see the Death of Nero portrayed on stage. Much better than Cleopatra. My wife doesn't think much of her, you know.'

For a moment, Narcissus sat frozen with his mouth hanging open, then he recovered himself and forced a smile. 'Perhaps we could perform both stories,' he said stiffly.

'And Narcissus had another brilliant idea!' said Flavia brightly.

'Oh?' said the proconsul, his face alight with interest.

'If your wife doesn't mind, that is.'

'I don't see how she could object to anything you might ask,' he looked from Flavia to Narcissus and back. 'What is your request?'

Flavia took a deep breath. 'Narcissus was wondering,' she said, 'if we could borrow "Nero's Eye" for half an hour, for the performance. After all, it used to belong to Nero and perhaps the plebs would like to see it in a dance about him.'

Flavia held her breath and watched the governor. Everything depended upon his answer.

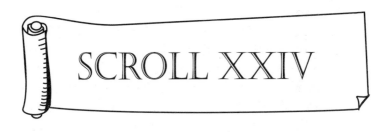

SCROLL XXIV

In the triclinium of the governor's villa it was quiet enough to hear a toothpick drop.

Then the procurator clapped his hands. 'What a brilliant idea!' he cried. 'Putting "Nero's Eye" in a play about Nero! And although it would only be on show for half an hour, it would give hundreds the chance to see it. I have been feeling guilty,' he added, 'for taking it out of circulation. This is the perfect solution. Well done, Narcissus! Well done.'

After dinner, Flavia asked Aufidius if she and her friends could go for a short walk.

'Of course,' he said. 'But take one of my Ethiopians as a torchbearer and bodyguard; it's getting dark. Perseus!' He snapped his fingers and immediately one of his jet-black slaves appeared.

'Yes, master?' said Perseus.

'Accompany these children wherever they want to go. See that no harm comes to them.'

Ten minutes later, Flavia stopped in front of Calypso's Caupona and turned to Perseus. 'Wait here,' she said. 'If we get into any trouble I'll give you a signal.'

'What signal, miss?' asked Perseus politely.

'I'll scream.'

'Very good.' The Ethiopian suppressed a smile. Clasping the torch in both hands, he adopted the pose of a sentry outside the tavern door.

The bead curtain clattered as Flavia led her friends into a dim, smoky space filled with the raucous babble of men, the exotic music of a local group of players and the clacking of a castanet dancer. As soon as Flavia and her friends appeared, the room went quiet for a moment. Flavia strode confidently forward. 'Stay close to me,' she said over her shoulder. 'Safety in numbers. Act like you belong.'

As the musicians struck up again and the woman resumed her rhythmic clacking, the men in the tavern began to speak, though not as loudly as before.

'Hey!' cried the innkeeper, pointing angrily. 'You can't come in here. We don't serve children.'

The music stopped again.

'We don't want anything to drink!' said Flavia imperiously, and wrinkled her nose at the sight of a little plate of roast locusts on one of the tables. 'And we don't want anything to eat, either.'

Beside her Lupus grunted and pointed. Flavia squinted through bluish clouds of lamp-smoke to see a man in a blue turban scowling at them.

'Hello, Uncle Gaius,' she said brightly, then looked around: 'We know this place is popular with you beast-hunters,' she said in a loud voice, 'and that's why we've come here. We're looking for someone who's good with animals.'

Beside her Jonathan held up a gold coin. 'We're looking for someone,' he echoed, 'who'd like to earn a hundred sesterces for an hour's work.'

After a moment's hesitation, half a dozen hands shot up.

Flavia turned to the nearest man. 'What kind of animals do you specialise in?'

'Leopards, lions, cheetahs. Cats of all descriptions.'

Flavia glanced at Nubia, who frowned and gave a tiny shake of her head.

'Sorry,' said Flavia. 'Sounds a bit dangerous.' She turned to another man and tried not to stare at his eye-patch.

'And you?'

'Rhinos and elephants,' said One-eye.

Out of the corner of her eye, Flavia saw Nubia's head shake again.

'Sorry. Too big and pointy.'

'Flavia,' said her uncle sternly. 'What are you doing?' He sounded like the Uncle Gaius she knew.

Flavia offered up a silent prayer of thanks, but continued to ignore him, according to her plan. She turned to a cheerful-looking man in a saffron-yellow turban. 'How about you?'

'Monkeys and apes,' said the man.

Flavia pursed her lips and nodded. 'That's a possibility. Stay right there.'

The man grinned at Gaius. 'Your niece is a bossy little thing, isn't she?'

Gaius nodded grimly. 'And rebellious.' His wooden chair legs scraped on the floor as he stood up. 'Flavia, what are you doing?'

Flavia brought her mouth close to his ear and whispered, 'We need an animal to make a surprise appearance at the theatre in a few days. One that will cause people to panic, but only a little.'

Her uncle sucked his breath in through his teeth. 'Panic is an unpredictable and dangerous thing.'

'I know. That's why we have to choose the right trainer, and the right animal. We only want a brief distraction, not pandemonium.' She turned to an ugly-looking thug in a tiger-skin cloak. 'What about you?' she said. 'What kind of animals do you train?'

'Dik-diks,' said Tiger-skin. 'You know: those little bitty gazelles. I like them because they're so cute,' he added.

'I have an idea,' said Gaius, stepping forward.

'No, Uncle Gaius,' said Flavia airily. 'You asked us to leave you alone and we will respect your request.'

Suddenly the castanet dancer appeared before them. She began to undulate and clack, and the band struck up an exotic tune with a strong beat.

Flavia covered Lupus's eyes with her hands. 'No, thank you,' she giggled. 'Too sexy.'

Lupus pushed her hands away, but now Gaius was standing between them and the castanet dancer.

'No, Uncle Gaius,' said Flavia patiently. 'We don't want your help.'

'You always were a rebellious girl,' he said, folding his hands across his chest. 'Now it's my turn to rebel. I'm going to help you whether you like it or not.'

When they returned from the tavern with Perseus, another of the ebony door-slaves bowed and said: 'The illustrious procurator requests your presence. He says you will be amazed. Follow me.'

Nubia heard the music as they passed through the lofty atrium and into one of the garden courtyards. It became louder as they approached the triclinium and suddenly she found her heart was pounding. She only knew one person who could play the lyre so beautifully: her tutor Aristo.

SCROLL XXV

As Nubia followed the others towards the procurator's triclinium, she heard the unmistakable notes of Aristo's lyre.

But it was a new song, one she had never heard him play before. And how could he be here, in the furthest outpost of the Roman Empire? And now she heard a man's light, raspy voice, singing in Greek.

Her heart sank. It was not Aristo. But whoever was playing was one of the best musicians she had ever heard.

The ebony door-slave stood to one side, gave a little bow and gestured for them to enter. Nubia was the last into the room and she followed the amazed stares of her friends.

'Isn't he wonderful?' Aufidius wore a wide grin. 'I'm so glad you brought him to my attention.'

On a dining couch next to the governor sat a shaven-headed man playing a lyre. It took Nubia a moment to recognise the man playing so beautifully. It was Mendicus, the beggar of Volubilis.

The next morning, Flavia pretended to go with the others to the theatre to rehearse, but as soon as they had turned the corner, she asked Narcissus if she could run back to bring the last sheet of the libretto for 'The Death of Nero'. She had finished it by lamplight the night before, and had the four sheets of papyrus hidden under her tunic, but she needed an excuse to escape for half an hour.

Narcissus coldly agreed; he was still angry with her for forcing him to learn a new pantomime in less than three days. She shrugged off his icy displeasure and as soon as he and the others were out of sight she made for the Eastern Gate.

Her uncle Gaius was waiting outside, as they had agreed the night before, and he led her to the pavilion of the Pentasii.

As they entered the tent, several men called out greetings to Gaius. He answered cheerfully and slapped one of them manfully on the back. He was wearing his blue turban, a very un-Roman blue-and-beige-striped caftan, and his strange little beard. She could hardly believe this was her grieving uncle.

'There she is,' he said at last, pointing to a wooden cage. 'Nissa. Sweet as a kitten. Wouldn't hurt a baby rabbit. Go on, you can stroke her.'

The lithe she-leopard stopped pacing in her cage, and regarded Flavia with large golden eyes. Flavia reached her hand through the wooden bars and tentatively stroked the big cat's head.

'Oh!' cried Flavia, snatching back her hand. 'She's growling at me!'

Her uncle laughed. 'She's not growling. She's purring. She likes you.'

Flavia cautiously extended her hand and stroked the cat behind her plush ear. 'Oh, Uncle Gaius, she's beautiful. And you think she'll play the part? Panic without pandemonium?'

'She'll be perfect,' he replied. 'Look! She's even been de-clawed. Unlike that creature.' He indicated a leopard in the cage next door. This cat had cold green eyes and she was extending and retracting razor-sharp claws.

Flavia bent forward to see the label on the cage: 'Ungula,' read Flavia, and looked at her uncle wide-eyed. 'That means "claw"!'

'Correct. She's the fiercest creature in this tent.' He chuckled. 'Do you know what enrages her?'

'What?' asked Flavia.

'She hates the sound of tambourines.'

'Tambourines?' echoed Flavia, and then gulped. 'I play the tambourine.'

'Well, whatever you do, don't ever bring one in here. The man who caught her used to beat her with a tambourine. Until one day she killed him and ate him. They say that's how she got her taste for human flesh.'

For the next three days they rehearsed 'The Death of Nero' morning and afternoon, with only a break at noon for a visit to the baths.

On the afternoon of the last day Jonathan showed Narcissus the apparatus that would raise him up for the finale of the Death of Antonius and Cleopatra.

Narcissus gave the rope an experimental tug and looked up at the lofty beam from which it hung. 'So. This is safe? I won't fall down?'

Jonathan nodded. 'It's safe. The old caretaker here told me they once used it to lower a four-horse chariot driven by the god Apollo. Not real horses, of course. And not the real Apollo. But it could easily support you. I'd bet my life on it.'

'Then you wouldn't mind trying it yourself?'

'Of course not,' said Jonathan, after the merest pause. 'In fact, why don't you go up and operate the winch? That's what I'll be doing tomorrow. You'll see how easy and safe it is.'

Narcissus nodded and disappeared behind the scaena. Presently he reappeared on the highest level, three stories up. His face seemed very high and remote.

'Do I just turn this handle?' he called down.

'Yes!' Jonathan shouted back. 'Do you see how you can flip the handle of the winch to lock it?'

'Come on then!' called back Narcissus. 'Get on. Let's try it out.'

Jonathan glanced at Flavia and the others. They were in the orchestra practising the comical, jolly finale from 'Venus and Vulcan'. Their backs were to him and they were intent on their song.

Jonathan shrugged and eased himself onto the piece of canvas between two ropes that joined further up.

'You're Antonius!' he called up to Narcissus. 'You're dying from a self-inflicted stab wound in your stomach. You're in great pain. You stretch out like this and lift your hands up toward Cleopatra. That will be me wearing a mask. Whoa!' he cried, as he felt himself pulled up into the air. 'Not so fast! Not so fast!'

'Sorry!' called Narcissus, not stopping. 'Am I going too fast? Is this too fast?'

'Yes!' yelped Jonathan. 'Too fast! Slow down!'

Narcissus abruptly stopped cranking and Jonathan came to a jerking halt, swinging twenty-five feet above the stage. Narcissus leaned out of the window in the scaena and looked down at Jonathan. There was something in his gaze that made Jonathan's stomach twist.

'I think it's all a bit dangerous,' said Narcissus, his kohl-rimmed blue eyes gazing steadily at Jonathan. 'What you're doing, I mean.'

'No,' wheezed Jonathan. 'It's perfectly safe. Really. Actors do it all the time ... *deus ex machina*.' His chest was tight. It was hard for him to breathe. Relax. He must relax.

'What are you doing here?' Narcissus's voice was cold.

'What?'

'The four of you. Not related to one another. No adult supervision. Imperial passes around your necks. As soon as I saw those I knew you were more than you pretended to be. So, what are you doing here?'

'We were looking for Flavia's uncle!' gasped Jonathan. 'And now we're doing a pantomime ... Pull me up and I'll ... show you how easy ... it is to get off.'

Down below his friends were still playing their jolly tune, oblivious.

'Tell me again, Jonathan, what happens if I let go of the crank?' asked Narcissus, almost casually.

'No! Don't do that! You don't want to let go.' Jonathan cautiously turned his head to look down and his stomach writhed. 'If you do ... I'll fall down ... go splat ... make big mess ... no show tomorrow.'

Suddenly he was falling. A heartbeat later he jerked to a stop.

'Why did you come to Africa?' asked Narcissus. 'The real reason. The truth.'

'I told you ... We came to find ... Flavia's uncle.' Jonathan could hear himself wheezing. 'We've done that now ... so if you'll just ... let me down now ... we can all ... go home.'

'You're not going anywhere,' said Narcissus. 'Not until you tell the truth.'

'Whoa! Stop!' cried Jonathan, as he fell another half foot downwards.

'Why is your bossy little friend so intent on me performing The Death of Nero?'

'She thought it would please the governor,' gasped Jonathan.

'Is it something to do with that big emerald? Or with the rumours that Nero never died?'

Down below, the jolly tune had stopped. Jonathan cautiously turned his head. He saw five concerned, distant faces gazing up at them. Jonathan turned back to look at Narcissus. The dancer's handsome face wore a smile, as if everything was normal. But there was a clear note of menace in his voice as he began to turn the winch. 'It doesn't matter,' he said, 'because by noon tomorrow, everything will have changed.'

'He *what*?' cried Flavia later that evening. 'He almost dropped you from the top of the scaena?'

They had practised all day long, with only a short break for lunch, then dined with the governor as usual. Now they were meeting by lamplight in the girls' room, alone for the first time that day.

'Yes,' said Jonathan. 'For a moment I thought he was going to drop me. If you hadn't looked up ...'

Lupus was giving Jonathan a look of disbelieving horror.

'You didn't betray our plan did you?' whispered Flavia.

'No, of course not. But he knows we're up to something.' Jonathan paused and took a breath. 'Flavia, I think Narcissus is up to something, too. He said that by noon tomorrow, everything would be different.'

'He said what?'

'He said that by noon tomorrow everything would be different. No. That everything will have changed.'

'What on earth can he mean by that?' mused Flavia.

Lupus sheepishly raised his hand.

'Yes, Lupus?' whispered Flavia. 'Do you know something?'

Lupus gave a queasy smile and nodded. He wrote on his wax tablet:

CASINA IS THE GREAT GREAT GRAND-
DAUGHTER OF ANTONIUS AND CLEO.
NARCISSUS GOING TO ANNOUNCE THIS
AFTER THEY PERFORM DEATH OF CLEO.
THEY WILL THEN TAKE OVER THE WORLD.

'What!?' gasped Flavia and Jonathan together.

OR MAYBE JUST CLAIM CLEO'S JEWELS, he
added with a shrug. I'M NOT SURE OF THE
EXACT PLAN

They all stared at him.

Then Nubia looked at Flavia. 'That is why Casina wears coin of Cleopatra.'

'And that's why she resembles Cleopatra,' breathed Flavia. 'Great Juno's peacock! Why didn't we realise it before?' She looked at Lupus. 'When did you find out about this? Recently?'

He waggled his hand, then nodded.

'And when did you say he's going to make the announcement?'

Lupus pointed to the part of this tablet where he had written: AFTER DEATH OF CLEO

'After the pantomime?'

Lupus nodded.

'I suppose it doesn't matter then,' said Flavia slowly. 'Because our pantomime is first on the programme. And by then, if everything goes according to plan, we'll have the object of our quest.'

It was the first day of the new governor's festival, and the theatre of Volubilis was filled with an excited throng of people. Like the theatre at Sabratha, it had a monumental three-story scaena, with hidden peepholes for cast and crew waiting backstage.

Nubia stood at one of these peepholes, next to Flavia and Lupus, who each had a peephole, too. Jonathan was up above them, double-checking the winch that would lift Narcissus up for the final scene in the Death of Cleopatra. Nubia stepped back and looked up at him. He waved down at her and gave her a thumbs-up.

Nubia put her eye back to her spy-hole. She could see Aufidius sitting in the front row beside the other magistrates. They had their own armchairs and slaves to fan them. Glycera and their three children sat in the row directly behind him, with other wives and children of dignitaries. In the rows behind them sat rich merchants and their families, with slaves and freedmen further back and higher up.

'Some of them have been here since before dawn,' said a voice behind them. Nubia turned to see Casina, whose face was white as parchment. 'Not the magistrates,' she added, 'their seats are reserved.'

'Are you all right?' Nubia asked her. 'You look most pale.'

'I'm fine,' said Casina.

'You do not look fine. You looked terrified,' said Nubia.

The singer gave a false laugh. 'Just a bit of stage-fright,' she said. 'It will pass as soon as we start.'

Nubia was nervous, too, but her fear was more than stage fright. They were about to execute a complicated theft of a valuable jewel.

She glanced around. To her left and to her right – at the stage doors – stood soldiers acting as guards. She knew there were also guards standing at each of the vomitoria, or exits, to keep the crowd moving. The world grew suddenly dimmer and Nubia looked up to see a small cloud pass before the sun.

'Look!' hissed Flavia from her peephole. 'It's Mendicus. He wants to sit in the magistrate's seats.'

Nubia and Casina both put their eyes to the peepholes.

'Behold!' said Nubia. 'Aufidius tells them to let him stay.'

'That's nice of him!' said Flavia. 'He's letting him have a cushion at his feet.'

A shape blotted out Nubia's peephole and a moment later she heard the distinctive sound of the herald's bronze staff striking marble.

'Honoured Magistrates, Esteemed Citizens, Residents of Volubilis!' began the herald. 'Respected Visitors, Women and Children ... Welcome! Welcome to our festival in honour of the goddess Minerva, patroness of our new procurator, Gnaeus Aufidius Chius. It is he who has sponsored these games.'

Nubia heard the crowd cheer and clap.

'He prays,' continued the herald in his huge voice, 'that this festival will find favour with the goddess of wisdom and warfare, and with all of you, also! This festival is for your edification, education and enjoyment.'

The crowd cheered again and Nubia heard a woman cry 'Narcissus! We want Narcissus!'

'Narcissus can edificate me any time!' quipped another female voice from the back rows, and the crowd laughed.

'And now,' blared the herald, 'I have great pleasure in introducing the great Narcissus and his troupe of musicians, all the way from Alexandria. Today they will perform a double bill beginning with ...' here he paused for dramatic effect: '"The Death of Nero!"'

SCROLL XXVI

As Nubia followed Hanno and Barbarus out from behind the scaena, the roar of the crowd struck her as forcibly as the blast of heat from the glassmaker's furnace. She could physically feel a wave of adoration and anticipation washing over her. She followed the two musicians down the six marble steps to the circle of the orchestra, aware of Flavia and Lupus coming behind her.

Nubia stared around in wonder. She had been used to practising in an empty theatre, and now the cavea was packed with people of all ages and colours and backgrounds, their happy expectant faces the only thing they all had in common.

Hanno and Barbarus were looking at her with encouraging smiles, so Nubia took a deep breath and lifted her flute to her lips. In a single heartbeat the theatre was silent, and she could hear the pure notes of her flute thrown back to her from the giant shell full of people. It was like listening to someone else, and it sounded so wonderful that she almost laughed with pleasure. Then Hanno began to buzz his aulos, Barbarus to strum his cithara and Flavia to jingle her tambourine. Lupus patted a goatskin drum on a strap round his chest and kept beat with his iron-soled right shoe. As Nubia looked out over the audience she could already see hands twitching, feet tapping and heads nodding to the rhythm.

She glanced at the back of the proscaenium. A small square table stood there, laid out with masks, garlands and other props. Her sharp eyes caught the gleam of green: the governor had put Nero's Eye on the table as requested.

Still playing her flute, Nubia turned back to look at the governor. His face was cheerful and expectant. Behind him Glycera was consoling her youngest son, Marcus, who was crying. Mendicus sat happily on a cushion at the governor's feet, holding Marcus's toy lyre.

A fresh burst of applause welcomed Casina as she came down the steps and took her place before the musicians. Once again, the applause ceased the moment the Egyptian girl began to sing. Her pure voice soared above the music and filled the whole world.

'*Help me, Polyhymnia,*' Casina sang the words which Flavia had written, '*Inspire me to sing, and these to play, and him to dance, the Song of Nero. Some called Nero a monster, others a saviour. Which was he? Tell us, O Muse! Reveal the Truth!*'

Nubia turned and tried to smile at Flavia but it was difficult to play the flute and smile at the same time.

The crowd gave the loudest roar yet as Narcissus leapt onto the stage.

Because Nubia and the others stood to one side of the proscaenium, they could see him perfectly. He wore a short white tunic over flesh-coloured silk leggings. A toga of purple silk billowed out behind him as he ran to centre stage. He wore a mask of a handsome young man.

'Nero was an artist in his heart and in his soul,' sang Casina, 'Accomplished at lyre and cithara.'

On stage, Narcissus used his hands to perfectly mimic someone playing a lyre. From the front row came the sound of one person clapping enthusiastically. Nubia turned her body a little as she played. She saw the lone clapper was Mendicus the beggar. Governor Aufidius patted him benevolently on the shoulder and leaned forward to say something in his ear. Mendicus stopped clapping and picked up the toy lyre.

Casina sang: 'Not content with the blessings of the Muses, Nero claimed the gifts of an athlete, too. Skilled at racing chariots was he, and once he rode a chariot pulled by ten horses, ungelded stallions all!'

Now Narcissus mimed stepping into an invisible chariot. The music was still joyful and quick, but Nubia picked up the pace even more as Narcissus burst from the stalls. Beside Nubia, Lupus had pushed aside his drum and was using wooden sticks on the marble lip of the stage to make the sound of horses' hooves. The crowd laughed and cheered and clapped. In the front row, Mendicus had risen to his feet and was jumping up and down like an excited child. With his shaven head, bulging blue eyes and potbelly, he looked like an oversized toddler.

Nubia turned back to watch Narcissus. His whole body leaned forward, his left hand twitching imaginary reins, his right wielding the whip. She could almost see the wind tugging his hair. The music they were playing was racing music, with an urgent jingling beat that conveyed a sense of speed and excitement. Nubia had composed this piece by remembering the time she had ridden on the back of a chariot in the Circus Maximus in Rome.

Suddenly, Narcissus took the imaginary turn too sharply and mimed being thrown out of the chariot. Lupus clashed the cymbals a fraction of a second too early, but it didn't matter. The whole crowd gasped, then cried out in alarm as Narcissus tumbled violently over and over, finally coming to a rest at the very precipice of the stage.

For a moment a perfect hush fell over the theatre. Was he really injured?

Then Narcissus leapt to his feet, and the real crowd cheered as he bowed to an imaginary one.

Nubia brought her flute to her lips and gave a nod and the music began again.

'*Nero won many crowns,*' sang Casina, '*and many wreaths of laurel.*' As she sang, Jonathan tossed garlands down from his hiding place behind a column on the second story of the backdrop.

Narcissus ran back and forth, so that the garlands fell onto his upraised arms like hoops on a pole. As the last garland fell, he positioned himself beneath it so that it landed neatly on his head, only a little askew.

'*He won many crowns,*' Casina was singing, '*not just for his prowess at racing chariots, but for song, dance and even pantomime.*' As she sang this last phrase, Narcissus bowed. As he bent his masked head, the garland fell. He deftly caught it on the toe of his bare foot, then kicked it out into the audience.

The audience cheered as he spun out the other garlands, making sure some reached the poorer patrons at the back of the theatre, as well as the rich ones at the front.

Nubia sighed. They had stayed up late the night before weaving those garlands. Abruptly a scuffle broke out in the second and third rows on the left. Finally Mendicus emerged, waving his trophy – a tattered garland. 'It's mine,' he exulted, 'I won the crown again!'

As the guards moved forward to restrain him, the beggar pulled the garland onto his head and sat quickly at the governor's feet, then gave them a look of such triumphant defiance that Nubia almost giggled into the mouthpiece of her flute.

'*Nero was always generous,*' sang Casina, as Narcissus tossed away the last garland, '*caring for his subjects as a mother cares for her child.*'

Nubia glanced at Hanno and raised her eyebrows. That was their cue to change to a minor key. Together they played a chord so poignant that it made the tiny hairs on her neck prickle as she heard it resonate back.

This key change marked the next movement of the piece. Flavia stopped jingling and Lupus slowed down the beat.

'*As a mother cares for her child,*' Casina was singing, her voice low and full of yearning. '*A mother, a mother, a mother . . . Nero's mother: Agrippina. A mother cares for her child but this mother had no care for her little boy.*'

Narcissus was at the little marble table near the scaena, his back to the audience, his shoulders slumped in the very picture of a rejected child. Nubia had seen him rehearse this many times, but even so a lump came to her throat and she had to look away. She saw Mendicus sitting in the front row, his head down and his shoulders shaking, weeping as if his heart would break.

'*Agrippina was evil,*' sang Casina, and her tone was ominous now. '*She was cruel, devoid of that natural softness which all women have. She was a Medea, one who would kill her own offspring, just to spite her enemies.*'

Nubia knew Narcissus's posture was changing and that he had taken off one mask and replaced it with another. The audience gasped when he turned to suddenly face them. It was a mask of evil female beauty and Nubia did not like to look at it.

'Agrippina, mother of Nero,' sang Casina. In the blue sky, a small cloud passed before the sun, dimming the bright day. 'Agrippina plotted and poisoned and killed, and finally had to be removed, as the surgeon cuts away the tumour, or lances the boil, or burns the leprous flesh.'

In the front row, Mendicus moaned audibly. Nubia knew without looking that Narcissus was writhing in an obscene dance, moving back towards the table.

The crowd cheered as Narcissus turned to show them the Nero mask again.

'Nero Caesar,' sang Casina, 'did the gods' bidding. Just as Orestes obeyed Apollo. It was the bravest thing he had ever done: to rid Rome of that Harpy. She fed on scraps of decayed rumour and poisoned men with her vomitings. Nobody understood what a great sacrifice it was for him to sacrifice her. Even though she had only ever given him bad things. The only good thing she ever gave Nero was his life. His life and an emerald.'

An excited murmur rippled through the theatre as Narcissus lifted the emerald from the props table, and Nubia turned just in time to see its green flash as the sun emerged from behind the cloud. The audience buzzed with excitement.

But now there was a commotion in the front row. Aufidius and another magistrate were holding back Mendicus, who was struggling and twisting, his arms stretched towards the emerald. 'The Seeing-thing!' he cried. 'It's my Seeing-thing!'

The guards started towards him, then one of them cried out and Nubia saw their eyes turn in disbelief toward the proscaenium. A she-leopard had appeared from stage right and she was pacing directly towards Narcissus.

SCROLL XXVII

Women screamed and men yelled as the leopard padded across the stage. Narcissus dropped the emerald on the table and backed towards the scaena, his eyes behind the smiling mask wide with terror.

Flavia tried not to smile. This was part of their plan.

'Don't be alarmed!' came a man's voice, and her Uncle Gaius strode out onto the stage, right on cue. 'Nissa is not fierce. She is tame.' He looked at the audience and gestured for them to stay seated. 'Nobody move!' he continued, in a voice full of authority. 'She is tame and perfectly harmless, but like most animals, she dislikes panic or noise.' He pointed at Narcissus, who stood visibly trembling. 'You! Play dead.' He turned to Flavia and her friends: 'You! Play calming music.' He gave Flavia a quick wink. 'Nissa likes calming music.'

Flavia suppressed a grin as Nubia played a soft deep tune on her flute. Lupus pattered a soft beat. Flavia jingled her tambourine.

The leopard turned towards Flavia and snarled.

'Back, creature!' cried Gaius cheerfully. 'I will need a chair or table.' He looked around and pretended to spot the table for the first time. 'There. A table!' He went to the table and tipped off the masks and the other props.

Flavia knew this was the moment for him to switch the gemstones. For a moment he had his back to the audience.

Flavia jingled her tambourine again, and again Nissa snarled and turned cold, green eyes towards her.

But now Gaius was brandishing the table with the legs pointing towards the leopard. 'Back, beast!' he cried. 'Back against the scaena!'

Flavia jingled softly and the leopard slashed out at her uncle.

The flute music stopped. 'Flavia!' hissed Nubia. 'Behold that is not Nissa. It is Ungula!'

'What?' gasped Flavia.

'I hear claws scratching on marble. You were telling me Nissa has no claws. It is Ungula, the fierce one.'

Up on stage Gaius was driving the snarling leopard towards the tall stone scaena.

'Ungula the man-eater?' said Flavia. 'The one who hates tambourines?'

Nubia nodded and Flavia squealed and dropped her tambourine in horror.

The tambourine clattered onto the ground and once again the leopard lashed out.

'Whoa! Kitty!' cried Gaius, jumping back just in time. 'Whoa!'

A ripple of laughter ran through the audience and Nubia began to play a soft and soothing melody. Casina began to sing 'la-la-la' in a tremulous voice.

'We've got to warn him!' hissed Flavia. Lupus nodded but Casina, still doing her la-la's looked at Flavia with a frown.

'That's not the tame leopard!' cried Flavia. 'It's a man-eater! You must warn my uncle!'

Casina stopped singing la-la. 'You know that leopard?' she gasped.

'Yes, but it's the wrong leopard. It was supposed to be a tame one. Please, Casina. Sing a song to warn him! We don't want the people to panic.'

Casina nodded. '*Sometimes*,' she sang, but her voice cracked and she had to begin again: '*Sometimes things are not what they seem. Sometimes a duplicate appears, a dangerous one takes the place of the real. Sometimes False appears instead of True. And so I cry: Beware! All is not what it seems!*'

'Come here, Kitty,' Gaius was saying. He had put down the table and was leaning forward to put the leash around Ungula's neck. Flavia's heart was thudding. He had not heard their warning. She opened her mouth to call a warning but before she could a voice came from her left.

'No! I'm not false. I'm the true one!' With a cry, Mendicus broke free of the guards' restraint, leapt up onto the proscaenium and ran for the objects that had scattered on the stage. 'Where's my seeing-thing?' he cried. He did not seem to notice the leopard, but she noticed him. As Mendicus barged past, the big cat swiped at him with her paw.

And suddenly Mendicus was down on the stage, screaming and clutching his thigh. People in the upper rows of the theatre began to scream and point. And Flavia's eyes widened in horror as she saw what they saw: a pool of red was spreading across the stage. And this was no silk scarf. It was human blood.

Up on stage, Flavia's Uncle Gaius was white as chalk: 'Great Jupiter's eyebrows!' he cried, backing away. 'It's not Nissa. It's Ungula. It's the man-eater!' He bumped into the table, hesitated, then reached behind him and lifted it. With the legs pointing towards the creature, Gaius slowly approached. With one lazy motion the leopard batted a leg of the table, knocking Gaius back against the scaena. His head flew back and struck a marble column, then he slowly sank to the stage, unconscious.

'Ow, it hurts!' Mendicus was screaming and leaving a glistening smear of blood as he pulled himself backwards across the stage. 'Ow, it hurts!'

But the she-leopard Ungula was no longer concerned with the beggar or with Gaius, she was approaching Narcissus. The pantomime dancer stood pinned against the scaena. His mask still wore its incongruous frozen smile, but Flavia was close enough to see the stark terror in his eyes. The whole theatre was suddenly still and silent as the leopard crouched, reading herself for the spring to his throat. Even Mendicus had stopped moving, and watched the big cat in horrified fascination.

'No! Leave him alone!' Casina was suddenly on stage, the tambourine in her hand, banging it hard against her thigh.

With a snarl of fury the leopard turned towards Casina, crouched and launched itself at the girl.

The she-leopard had sunk her teeth into Casina's shoulder and was shaking the screaming girl from side to side, like a dog with rabbit.

Lupus knew he had to act now. He vaulted onto the stage and ran for the net that lay beneath Gaius's shoulder. Ignoring the blood, he tugged the net free and ran towards the leopard, now dragging Casina towards the exit. With a quick prayer, Lupus tossed the net.

The big cat dropped Casina and batted the net away. But one of her claws caught the rope and soon both forepaws were entangled. The she-leopard snarled as she fought the strange ropy creature and now the guards had finally come to their senses. They were rushing forward with their swords and one of them darted in to have a swipe.

The she-leopard snarled and in trying to bat him she overbalanced and rolled back onto the stage.

The crowd cheered. This was better than any pantomime or wild beast hunt they had ever seen.

Lupus looked around frantically for something he could use as a weapon: a bow, a blunt object, a stone for his sling belt, anything.

'Lupus!' called a voice from up above. 'The table.'

Lupus looked up to see a canvas strap descending

on ropes suspended from a beam. This was Jonathan's method for lifting Antonius up to Cleopatra.

'Hang the table from the harness by one leg!' called Jonathan.

Instantly, Lupus understood Jonathan's plan. He ran to the small props table, and lifted it. He was surprised by how heavy it was: the polished top must be solid marble. The harness swung back, then down towards Lupus, and he was easily able to pull the canvas strap under one of the bronze legs of the table.

At once the table rose into the air and moved across the stage – swinging precariously – until it hung directly above the netted leopard.

Ungula stopped struggling with the net and tried to bat the table's shadow. Then she looked up. For an impossibly long moment, the whole theatre held its breath. Then the table fell on the she-leopard, and she lay still, stunned by the direct hit.

The crowd cheered then grew silent again as Narcissus tore off his mask and ran to Casina.

'Casina! My love!' he cried, and lifted her onto his lap. 'Are you all right?'

She nodded her head weakly. 'I think so,' she groaned. 'Are you?'

Flavia saw him close his eyes in relief. Then he raised his face and looked out at the crowd. 'Have you ever seen anything so brave?' he said in a voice that must have carried to the furthest seats. 'She risked her life for mine!' He looked round at the audience. 'Such bravery can only come from noble stock.'

He smeared his palm into the blood pooling beneath her shoulder and held up his red and dripping hand.

'This blood,' he cried, 'the blood of this girl, is royal blood! Although her father was illegitimate, his blood and hers also is royal.' Narcissus filled his lungs. 'For this brave girl is a descendant of—'

'No!' cried Casina, catching his wrist. 'I'm not her descendant! Stop it!'

'You what?'

Casina was crying. 'I only said that to make you like me. I never thought it would go this far. I never thought you would really do it.'

'You mean you're not the great, great-granddaughter of Marcus Antonius and Cleopatra?' He was whispering but Flavia was close enough to hear him. 'Their blood doesn't run in your veins?'

Casina shook her head. 'My grandmother wasn't Julia Urania, and my mother wasn't Drusilla. She's just a seamstress from Alexandria. And my father owns a fuller's shop.' Tears were running down her cheeks. 'I'm just an ugly girl with a big nose and frizzy hair. None of the boys would even look at me. Then one day my best friend showed me a picture of Cleopatra on a coin. That's what gave me the idea.'

He stared at her aghast.

'I looked just like Cleopatra on the coin,' she sobbed. 'She had frizzy hair and a big nose, too. But men adored her. That's what gave me the idea.'

Narcissus stood up, allowing her head to fall with a crack onto the stage. 'You lied to me?'

'Only to make you notice me!' She lifted up her arms. 'Narcissus, I love you! I'd do anything for you. But I can't pretend to be who I'm not.'

'You let me come two thousand miles to this bar-barian backwater, practising the story of Cleopatra every night, just to tell me you're a fuller's daughter?' He took a step back. 'You deceiving harpy! How could you do this to me?'

Casina allowed her wounded arm to fall back to the stage. 'Narcissus! Don't leave me! I love you. I would die for you.'

He took a step away, then turned back and bent down. His tawny hair covered his face but Flavia heard him hiss, 'You made a fool of me. I hope you *do* die.'

Then he turned and hurried to where Mendicus lay moaning on the stage.

Nubia ran up the half dozen steps to the stage in order to help the sobbing Casina. Flavia followed to attend to her uncle. She almost slipped on a pool of blood beneath his head. A moment later the crowd cheered. Flavia turned to see some of her uncle's beast-hunter friends rolling a wheeled wooden cage towards the stunned she-leopard.

And now everything happened at once. Men and women swarmed onto the stage, the beast-hunters gingerly lifted Ungula into the cage and lictors arrived to calm the crowd and usher people out of the theatre. Several doctors had rushed onto the stage, too. Flavia saw a turbaned man attending to Casina, and a bald one had just finished binding Mendicus's thigh. And now a man was standing over her uncle's unconscious form.

'I am a doctor,' he said in Greek-accented Latin. 'May I help?'

'Oh please!' cried Flavia. She eased her uncle's head onto her lap and allowed the doctor to feel a pulse in his neck and pull back one of his eyelids. Gaius groaned and his eyelids fluttered.

'He's going to be all right,' said the doctor. 'But I

must apply styptic to staunch the flow of blood, and I must bind his wound. Then he must rest.'

A shadow fell across her and she looked up to see Jonathan standing beside the doctor, he had come down from the scaena.

'He's going to be all right,' said Flavia. 'The doctor's going to bind his head.'

Jonathan nodded. 'Yes,' he said. 'He's regaining consciousness. I'm going to see how Casina is. That leopard was chewing her shoulder. What on earth happened?' he began, then caught himself, shook his head and ran to Casina.

Flavia looked back down at her uncle. His face was very pale but his eyes were open. He winced as the doctor tied off the strip of linen around his head.

'You'll be all right,' said the doctor in Greek, and he stood up. 'Just make sure you get plenty of rest. My name is Eudynamos,' he added. 'I live near the tanners' quarter if you feel you need further attention.'

'Flavia,' muttered her uncle, 'please give the doctor some money. In my belt pouch.'

Flavia nodded and reached into his coin purse. Her fingers encountered the cool polished surface of the emerald with a shock. In the chaos she had forgotten all about their mission.

'How could I have taken the wrong leopard?' he whispered, when the doctor had gone. 'The label on the cage said "Nissa".'

Flavia looked up at Lupus, Jonathan and Nubia, who had come to stand in a semi-circle around her uncle. Nubia's yellow silk caftan was stained with blood.

'They've taken Casina to the procurator's house,' said Jonathan. 'The doctor says it's a miracle that she's alive.'

'I'm sure it was the right leopard,' whispered Gaius again. 'I don't understand.'

Jonathan squatted beside Gaius. 'Don't worry, sir. She's going to be fine.'

Suddenly a woman screamed and Flavia heard someone cry: 'It's gone! Someone has stolen Nero's Eye!' The voice was Glycera's.

Flavia looked at her uncle. 'Didn't you leave the replica among the other props?' she asked in a low voice.

'Of course,' he said, his voice so faint she could barely hear. 'With the garlands and the masks. I put it down carefully, so as not to break it.'

'Great Juno's peacock!' Flavia breathed. 'We've got the real one but now someone's stolen the replica!'

'Stop!' cried Aufidius in a huge voice. 'No person is to leave this theatre until we have searched everyone. Lictors! Guard the exits.'

Flavia looked wide-eyed at her uncle. If they found the emerald on his person they might crucify him.

An urgent grunt from Lupus. She looked up at him. He was opening and closing his hand very rapidly, as if to say: Give it to me.

Flavia reached over to her uncle's leather coin purse and opened it. Lupus nodded, glanced around and reached into the purse. A moment later he was gone. When Flavia saw him again, he was standing on the other side of the wheeled wooden cage containing Ungula, which four men from the Pentasii Beast Hunting Corporation were wheeling away.

Presently Lupus was beside them again, helping Flavia and Jonathan assist Gaius to his feet. Flavia caught his eye, then glanced at the cage and raised her eyebrows. Lupus nodded.

And now they were in the queue to leave the theatre, supporting Gaius, who was still unsteady. Up ahead the lictors were searching those leaving.

Flavia watched them pat down the four beast-hunters, then held her breath as they glanced at the cage. Ungula was still entangled in the net, but blood stained her muzzle, and her green eyes gazed coldly at the two lictors. They glanced at each other, then waved the cage on. Flavia breathed a sigh of relief.

A moment later she and her uncle were patted down, and his belt-pouch searched, and then they were through.

'Come on, Uncle Gaius,' she said. 'Let's get you back to your lodgings.'

They were halfway to Calypso's Caupona when an empty litter jogged up beside them. Flavia recognised the four litter bearers: they were black as ebony and wore only red loincloths and matching turbans.

'Our master says the brave beast-fighter must come to stay at his villa,' said the one called Jason. They put down the litter and helped her uncle in. When Gaius was installed, the four Ethiopians lifted the poles and trotted back towards the governor's villa.

Flavia and her friends hurried after them.

'What happened to Narcissus?' Flavia asked Jonathan. 'Did you see?'

'Narcissus left just before the soldiers started searching people,' said Jonathan. 'I saw him helping Mendicus out of the theatre.'

'He abandons poor Casina,' said Nubia.

'I know,' said Flavia. 'I guess he only liked her when

he thought she was descended from Cleopatra. Poor girl.'

Suddenly a turbaned man clamped his hand on Flavia's forearm. She gasped and looked up into the face of a stocky man in a cream turban. Behind him loomed his bodyguard: a man in a one-sleeved pink tunic with a head like an upside-down egg.

'Taurus!' cried Flavia. 'And Pullo. You're here!'

Taurus nodded. 'We just arrived. Heard there was a commotion at the theatre. Came straight here to find lictors searching people at the exits and everyone talking about a stolen gem.' He lowered his voice. 'Did you really do it? Did you get it? Where is it?'

Flavia stared at him. He had deserted them over a month ago, and now he wanted the fruit of their labours.

'Why did you sail without us?' she cried. 'And where are all our things? Our clothes, our money, our musical instruments? You abandoned us in Sabratha!'

'My dear girl, we didn't abandon you. We all thought you were on board, down in the hold. When we realised our mistake we returned to Sabratha.'

'You did?'

'Of course. We spent a week scouring the town for you but had no luck. So we set sail again for Lixus, intending to meet you here. Contrary winds delayed us, but as you can see, we got here eventually.' He bent closer. 'Did you succeed in your mission?'

'Yes,' said Flavia. 'Only we didn't mean for the theft to be discovered so soon. We made a glass replica and switched it for the real thing. But someone stole the replica. They probably think they have the real gem.'

'Two thefts!' he said. 'And one of them deceived.' He

221

chuckled and then stopped. 'But where is the real gem? Do you have it on you?'

Flavia glanced at Lupus. He gave her a tiny shrug.

'They were searching everyone,' she explained. 'So we hid it under the straw in the leopard's cage.'

'What? That cage they were wheeling past a few moments ago?'

'Yes. They didn't think to search there. We were going to get it later.'

Taurus gave Pullo a rapid but meaningful glance, then turned back to Flavia. 'Don't worry,' he said. 'You've done your part. We will take over from here.'

'What?' gasped Flavia.

'But the emperor!' protested Jonathan. 'He asked us to bring it to him in Rome.'

'Of course,' said Taurus, his red mouth curving in a smile. 'And I am on my way to Rome now, with fast imperial horses up to Tingis and then an oared warship to Ostia.'

'Then you can take us home!' cried Flavia.

'I'm sorry,' said Taurus smoothly, 'but I don't have room to take all of you. However, here's enough gold to pay for your passage back. And I'll have your belongings sent to the governor's villa.'

'Wait!' cried Flavia.

He patted her arm: 'Speed is essential, dear girl. I must get that gem to Rome. Once again, well done all!'

He turned and hurried after Pullo, and within moments they were out of sight.

The four friends looked at each other.

'What just happened?' said Jonathan.

Flavia shook her head. 'I'm not sure.' Suddenly a

terrible thought occurred to her: 'You don't think he's going to steal the gem for himself, do you?'

'I don't think so,' said Jonathan after a short pause. 'He knows we know he has it. And besides, he was our contact, and also Titus's cousin and agent. No,' he said. 'He'll give it to Titus. And he'll get all the glory.'

'You did not warn them of savage she-leopard Ungula,' said Nubia.

'I tried to just now...' said Flavia. 'But he wouldn't listen.' She allowed herself a grim smile. 'I almost hope he finds out the hard way.'

SCROLL XXIX

Flavia found her uncle resting in a bed in an upper guest room of the proconsul's villa. His head was wrapped in linen strips and his face was pale. The red light of the setting sun punched through the latticework screen to make pink lozenges of light on the white marble wall. Above him hung a wicker cage, and in it a blue and yellow bird sang with piercing sweetness.

'Hello, Uncle Gaius,' said Flavia, pulling up an ivory stool. 'How are you feeling?'

'Terrible. That poor girl almost died because of me. Is she all right?'

'Yes. The governor's wife is looking after her in a room downstairs. They're very kind here.' She frowned. 'Uncle Gaius, how on earth did you get the wrong leopard?'

'I've no idea. The only explanation I can think of is that one of my colleagues switched the signs on the cages.'

'But why would they do such a thing?'

He gave her a rueful look. 'They were always playing practical jokes on me. They probably had no idea I intended to take Nissa on an outing. Probably just wanted to give me a fright when I went to toss her an antelope steak. But tell me about that poor girl ... what was her name?'

'Casina. I think she's suffering more from a broken heart than from the leopard bite. How do you feel? How's your head?'

'Feels like a bull elephant stamped on it.'

Flavia tried not to giggle. 'Oh, Uncle Gaius!' Then she grew serious. 'Uncle Gaius, why did you run away from Ostia? Was it because you couldn't bear the grief of losing Miriam?'

He closed his eyes and nodded. 'Since she died, I've felt so empty. And everything in Ostia seemed grey and damp and cold.'

'Everything in Ostia *was* grey and damp and cold. It was the most miserable winter ever.'

He smiled weakly. 'Maybe. But it felt as if the sun would never shine again.' He opened his eyes and blinked up at the birdcage, as if it held some answer. 'All my life,' he said, 'I've done what was right. I've acted responsibly. When I fell in love the first time and she chose someone else, I didn't fight back. I blessed their marriage. I ran my farm diligently. Treated slaves and freedmen with fairness. Paid my taxes without a murmur. And how did the gods repay me? With a volcano that destroyed everything I ever achieved. I had to move somewhere new and I had to take charity from young Pliny. I started to take out loans. Then the interest became too great. Didn't you ever wonder why I went up to Rome so frequently last year? I owe thousands. Hundreds of thousands.'

'Why didn't you ask pater for help? Or Doctor Mordecai. Or me? I have seventy thousand on deposit with Egrilius and Son.'

'Because I was ashamed. I'm a grown man. How could I ask you for help?'

Above him the bird trilled.

'I felt like that bird. Trapped in a cage. The week after we buried Miriam, two men came to see me. They threatened me. Do you know what I did? I gave them the deeds to the Lodge. The Lodge paid for by my wife's faithful friend.'

'Great Juno's peacock!' breathed Flavia. 'That's why they came to live at Jonathan's house.'

He winced as he tried to sit up. 'Who?'

'Hephzibah and the babies. And the two wet-nurses. They moved in with Jonathan about a week after you disappeared. Hephzibah didn't say anything, but I could see she was upset.'

'That's because Miriam wanted the boys raised in the country, far from the immorality and decadence of Rome. I couldn't even grant her that one last wish. I was a failure as a husband. And as a father.' He shook his head. 'So I ran away. I left my children and my household and I ran away. To a life of adventure. I wanted to be good at something. I wanted to be brave.'

'So you pretended to be dead?'

He nodded. 'In case I still owed money ... I lost count of my creditors.' He gave a bitter laugh. 'Very brave of me, wasn't it?'

'Oh, Uncle Gaius.'

He turned his head to look at her. 'I thought I was being brave. Taking the first ship out of Ostia. I hate sailing. I was seasick the whole way. I thought I was being brave by riding out into the desert with a company of beast-fighters. The only beast I caught was a scorpion in my boot. I was trying to be something I never could be.'

'You know,' said Flavia thoughtfully. 'Almost everyone we've met on this trip was pretending to be someone they weren't.'

'Really?'

'Yes. Narcissus was pretending to be a pantomime dancer when really he wanted to rule the Roman Empire with Cleopatra's great-great-granddaughter by his side. Casina was pretending to be Cleopatra's descendant when really she was just a pantomime singer. And you were pretending to be a beast-hunter!'

He nodded. 'You're right. I was pretending. And you were right to call me a coward. The brave thing to do is to embrace life. And love. And if you suffer, then you suffer. I thought being a hunter of beasts was the brave thing. It was cowardly.'

Flavia sighed. 'I wanted to be a hunter, too.'

He raised an eyebrow at her. 'You did?'

Flavia grinned. 'For about a day. Nubia and I renounced men and decided to become virgin huntresses of Diana, stalking our prey with bow and arrow. *A painted quiver on her back she wore, and at full cry pursued the tusky boar*,' she quoted.

'What happened?'

'I shot a poor sailor having his lunch. Got him in the calf. But only a little,' she added.

Her uncle looked at her and suddenly they burst out laughing.

'No!' he cried. 'Don't make me laugh. It hurts!'

When they had recovered he lay back on the pillow, his eyes closed.

'Uncle Gaius,' said Flavia presently, 'if the brave thing is to face responsibility, does that mean you'll go back to Ostia? And be a father to your little boys?'

He opened one eye and looked at her. 'Do they still cry?'

Flavia nodded. 'Night and day.'

He groaned.

'But maybe that's because they miss their father.'

'If you do it, I'll do it.'

'If I do what?'

'If you face your responsibilities.'

'What do you mean?'

'Jonathan told me the most eligible bachelor in the Roman empire proposed marriage to you, but that you turned him down. Is that true?'

Flavia nodded.

He grinned. 'Coward, yourself!' Then his expression grew serious again. 'If you renounce your vow of chastity and face your responsibility, then I will, too.'

'But Uncle Gaius, I can't just break a solemn vow! I dedicated a rabbit at the Temple of Diana. And she sent me on the quest to find you.'

'Then give her a thanksgiving offering and ask her to release you from the first vow.' He paused and then said, 'It's our munus. Our duty.'

'What is?'

'To have descendants.'

She suddenly remembered the dream from the desert, of Diana and the woman with the baby. Suddenly she knew who all the people were in the woman's procession. 'They were her descendants,' she murmured. 'Thousands and thousands of descendants.'

'What?' said her uncle wearily. His eyes were closed.

Flavia looked at him fondly and shook her head. 'Nothing,' she said.

One of the Ethiopian slaves entered the room on

silent bare feet and began to light the lamps. Flavia realised the sun had set and it was almost dark.

'Very well, Uncle Gaius,' she said softly.

He opened his eyes. 'Very well what?'

'As soon as you're better,' said Flavia, 'we'll go to the Temple of Castor and Pollux here in Volubilis and make new vows. But rest now. It's dark and you're tired.'

'Good girl. You're a good girl,' said Gaius. He squeezed her hand, released it, closed his eyes and smiled. Soon his breathing was deep and steady, and Flavia knew he was asleep.

'Is your uncle resting comfortably?' asked Governor Aufidius from his dining couch. Apart from two ebony slaves and three-year old Marcus – asleep on the couch beside him – he was alone in the triclinium.

'Yes, thank you,' said Flavia. 'Thank you for taking him in. You're very kind.' Suddenly realization dawned. 'How did you know he was my uncle?' she asked.

'You cried out "Uncle Gaius!" when the big cat batted him.'

'I did?'

He nodded and gestured for her to recline. 'Curious that you never mentioned your uncle ...'

Flavia glanced around nervously. 'Where is everybody?'

'Quite a coincidence. Him being here in Volubilis.'

'Have they finished dinner?' asked Flavia.

'I did a bit of digging,' said Aufidius. 'You're a highborn Roman girl, not a pantomime musician. And apparently your uncle arrived last week with a company of beast-hunters. Did you know he was here?'

'Not at first,' said Flavia. 'We've been searching for

him for over a month. The only way we could get here was with Narcissus. We agreed to perform for him if he paid for our passage.' That at least wasn't a lie.

The governor nodded – apparently satisfied – and looked down at his sleeping son. 'My wife went back to the theatre to hunt for her gem by torchlight. Your three friends generously offered to help her search.' He clicked his fingers. 'Have some fruit.'

Instantly a slave was extending a plate of fruit. Flavia took a small bunch of red grapes but she did not eat any. 'Sir, I'm very sorry we lost your wife's necklace. She obviously loves her jewels.'

'Wasn't the stone she loved,' said Aufidius and looked affectionately at his son. 'It's her boys she loves.'

'What?'

'They're both extremely short-sighted,' he explained. 'Like my wife. Almost blind, in fact.' He glanced up at her. 'You didn't know that, did you?'

Flavia did not know what to say.

'She blames herself, I believe,' said Aufidius. 'That emerald helped them to see things more than a few feet away: a stork on the roof, the people in the forum, a pantomime on stage.'

Flavia sat up straight. 'Then she didn't love the emerald because it was a beautiful bauble worth a fortune?'

He shook his head. 'The only value it had in her eyes was that it helped our boys see. She wore it round her neck. So it wouldn't get lost,' he added.

'Sir,' said Flavia, 'I know of a man on Glassmakers' Street who can make you dozens of lentil-shaped gems like that, but of almost clear glass: much better than green.'

'By Jove! Do you?' He sat up carefully, to avoid waking his son. 'Do you really?' He looked at her with such boyish eagerness that Flavia laughed.

'Yes,' she said. 'Your wife and sons can each have one.'

'Jason!' called Aufidius. 'Fetch Philo at once.'

A moment later the governor's secretary stood in the wide doorway of the triclinium.

'Philo,' said Aufidius. 'Go with Jason here and tell my wife to come home. Tell her not to waste any more time looking for that green bauble.' He smiled at Flavia. 'Tell her we shall soon have something even better.'

SCROLL XXX

'Domina,' said Flavia three days later, 'we have something for you.'

Glycera looked up at them and smiled. She was sitting beside Casina's sickbed in a cool bedroom with frescoes of gardens on the wall. She had been speaking softly to the Alexandrian girl, who was still weak but recovering well.

Flavia and her friends stood shyly in the bedroom doorway.

Glycera kissed Casina's forehead, stood and moved gracefully across the marble floor of the bedroom. She pulled the gauzy curtain across its wooden ring then turned to face the four friends, standing in the shady peristyle. Each of them extended a pouch of coloured silk.

Tears filled her green eyes when she opened the first pouch and lifted out a clear glass lentil on a chain. 'Oh, children!' She said. 'Thank you! Are these all ...?'

They all nodded and Flavia said, 'Actually it was your husband who paid for them.'

'There is one for little Marcus and Gaius,' said Nubia. 'With one being left over in case of breaking.'

Jonathan said. 'But if you do break one, you can get a replacement from a man on Glassmakers' Street.

He's called Vitrarius. He grinds them from chunks of glass.'

Lupus nodded and gave Glycera a thumbs-up.

'Oh, children!' Glycera stepped forward and kissed each of them on the cheek. Her skin was smooth and cool and she smelled of roses.

Suddenly she took the signet-ring from her finger. 'Flavia, I want you to have this,' she said.

'Your signet-ring of Octavia!' breathed Flavia. 'I couldn't accept that.'

'Please do. Nubia said you had to trade your own signet-ring to a bath slave in Sabratha, when your things were stolen. Please? Please accept it?'

Flavia gazed up into Glycera's liquid eyes, then accepted the ring with a smile. It fit her left forefinger perfectly.

'Mummy! Mummy!' Gaius and Marcus ran into the room. They hugged Glycera's legs and little Marcus reached out a chubby arm to squeeze one of Flavia's legs, too.

She reached down to touch his silky curls and suddenly had an irrational and almost overpowering impulse to cry.

A week later, on the Kalends of May, the merchant ship *Tyche* set sail for Rome from the port of Lixus. For two days they beat up along the west coast of Africa, then finally sailed through the Pillars of Hercules into the relative calm of the Mediterranean. Presently Africa became a violet smudge on the horizon and Hispania loomed tawny and clear on the left. It was a bright morning, warm but not hot, and the ship was making good time. Gaius was chatting with the captain at the prow, and Lupus had climbed up into the rigging, so Jonathan went looking for Flavia and Nubia.

'There you are,' he said at last. 'I've been looking all over for you.'

'We like it back here by the altar,' said Flavia. 'We feel safe under the swan's head.' She was writing on her wax tablet and Nubia was cleaning her flute with a stick and a scrap of rag.

'It is not so windy here,' said Nubia.

'Then I'll leave you to your protective peace.'

'No. Come and sit beside us,' said Flavia. She patted the warm, wooden deck and Nubia moved over so that he could sit between them.

He sat on the silky deck and picked absently at the gummy line of pine pitch between the planks.

'Jonathan,' said Flavia, looking up from her wax tablet, 'do you think that beggar could have been Nero? If Nero hadn't died he would be about forty years old. Do you think he could have been forty-three?'

'I don't know. Living rough for ten years can make someone look old. If you imagine him with brown hair and all his teeth then I think he would look more like forty.'

'He did have bulging blue eyes like Nero. And a short, thick neck.'

Jonathan fished in his coin purse and brought out a sestertius. 'I found this in my money pouch,' he said. 'Look. It's got Nero on one side.' He handed it to Flavia. 'What do you think?'

She looked at it for a few moments, then nodded. 'It could be him.' She handed the coin to Nubia and said, 'Wouldn't that be strange? If we'd met Nero without knowing it?'

'Maybe he is person who takes glass eye of Nero,' said Nubia. 'He is always calling it My Seeing Thing.'

'Great Neptune's beard!' breathed Flavia. 'I hope not. Titus sent us to get the emerald to avoid a pretend Nero challenging his power. What if it turns out we've put a replica of that emerald in the hands of the real Nero? What do they call that? Something beginning with "I"?'

'"I think we made a big mistake"?' suggested Jonathan.

'Irony!' said Flavia. 'It would be ironic if we've done the very thing Titus wanted to prevent.'

'It's not as if that hasn't happened before,' said Jonathan grimly.

'And now "Nero" has Narcissus as his manager!' said Flavia. 'A man with an insane craving for power. According to Lupus.' She looked at her two friends. 'Do you think we should warn Titus?'

'No,' said Jonathan. 'Don't disturb the hornets, as they say.'

From above them came the cry of a giant seagull. They all turned and looked up. High on the mainmast Lupus was leaning out and flapping his arms like wings.

They waved up at him and Flavia shouted, 'Don't fall or you'll kill one of us.'

Lupus nodded and made the seagull sound again.

They laughed.

'Are you glad to be going home, Lupus?' called Flavia.

He nodded and flapped enthusiastically.

Flavia looked at Jonathan. 'How about you, Jonathan. Are you glad to be going home?'

'To Ostia?'

She nodded.

'Yes and no. Mostly yes.' He flicked a tiny ball of pine pitch over the back rail of the ship. 'And you?'

'Yes.' She gazed out over the blue horizon, and the tawny shoulder of land to her right. 'There are some things I have to do. People to see. Apologies to make. Many, many apologies ...'

He glanced at her. 'And a proposal to accept?'

Flavia and Nubia just looked at each other and giggled.

Jonathan rolled his eyes and grinned. 'How about you, Nubia?'

'I am missing Nipur and Tigris and Scuto,' she said.

'And Aristo?'

'Yes. And Aristo.'

For a while they all gazed out towards the fading smudge of land on the horizon.

'What will you miss most about it?' Jonathan asked the girls. 'About Africa, I mean.'

'Camels,' said Nubia, without hesitation. 'And other animals.'

'The sand sea at dusk,' said Flavia, 'with an oasis on the horizon and a crescent moon floating above the palms.'

'Very poetic,' said Jonathan. 'What will you miss least?'

'The flies,' said Flavia. 'And the lack of proper latrines.'

'Cruel slavery,' said Nubia.

'What about you?' asked Flavia.

Jonathan considered. 'I will certainly *not* miss the sight of decapitated heads bouncing in the dust. But I will miss the silence of the desert. And the stars at night. And the comforting swaying rhythm of the camels.'

'Just think,' said Flavia. 'If we hadn't missed the boat in Sabratha, we'd never have known what it was like to ride a camel in the silence of the desert.'

'Alas,' said Nubia softly, pointing with her chin towards the horizon. 'Africa is now gone.'

'Don't be melancholy, Nubia,' said Flavia. 'We might go back one day, maybe with Aristo and the dogs.'

Nubia smiled sadly and raised the flute to her lips and began to play. It was a new song. A haunting, exotic farewell to Africa.

Jonathan closed his eyes and let the sun warm his face. Presently he heard the sticky click of Flavia's stylus on the wax tablet.

'What are you writing?' he asked. 'Your journal?'

'No,' said Flavia. 'I'm writing another pantomime.'

Jonathan opened his eyes. 'What's the subject?'

Flavia looked at him and smiled: 'Octavia, the stepmother of Cleopatra Selene,' she said. 'I'm writing about Octavia.'

FINIS

ARISTO'S SCROLL

Actaeon (*ak*-tee-on)

mythical hunter who accidentally came upon the
goddess Diana while she was bathing in a forest
pool; in anger, the goddess turned him into a deer so
that his own hunting dogs would tear him to pieces

Africa

In AD 80, the time of this story, Africa was the
Roman name for the coastal strip of North Africa,
rather than the whole continent; it was divided
into five Roman provinces; from west to east:
Mauretania Tingitana, Mauretania Caesariensis,
Africa Proconsularis, Cyrenaica and Egypt (see map
at front of book)

Alexander Helios

(c. 40–c. 25 BC) son of Marcus Antonius and
Cleopatra, and twin brother of Cleopatra Selene, he
probably died of a fever in Rome around the age of
fifteen

amphitheatre (*am*-fee-theatre)

oval-shaped stadium for watching gladiator shows,
beast fights and the execution of criminals

amphora (*am*-for-uh)

large clay storage jar for holding wine, oil or grain

Antonius (see Marcus Antonius)

as (ass)

a copper coin worth a quarter of a sestertius in the
first century AD

Atlas Mountains

mountains in what is now Morocco; named
after the mythical titan who 'held' the sky on his
shoulders; the Middle Atlas range are the furthest
north

atrium (*eh*-tree-um)

the reception room in larger Roman homes, often
with skylight and pool

aulos (*owl*-oss)

wind instrument with double pipes and reeds that
made a buzzy sound

Augustus (awe-*guss*-tuss) (63 BC–AD 14)

Julius Caesar's adopted grand-nephew (son of
Caesar's niece, Atia) and first emperor of Rome; his
given name was Octavian; the Octavia mentioned
in this story was his older sister

basilica (ba-*sill*-ik-uh)

large public building in the forum of most Roman
towns, it served as a court of law and meeting place

bath-set

a ring (usually bronze) with various bath-
implements (also bronze) hanging from it: strigil,
oil flask, tweezers and ear scoop; you would hold it
or wear it around your wrist whenever you went to
the baths

caelum (*kai*-lum)

Latin for 'heavens' or 'sky'; *homo ad caelum* means
'man to the sky'

Caesarea (kai-zah-*ree*-uh)

(modern Cherchell) port town capital of the

239

client kingdom of Mauretania, then of the Roman
province of Mauretania Caesariensis (see next entry)

Caesariensis (kai-zar-ee-*en*-siss)

Mauretania Caesariensis (modern Algeria) was a
Roman province in North Africa, named after its
capital Caesarea (modern Cherchell)

Caesarion (kai-*zar*-ee-on)

(47–30 BC) son of Julius Caesar and Cleopatra,
he was murdered by Octavian (who would later
become Augustus) when he was seventeen

caftan (*kaf*-tan)

long-sleeved loose robe, worn by men and women
in hot countries

Capitolium (kap-it-*toll*-ee-um)

temple of Jupiter, Juno and Minerva, usually
located in the forum of a town

Carthage (*kar*-thaj)

Phoenician port town founded by the mythical
Queen Dido; the Romans destroyed it in 146 BC but
soon realised the value of its location and rebuilt it

Castor (*kas*-tor)

one of the famous twins of Greek mythology
(Pollux being the other)

caupona (cow-*pone*-uh)

inn, tavern or shop, usually the former

cavea (*kah*-vay-uh)

the curved seating of a Roman theatre, often
divided into three sections

Circus Maximus

famous oval course for chariot races, located in
Rome near the imperial palace

Cleopatra (klee-oh-*pat*-ra)

(69–30 BC) Cleopatra VII was the Greek ruler of

Egypt during part of the first century BC; she bore
children to Julius Caesar and Marcus Antonius

Cleopatra Selene (c. 40 BC–AD 5)

daughter of Cleopatra VII (above) and Marcus
Antonius, she married the Numidian King Juba II
and ruled Mauretania with him until her death

Cydamus (*kid*-a-mus)

(modern Ghadames) an oasis town in Libya which
was on the Saharan caravan route from Roman
times; it has covered streets and thick, bread-like
walls

deus (*day*-ooss)

Latin for 'god' the expression *deus ex machina* means
'god from a crane'

Diana aka Artemis

virgin goddess of the hunt and of the moon: she
despises men and loves her independent life of
adventure, hunting with her maiden friends and her
hounds

domina (*dom*-in-ah)

Latin word meaning 'mistress'; a polite form of
address for a woman

Drusilla (droo-*sill*-uh)

(born c. 38 AD) daughter of Ptolemy and Julia
Urania of Mauretania

euge! (*oh*-gay)

Latin exclamation: 'hurray!'

Flavia (*flay*-vee-uh)

a name, meaning 'fair-haired'; Flavius is the
masculine form of this name

Flavia Domitilla (*flay*-vee-uh dom-ee-*till*-uh)

wife of Vespasian and mother of Titus; she lived in
Sabratha for a time

forum (*for*-um)

ancient marketplace and civic centre in Roman towns

Forum of the Corporations

Ostia's special forum for businesses associated with ships, import and export

Fulvia (*full*-vee-uh)

(75?–40 BC) a colourful Roman matron, she was a wife of Marcus Antonius (he was her third husband) and an enemy of Cicero

ghul (gool)

Arabic for 'demon', especially of the desert

gladiator (*glad*-ee-ate-or)

man trained to fight other men in the arena, sometimes to the death

gratis (*grat*-iss)

Latin for 'free' or 'no charge'

Helios (*heel*-ee-oss)

Greek for 'sun'; a popular name for boys and men in Roman Egypt

Hercules (*her*-kyoo-leez)

very popular Roman demi-god, the equivalent of Greek Herakles

homo (*ho*-mo)

Latin for 'man'; *homo ad caelum* means 'man to the sky'

Ides (eyedz)

thirteenth day of most months in the Roman calendar; in March, May, July and October the Ides occur on the fifteenth day of the month

Isis (*eye*-siss)

Egyptian goddess often shown with her baby son Horus and a sacred rattle, or sistrum; in the Roman period she became associated with Venus

Italia (it-*al*-ya)

    Latin word for Italy, the famous boot-shaped peninsula

jinn (gin)

    Arabic for a kind of demon who can take on the shape of man or beast

Juba II (*joo*-ba)

    (c.50 BC–AD 23) king and scholar of Numidian birth who was raised in Rome after the defeat of his father Juba I by Julius Caesar; Juba II became a friend of Augustus, married the daughter of Cleopatra and ruled the client kingdom of Mauretania from Caesarea (Cherchell) and especially Volubilis

Julia Urania (*jool*-ya yur-*an*-ya)

    wife of Ptolemy of Mauretania and mother of Drusilla of Mauretania

Juno (*joo*-no)

    queen of the Roman gods and wife of the god Jupiter

Jupiter (*joo*-pit-er)

    king of the Roman gods, husband of Juno and brother of Pluto and Neptune

kohl (coal)

    dark powder used to darken eyelids or outline eyes

Laurentum (lore-*ent*-um)

    village on the coast of Italy a few miles south of Ostia and site of a villa belonging to Pliny the Younger

lemures (lay-*myoor*-aze)

    ghosts of the dead

Leptis Magna (*lep*-tiss *mag*-nuh)

    one of the three port towns comprising Tripolitania'

in the province of Africa Proconsularis (the other
two being Oea and Sabratha); this is the Latin
spelling: the Phoenician spelling is Lepcis Magna

libretto (lib-*ret*-oh)

Italian word from the diminutive of Latin 'liber'
(book), meaning the text of a long musical vocal
piece

Liber Pater (*lee*-bare *pah*-tare)

an Italian fertility god who was often identified with
Greek Dionysus and African Shadrapa; he was the
male equivalent of Ceres, goddess of grain

Libya

the Greek word for Africa in the first century AD

lictor (*lick*-tor)

official who holds fasces – sticks and an axe – and
who usually precedes a magistrate

Lixus (*licks*-uss)

(modern Larach) Phoenician trading port on the
Atlantic coast of Mauretania Tingitana (modern
Morocco)

machina (*mak*-ee-nuh)

Latin for 'crane' the expression *deus ex machina*
means 'god from a crane'

Macedonian (mass-uh-*doe*-nee-un)

anyone from the part of Northern Greece called
Macedonia; Cleopatra's ancestors were from
Macedonia, so she was Macedonian not Egyptian

Marcus Antonius (*mar*-kuss an-*tone*-ee-uss)

(82–30 BC) aka Mark Anthony, a soldier and statesman
who lived during the time of Julius Caesar; he was an
enemy of Augustus and a lover of Cleopatra

Mauretania (more-it-*tan*-ya)

region corresponding to northwest Africa; in the

first century BC, it was a client kingdom of Rome, ruled by kings subject to Rome; after the murder of King Juba II's son Ptolemy by Caligula in AD 40, it became a Roman province with a governor rather than a king

meander (mee-*and*-er)
Greek pattern of straight boxy lines which imitates a winding or meandering river; often resembling a maze, it was a popular border for clothing and architecture

mendicus (men-*dee*-kooss)
Latin for 'beggar'

Medusa (m'-*dyoo*-suh)
mythical female monster with a face so ugly she turned people to stone

Minerva (m'-*nerv*-uh)
Roman equivalent of Athena, goddess of wisdom, war and weaving

munus (*myoon*-uss)
the Latin word for 'duty' or 'responsibility'

Neptune (*nep*-tyoon)
god of the sea and also of horses; his Greek equivalent is Poseidon

Nero (*near*-oh)
(AD 37–68) notorious emperor who was reported to have strummed his lyre while Rome burned in the great fire of AD 64; he ruled from AD 54–68

Nones (nonz)
Seventh day of March, May, July, October; fifth day of all the other months

Numidians (new-*mid*-ee-uns)
an ancient ethnic group occupying Northwest Africa, now known as Berbers

Octavia (ok-*tave*-ee-uh)

(c. 69–11 BC) also known as 'Octavia Minor', older sister of Octavian (aka Augustus, the first emperor of Rome) and fourth wife of Marcus Antonius

Octavian (see Augustus)

Oea (oh-*eh*-uh)

(modern Tripoli, capital of Libya) along with Sabratha and Leptis Magna, Oea was one of the three ports collectively called 'Tripolitania' (lit. the three cities); the name Oea is Phoenician and Tripolitania is Greek

Orestes (or-*ess*-teez)

a mythical hero who killed his mother and was then driven mad by the Furies

Ostia (*oss*-tee-uh)

port about 16 miles southwest of Rome; Ostia is Flavia's home town

orchestra (*or*-kess-tra)

semi-circular space between the scaena (stage) and cavea (seating) of a theatre

pantomime (*pan*-toe-mime)

Roman theatrical performance in which a man (or sometimes woman) illustrated a sung story through dance; the dancer could also be called a 'pantomime'

Parthian (*parth*-ee-un)

someone from Parthia, an ancient region of Asia now comprising parts of modern Iran, Afganistan, Pakistan and Arabia, to name just a few

pater (*pa*-tare)

Latin for 'father'

paterfamilias (*pa*-tare fa-*mill*-ee-as)

father or head of the household, with absolute

control over his children and slaves

Pentasii (pen-*tah*-zee)

one of several corporations of North African beast-hunters known in Roman times; their symbol was a five-pointed crown with a fish in the centre

peristyle (*perry*-style)

a columned walkway around an inner garden or courtyard

Phoenicians (fuh-*neesh*-unz)

Semitic sea-people who established trading posts in coastal positions all over the Mediterranean; they are described by the word Punic

plebs (plebz)

term for the 'common people' or 'lower classes', as opposed to those of the equestrian and patrician class

Pollux (*pol*-luks)

one of the famous twins of Greek mythology (Castor being the other)

proconsul (pro-*kon*-sul)

Latin term for the governor of a senatorial province

procurator (prok-yur-*ate*-or)

governor of an imperial province, usually a man of the equestrian class

proscaenium (pro-*sky*-nee-um)

the stage of a theatre, literally: the bit in front of the scaena (backing wall); in many theatres the proscaenium was wooden, and acted as a sounding board

province (*pra*-vince)

a division of the Roman Empire; in the first century AD senatorial provinces were governed by a proconsul appointed by the senate, imperial

provinces were governed by a propraetor appointed
by the Emperor

Ptolemy (*tall*-eh-mee) of Mauretania
(c. 5 BC–AD 40) son of Juba II and Cleopatra Selene,
grandson of Cleopatra and Marcus Antonius, he
was the last client king of Mauretania; his execution
by order of the emperor Caligula sparked a revolt
in Mauretania which resulted in that client kingdom
becoming a Roman province

quadrans (*kwad*-ranz)
tiny bronze coin worth one sixteenth of a sestertius
or quarter of an as (hence quadrans); in the first
century it was the lowest value Roman coin in
production

Sabratha (sah-*brah*-tah)
(modern Tripoli Vecchia or Zouagha or Sabrata)
originally a Phoenician trading post, it became one
of the 'three cities' of Tripolitania in the North
African province of Africa Proconsularis (modern
Libya)

scaena (*sky*-nuh)
the monumental wall behind the stage in a Roman
or Greek theatre; it often had up to three levels
with columns, windows and doors leading
backstage

scroll (skrole)
papyrus or parchment 'book', unrolled from side to
side as it was read

Selene (s'-*lay*-nay)
Greek for 'moon'; a popular name for girls and
women in Roman Egypt

senna (*sen*-uh)
a leaf with laxative effect

sesterces (sess-*tur*-seez)

    more than one sestertius, a brass coin; about a day's
    wage for a labourer

sistrum (*siss*-trum)

    bronze rattle used as an instrument, often linked to
    worship of the goddess Isis

SPQR

    famous abbreviation for senatus populusque
    romanus – the senate and people of Rome

stola (*stole*-uh)

    a long tunic worn by Roman matrons and
    respectable women

stylus (*stile*-us)

    metal, wood or ivory tool for writing on wax tablets

succubae (*suck*-you-bye)

    from the Latin succumbo, to lie down; female
    demons who lie down with men

tablinum (tab-*leen*-um)

    room in wealthier Roman houses used as the
    master's study or office, often looking out onto the
    atrium or inner garden, or both

Tiber (*tie*-bur)

    the river that flows through Rome and enters the
    sea at Ostia

Tingis (*tin*-giss)

    (modern Tangier) port town and capital of the
    Roman province of Mauretania Tingitana

Tingitana (tin-gee-*tah*-nah)

    Mauretania Tingitana (modern Morocco) was the
    westernmost Roman province of North Africa, and
    was named after its capital Tingis

Titus (*tie*-tuss)

    Titus Flavius Vespasianus has been Emperor of

Rome for almost two years when this story takes
place

triclinium (tri-*klin*-ee-um)

ancient Roman dining room, usually with three
couches to recline on

tunic (*tew*-nic)

piece of clothing like a big T-shirt; children often
wore a long-sleeved one

Ursa Minor (*er*-sa *mine*-or)

Latin for 'Little Bear', a constellation known today
as the 'Little Dipper'; the north star is part of it

Venus (*vee*-nuss)

Roman goddess of love, Aphrodite is her Greek
equivalent

Vespasian (vess-*pay*-zhun)

aka Titus Flavius Vespasianus, Roman Emperor
from AD 69–AD 79

vivarium (vee-*var*-ee-um)

a place where wild animals were kept awaiting
transport to the ampitheatre; there was an Imperial
vivarium south of Ostia, near Laurentum

Volubilis (vo-*loo*-bill-iss)

founded by Carthaginians in the third century BC,
this city was one of the capitals of the territory
ruled by King Juba II of Mauretania in the first
century BC

vomitoria (vom-it-*ore*-ee-uh)

Latin word meaning 'entrances' to the theatres or
amphitheatres

Vulcan (*vul*-kan)

crippled god of forge and fire, he was married to
Venus

wadi (*wad*-ee)

riverbed in the desert; usually dry

wax tablet

wax-coated rectangular piece of wood used for making notes

THE LAST SCROLL

'Africam Graeci Libyam appellavere ...'

The Greeks call Africa Libya ... So begins the fifth scroll of Pliny's *Natural History*.

In the first century AD, the fertile coastal region of North Africa was part of the great Roman Empire. This region was often called 'Rome's breadbasket', because of the great quantities of wheat grown here and then shipped to Rome. The wheat needed to be shipped to Rome, and so several port towns sprang up. These were usually built according to the Roman layout and would have seemed quite familiar to a Roman traveler.

Sabratha, for example, was a port town about the same size and shape as Ostia. Its wild beast importers had their own office in Ostia's famous Forum of the Corporations (with a mosaic of an elephant as their trademark.) If you visit Sabratha today, you can still see the forum with its Capitolium and basilica, very much like Ostia's. You can also see ruins of a massive sandstone temple to the Egyptian goddess Isis, as well as a reconstructed Roman theatre, with an imposing three-story scaena.

Even Volubilis, one of the furthest outposts of the Roman Empire and several hundred miles inland, would have felt Roman. In the first century BC, Volubilis was one of the capitals of King Juba's client kingdom of Mauretania.

The part of Africa which would have seemed exotic to a Roman was the great inland desert. Then as now, the Sahara spread over a great area of North Africa. But in Roman times much of the Sahara was savannah, providing habitat for exotic animals like giraffe, zebra, antelope and lions. Catching game for the arena was a huge industry in the first century AD, and the Romans hunted these wild animals virtually to extinction.

Pantomime in Roman times was nothing like modern pantomime. The pantomime dancer of Roman times wore a mask and danced the actions of a story, which was sung by a singer and accompanied by music.

Narcissus the pantomime dancer is a made-up character, but there really was a famous pantomime dancer in Rome named Paris.

The man who claimed to be Nero was also a real person. We have several accounts of him appearing during the reign of Titus. According to these accounts, the real Nero did not die – but rather a look-alike – and the real Nero went into hiding and waited for the right time to reappear!